Run Like **JÄGER**

Karen **BASS**

Enjoy! KBass '08

COTEAU
BOOKS
FOR TEENS

Edited by Laura Peetoom.
Cover image by Masterfile.
Cover and book design by Duncan Campbell.
Printed and bound in Canada by Gauvin Press.
This book is printed on 100% recycled paper.

Recycled
Supporting responsible use
of forest resources
www.fsc.org Cert no. SGS-COC-2624
© 1996 Forest Stewardship Council

Library and Archives Canada Cataloguing in Publication

Bass, Karen, 1962–
Run like Jäger / Karen Bass.

Includes bibliographical references.
ISBN 978-1-55050-377-7

I. Title.
PS8603.A795R85 2008   C813'.6   C2008-900239-3

10 9 8 7 6 5 4 3 2 1

2517 Victoria Ave.
Regina, Saskatchewan
Canada   S4P 0T2

Available in Canada & the US from
Fitzhenry & Whiteside
195 Allstate Parkway
Markham, ON, L3R 4T8

The publisher gratefully acknowledges the financial support of its publishing program by: the Saskatchewan Arts Board, the Canada Council for the Arts, the Government of Canada through the Book Publishing Industry Development Program (BPIDP), Association for the Export of Canadian Books and the City of Regina Arts Commission.

Canada Council   Conseil des Arts
for the Arts   du Canada

SASKATCHEWAN
ARTS BOARD

Canada

CITY OF REGINA

To my husband, Michael,
for being my "Patron of the Arts."

Chapter One
Southeast of Berlin, Spring

Large knuckles pressed against Kurt's windpipe as Peter twisted his fingers in Kurt's collar. *"Lass mich los, Neumeyer!"* Kurt choked. "Let me go." He could feel heat painting his cheeks as Peter's grip tightened and less air trickled down his throat.

Peter, taller than Kurt by half a head and much broader, stuck out his square chin, as if offering a target. *"Versuch es doch mal!"*

Try to make me? You'd like that, Kurt thought. The stranglehold tightened. Spots danced on the outside edges of Kurt's vision and he realized Peter wouldn't let go until he passed out. If then. Desperate for air, Kurt lashed out, the back of his fist catching Peter's wrist and knocking his hand away. A ripping sound accompanied the air rushing into Kurt's lungs. He spun and barged through the circle of Peter's friends before he could be grabbed again.

"Du bist ein Feigling, Schreiber," Peter called.

The group of young men laughed, repeating Peter's taunt with glee.

Peter's voice rang above the clamour. *"Genau wie Dein Grossvater."*

The words chased Kurt down the street. He strode, head down, rubbing his neck, refusing to look back, refusing to show any sign he had heard Peter. Over the rapid tattoo of his heart, he listened for footsteps that didn't materialize. Though his tormentors hadn't pursued him, the accusation ricocheted through his mind, taunting him, driving him forward.

You are a coward, Schreiber.

Just like your grandfather.

Kurt bumped into someone, apologized, charged ahead. Minutes later he arrived at the lake. The toes of his sneakers hung over the lip of the grassy bank as he stared at the waves lapping the shore. Calm seeped back into his thoughts and he retreated to a bench in the shade of a maple tree.

An unruly strand of dark blond hair flopped into Kurt's left eye. He brushed it back. His "James Dean curl," his mother called it. The thought made him long for one of their classic-movie nights; he hadn't seen an old movie since arriving in Germany. Slouching, hands in pockets, Kurt rested his head on the back of the bench. Above, light danced through leaves in flashes of white gold. From the corner of his eye, he noted the white triangle of a boat sail.

No question, Germany was a beautiful country. Kurt sometimes missed his parents, even his little sister, Emily. Despite homesickness, despite being teased when he mixed up German words or sentences, despite being hassled by Peter, he wasn't sorry he had come to Germany on this exchange program. It meant he would have to do an extra half year of school when he returned to Calgary, to pick up Chemistry and Math, the two subjects he hadn't thought he could handle in German. Still, it was worth it to get to spend a year in Europe. Getting his request to be billeted in the town where his grandfather had lived as a child had been a bonus. Except for days like today.

Feigling.

"Kurt?"

He turned his head to see Marta Fischer hiking toward him, arms swinging broadly. Kurt said hello and returned to staring at the leaves overhead.

Marta plopped down on the bench, smoothed her skirt and peered upward. She had become Kurt's best friend over the last seven months. He figured she had invited him into her life because, as the strange guy from Canada with the bad accent, he qualified as a stray – and Marta was forever taking in strays. Unlike some others, she never laughed when he made mistakes speaking German, just corrected him and continued on, though he rarely needed correcting any more. These days, he even found himself thinking in German, which was the point of living with a German family, going to a German school, speaking German all the time.

A moment later Marta broke the comfortable silence. "Are we looking at something?"

"No."

"Good. Because if we are, I'm too blind to see it."

Kurt smiled, but said nothing.

Marta turned toward him. "What were Peter and his friends bothering you about after class?"

Kurt shrugged. "Neumeyer has been daring me to fight him ever since I scored that goal against him in Sports class."

"That was a beautiful goal. I'm glad I got to see it."

"It was lucky. I can run, but I'm no soccer player. Neumeyer knows that. I think it made him even more angry that I faked him out."

"Peter has been a bully ever since kindergarten. He learned it from his father." Marta laid her hand on Kurt's shoulder and tilted her head. "I was inside and couldn't hear. What was he saying?"

Kurt pulled away from Marta's touch. Elbows on his knees, he clenched his fists as the urge to hit something surfaced. Walking away from that word – *Feigling* (coward) – had been very hard.

"Kurt?" Marta's voice was soft, compassionate.

"He called me a coward."

"Does it matter what he calls you? Name-calling is so...juvenile."

"It didn't bother me." A bald lie. Of course it bothered him, but he couldn't let anyone see that. The old saying about names not hurting was wrong, especially when he didn't know if it was true. The exchange program rules were very strict and, unless Kurt wanted to be sent home, he couldn't fight no matter what they called him. He didn't want to be sent home...but would he fight, if he could? Peter didn't seem to think so.

"So what's bothering you?" Marta asked.

Kurt relaxed his fists and stretched his fingers. "He said I was just like my grandfather." Kurt loved his grandfather, who shared his name and would talk about anything with Kurt. Almost anything. The first twenty-three years of his life were a mystery. That mystery was part of the reason he was here – maybe even the reason he had taken German instead of French ever since seventh grade. Now, to have someone like Peter know something Kurt himself didn't...something shameful...

He jumped to his feet. "Are you working this afternoon?" Marta worked part-time at the local pharmacy, *Gunter's Apotheke*.

"No."

"Good. I want an ice cream. All winter you've been telling me about that *Eiscafe* in Berlin. The best ice cream in Europe, or so you claim."

Raising her eyebrows, Marta said, "Are you calling me a liar, Kurt Schreiber?"

"No. I'm saying that today is the day you get to prove it." Kurt forced a smile. "I'm buying."

Marta stood. "How can I refuse that? Let me phone my mother." She hesitated, then pointed at Kurt's neck. "Did Peter do that?"

Kurt felt the torn collar and shrugged. "I'll stop at the Klassens', let them know where we're going and change shirts."

Marta scowled at the offending collar, then fished her cellphone out of her backpack and called home. Kurt eyed the water. What he longed to do was jog the eight kilometres around the lake instead of pretending cheerfulness with Marta, but he didn't want to be alone with his muddled thoughts – far easier to push them aside by filling his mind with the sights and sounds of Berlin.

At the house, Marta chatted with Frau Klassen while Kurt bounded up the stairs and switched his torn blue shirt for a light grey one. He buttoned and tucked it in as he descended the narrow staircase. Frau Klassen fussed over him at the door, sweeping his hair out of his eyes and warning him to stay away from Peter Neumeyer. Kurt gave Marta an irritated glance; why had she told? Marta looked totally unrepentant. The kindly woman, at least a decade older than Kurt's mother, her own children grown, waved the two young people off with an order to have fun.

When they were a block away, Kurt said, "You realize that next time Frau Klassen sees Neumeyer, she'll lecture him, probably in front of his friends, and embarrass him. Then he won't just invite me to fight, he'll pound me flat."

"Peter wouldn't dare..."

"Oh? You're the one who said he's always been a bully."

Marta sniffed, as she always did when she knew she was wrong. Kurt shrugged and raised his eyebrows, then had to jump aside to avoid Marta's swinging elbow. He laughed, though he wasn't sure why, since the prospect of being hammered by Peter Neumeyer was a grim one.

They descended into the pedestrian tunnel that dipped under the train tracks, then jogged up the steps to the platform sandwiched between the two tracks. And there were Peter and three of his friends near the automated ticket machine. He almost suggested to Marta that they go for ice cream some other day. He steered her to the edge of the platform, as far away from Peter as possible. Maybe Peter wouldn't notice them.

Marta talked about one of her classes. The words droned together as Kurt's thoughts turned – as they often did in this place – to his grandfather. This was the same train station his grandfather had used when he was a teenager. Perhaps he had stood in this very spot, avoiding a bully, peering down the tracks, wishing the train would be early for a change. His grandfather would have ridden on a train like the one at Heritage Park in Calgary – a black hulking beast belching steam as it clacked along. The train coming into view was square, red and silent, except for the squealing brakes.

"Schreiber." Peter's voice spun Kurt around. The bully sneered. "You didn't answer me."

"You didn't ask a question." Kurt started to turn away, but Peter yanked him back.

Marta stepped between them. "Back off, Peter. We aren't bothering you."

Peter eyed her for a moment, then sneered. "Just what I would expect from your kind, Schreiber. Hiding behind a girl's skirt."

Kurt's cheeks blazed. Fist clenched, he stepped around Marta. She grabbed his arm. "Ignore him, Kurt. The train is here."

Kurt glared at Peter, whose scorn was etched deeply in his expression. Marta whispered, "Please." Kurt worked his jaw, wanting to wipe that smug look off Peter's face. Marta's sigh urged him to turn away. The quiet, "Just like your grandfather," followed Kurt onto the train, assaulting his mind like a kidney punch.

Marta sat beside Kurt instead of across from him. "Why would Peter think your grandfather was a coward?"

Kurt traced the graffiti etched into the window. "I don't know. Grandfather never talks about his life here in Germany. He didn't even want me to come. It's as if he's hiding something."

"I feel the same way sometimes. Opa will talk about different things from his childhood, but never anything to do with the war. All he ever says when I ask is, 'It's not important.'"

"If it's not important, why don't they tell us?" Marta didn't answer and Kurt fell silent.

A forty-minute train ride got them to the city. In central Berlin, he let Marta lead the way. He smiled and nodded at what she said, laughed when he thought he should and agreed the ice cream was great even though his mood seemed to rob it of any taste.

After cutting down two tree-lined side streets, they emerged onto busy Entlastungs Strasse and followed it into the Tiergarten, the sprawling park that Kurt always thought of as the heart of Berlin. Normally he enjoyed exploring the network of pathways. Today the shade harboured a chill and the fresh greens of spring seemed tarnished yellow. A cowardly colour.

Kurt paused at an intersection. Marta continued on, unaware he had stopped. On a bench beneath a statue of a horseman, someone was reading a newspaper called *Die Wahrheit*. It wasn't a paper Kurt ever recalled seeing. Probably a local paper put out by students or an activist group. He stared at the words. *Die Wahrheit*. The truth.

Marta nudged him. "Come on, Kurt! What's wrong with you? All afternoon you've been moping. Don't tell me you're still upset about meeting Peter at the train station."

Kurt shrugged.

"You can't believe what he said."

"I don't know what I believe." A frown crept across Kurt's brow. "But I know what I want, and that's to find out the truth."

"You told me your grandfather refuses to talk about when he lived in Germany. How do you expect to find out anything?"

"Someone said something to Peter – so someone knows what happened back then."

"You can bet Peter won't help you, so where can we look?"

Kurt pointed at the person on the bench, soaking in the sun and the truth. "Berlin had newspapers in the 1930s, didn't it?"

Marta's snort underlined the absurdity of Kurt's question. Of course they had had newspapers back then. And that's where his search would begin.

Chapter Two

"**I** thought being an investigator was supposed to be exciting." Marta sighed.

"Only in the movies, sweetheart." Kurt scanned the small print to the end of the microfiche column. He slid out the reader and removed the flimsy sheet used to store old records like newspapers. It reminded him of an oversized photographic negative. He picked up the next microfiche and prepared to load it.

Marta's tentative voice stopped his hand in mid-air. "Sweetheart?"

"I don't mean... Ahh... Don't mind me, Marta, I just had a Bogart moment." When Marta appeared confused, Kurt said, "You know, Humphrey Bogart, the old movie actor?" Marta shook her head. Kurt added, "His most famous role was as Rick in *Casablanca*, and in it he called everyone 'sweetheart.' Well, not everyone, just Ilsa, the woman he l –" Suddenly embarrassed, Kurt returned his attention to the microfiche. "Never mind."

"Why do you know so much about old movies?"

"I told you, my mom collects them. I've watched all the classics. Some of them were pretty..." Kurt tried to recall whether there was a German word for "corny." "You know, dumb. But that one – *Casablanca* – was all right." As he started to scan the next microfiche, he continued, "It took place during World War Two and was about this guy who outsmarted the Nazis..."

Kurt trailed off. He knew some Germans got upset when foreigners talked about that war – some tour books about Germany even warned visitors against discussing the Nazis – and, though Kurt knew Marta wouldn't care, the word seemed to hang in the air like cigarette smoke after the smoker has left the room. Maybe because they were searching newspapers from the 1930s and '40s, with stories about how wonderful *Das Reich* was and what a remarkable leader *Der Führer* was.

Hitler a great leader. The thought halted Kurt's hand, the microfiche stopping at a headline that declared, *Der Führer Richtig Noch Einmal* (The Führer Right Once Again). Even though Hitler had committed suicide in April of 1945, ice gripped Kurt's spine. He suddenly felt...trapped behind enemy lines. He shook his head to chase away the thought.

"What?" Marta said.

"Nothing." Kurt sat back and stretched his arms above his head. "My eyes are crossing and I'm starting to think it *is* 1937, reading all these weird old headlines." He let his head loll back and closed his eyes. "How is 1942 looking?"

"I'm into 1943 now."

"And what was happening in little old Zethen in 1943?" Zethen was practically a suburb of Berlin now, but it had once been a separate, small town. Still, it had never had its own newspaper and had always relied on Berlin's reports about surrounding communities.

"Most of the stories seem to be from the national propaganda department. I'm skipping over those and looking for local things like gossip columns, marriage announcements, obituaries."

Which was why Marta was making better progress, Kurt admitted to himself. He kept getting sidetracked by headline stories. Kurt had read up on Germany a lot before coming over last fall, so he knew the facts, but the picture drawn by these stories, of the country Germany had been under Hitler's leadership, was still alarming. Kurt shuddered, thankful that that government had been reduced long ago to white letters on a black microfiche. Black letters on white textbook pages.

Kurt frowned. To his grandfather, these words had been real. Like *Casablanca* in Technicolor, but rated 'R' for violence. Had his grandfather been afraid, living in such dark times? Is that why he wouldn't speak of them? *Feigling*. No, even the bravest man could have found Nazi Germany frightening, Kurt was sure. And to stand up for what was right, when wrong was in control...

"I think I've found something."

Kurt's eyes flew open. He scooted his chair sideways and leaned over Marta's reader, his shoulder brushing against hers. Marta directed him to the middle column.

> *Herr Hermann and Frau Nixie Brauer are pleased*
> *to announce the marriage of their daughter, Hedda,*
> *to Kurt Schreiber, son of Jakob and Else. The couple*
> *were wed in a small ceremony in Zethen on*
> *Tuesday, May 10th.*

"That's them." Kurt smiled at Marta, his nose almost bumping hers. "My grandparents. Kurt and Hedda. Dad's name is Jacob, too. He said they've done that for generations, alternate Kurt, Jacob, Kurt, Jacob. The oldest sons only have one name or the other."

He reread the announcement. "This doesn't tell me anything new, except the name of my great-grandmother. Why couldn't they have at least said what he did for a living? That he was a train conductor, or a store owner, or a newspaper reporter?" Kurt fell silent. That would be interesting. A newspaper reporter. Maybe that's what the older Kurt Schreiber had been. Maybe he had protested against the Nazis too loudly, had been threatened, and had stopped printing the truth, and *that* was why someone had decided he was a coward. He started paying close attention to the bylines, hoping to see the name, *Kurt Schreiber*, until he realized that in 1937 – the year he was scanning – his grandfather would have only been fourteen years old.

They took a midafternoon break and sat on the front steps to eat the sandwiches Marta's mother had made. They decided to keep searching for another hour. Twenty minutes later, Marta's quiet gasp interrupted Kurt as he skimmed a January 1938 article outlining Hitler's demand that the German people of Austria be reunited with their brothers in the Fatherland.

"What did you find?" Kurt jumped to his feet and leaned over Marta's shoulder.

She slid sideways and stood. "Look for yourself. First column."

Kurt gave Marta a puzzled glance and took her seat. The article jumped out at him. *10 November 1943: "Local Couple Dies."* The opening sentence read: "On Monday the 8th of November came a local couple through a car accident to their death." Kurt rubbed his neck. He was getting tired; it was taking longer to unscramble the sentence from German word order into English. He furrowed his brow and read the article carefully.

> *On Monday, November 8th, a motorcar accident claimed the lives of a local couple. Frau and Herr Jakob Schreiber were killed instantly when their vehicle crashed into the Hilde Bridge on the Spree River, three kilometres from Zethen. Officials say the bridge was icy at the time of the accident. The couple was preceded in death by their middle of three sons, Gottfried, when he was murdered by Dutch anarchists in a cowardly attack on a civilian convoy. Jakob and Else Schreiber will be interred at Zethen Lutheran Cemetery on February 12th.*

Kurt pushed the chair away from the counter and stretched out his legs. He had had a great-uncle named Gottfried. Had he been one of the civilians in that convoy, or a soldier guarding it? Dutch anarchists? Kurt blinked. They meant the Dutch Resistance, the people who had fought against the Nazis even after their country was taken over during the war.

"Should we keep looking?"

"Not if you're as tired of this as I am." Kurt reached for his notebook. "I'll record the dates we're leaving off at, and the date of this accident." November 8, 1944: the day his great-grandparents had died. Should he feel sad? It was hard to feel anything when he didn't even know what they had looked like. He tapped the paper with his pen. "I'd like to check out the cemetery."

"Why? What will a headstone tell you?"

Kurt shrugged. "Probably nothing. I'd like to see it, that's all."

"That was rude of me. I'm sorry, Kurt. Of course you'd like to see your great-grandparents' gravesite."

"It's no big deal. I'm just...curious." Kurt sketched a cross. "Is the cemetery very big? I mean, are we going to have to read thousands of headstones just to find one or two?" He drew an outline of a skull, the kind on pirate flags, shaped like a keyhole.

"I don't know. It's middle-sized compared to some here in Berlin. I'll ask my mother how you usually find a certain grave. Maybe there is a map or something."

"Sure. 'X' marks the spot." Kurt gave the skull two little x's for eyes.

Marta almost crowed when her mother told her she was right. She beamed across the table at Kurt while Frau Fischer explained about the cemetery registry at the town hall. Kurt, armed with names and the date of death, would get a map detailing the location of the grave. Kurt gave Marta a mock frown, rolling his eyes when her grin threatened to split her face.

The next day, Thursday, Marta had to work after class, so Kurt headed to the red brick *Rathaus* (town office) alone. Inside, even Kurt's soft-soled runners caused hollow echoes to bounce off the walls, up to the ceiling, where they faded to whispers. At the information desk, a double-chinned receptionist directed him to the second floor, where the records office was tucked into a corner. It was the third floor by Kurt's reckoning, but Europeans never seemed to count the ground floor as number one.

Two people were ahead of Kurt. He filled out a request form, then waited under buzzing fluorescent lights that gave the walls a sickly yellow tinge. When it was Kurt's turn, he listened for the third time while the zealous clerk explained how the cemetery was laid out according to time periods. Eighty minutes after entering the building, Kurt clutched his map, feeling as if it was gold after the ordeal he had endured to get it. There was no way he wanted to go through that again. He paused beside the oversized oak doors and examined the slightly crumpled paper.

The door swung open. Kurt grabbed the handle and stepped back to admit a woman with two toddlers in tow, one sucking a thumb, the other a lollipop. She thanked him. Kurt nodded. He turned to step outside, halting when he noticed the group lounging on the steps.

Peter Neumeyer, two friends, and his younger brother, Stephan. They were laughing and passing around a pack of cigarettes.

Kurt sidestepped into the shadows of the lobby, let the door swing closed and stuffed the map into the front pocket of his jeans. He didn't want a run-in with Peter today. Or any day for that matter. He was tired of the needling, which had become almost constant since Peter and his gang had latched onto that coward thing. The whispers, the disdainful looks. And at every opportunity, that word.

Feigling.

Sighing, Kurt wiped sweaty palms on his thighs and attempted to saunter back to the information desk. As he asked if there was a public washroom, he glanced around for other exits and spotted one at the end of the hall. Her voice echoing, the receptionist announced there were no facilities. Kurt thanked her anyway and strode toward the side exit like a man on a mission.

Several metres away, Kurt noticed a sign on the door: *Nur Arbeitnehmeren* (Employees Only). He leaned against the sill of the lone window by the exit and waited until the corridor was empty and the receptionist had her back turned, then he opened the forbidden door and paused in the stairwell to listen for signs of other people.

He could hardly hear above the hammering of his own heart. He chided himself for being stupid. He wasn't breaking the law; he was using an employee exit. A dozen steps below, a steel door beckoned. Somewhere above Kurt, another door slammed. Kurt flinched. He took a breath and jogged down the stairs, gaze fixed on his escape hatch.

Kurt burst outside and crashed into a man, solid as a wall, but wearing a suit and tie. Muttering, "sorry," he slipped from the man's grasp, darted up the stairs to the parking lot and through the scattering of cars, the man's rebuke chasing him. He loped around the corner and skidded to a halt.

Stephan Neumeyer stood at the mouth of the alley. The fifteen-year-old dropped his cigarette and ground it under his heel while Kurt watched in dismayed fascination. Stephan shouted, "You were right, Peter!"

Kurt spun and dashed towards the other end of the alley. Behind him, shouts and heavy footfalls sounded. Kurt sped up, confident the one thing he *could* do was outrun his pursuers. He emerged from the alley, narrowly missing a trio of girls, and swerved onto the bicycle path. Kurt ignored the few bikers who dinged their bells for him to get out of the way.

Kurt immediately fell into the rhythm. The slap of his shoes against the pavement. Air flowing in and out. Energy pumping through his limbs, carrying him to a place where the only thing that existed was running itself.

He didn't slow down or look back. He left the business district behind, turned off the bicycle path onto one shaded side street, then two more, until he arrived at the familiar two-storey white masonry house with its red roof and matching shutters. Kurt unlocked the front gate, flopped onto the steps of the Klassens' house and slowed his breathing as he clenched and unclenched his fists.

Instead of the release he usually felt after running, frustration spilled over and Kurt slapped his open palm against the top step. Pain flashed up his arm. He cradled his throbbing hand and dropped his chin onto his chest. His hair dangled in his eye, but he didn't brush it away.

Kurt knew what would have happened if Peter's gang had cornered him in that alley. If he let himself think about it, he could almost feel knuckles striking his flesh, shoes denting his shins. Still...maybe he should have let them beat him up. At least, then, one or two of them might have ended up with a few bruises.

As it was, the only thing bruised was Kurt's name. He had proved to Peter Neumeyer – and to himself – that Kurt Schreiber the younger was exactly what Peter had accused him of being: a coward.

Chapter Three

A few days ago Kurt had been in Zethen, running from Peter Neumeyer. Now he was dripping in Paris. It made him think of an old movie his mother had made him watch called *April in Paris*. A lame romance. Worse, a musical. She hadn't been impressed when he'd suggested that the Geneva Convention should list "watching 1950s musicals" as a form of torture – at least for guys.

A dozen exchange students and three supervisors got together once a month to tour different places in Europe. See Troop, they called themselves. The students of See Troop came from various points in North America: three from Canada, eight from the United States and one from Mexico. They were billeted in different places, too: one each in Italy, England, Denmark and Austria, two in Germany, three in Spain and three in France. They were all outgoing and smart (which had helped them get through the required essays and interviews to qualify for the exchange program), and Kurt enjoyed getting together with them. He also enjoyed the weekend of speaking and hearing English, since they were otherwise supposed to speak only the native languages of their hosts.

He usually enjoyed it, anyway. This four-day weekend was devoted to the City of Lights, but so far there wasn't much that was light about it. The skies matched Kurt's mood. Grey and overcast. According to the movie, and a lot of tourist booklets, April in Paris was the season of love, the ultimate in romance. Instead, they had a misty rain that hadn't let up since they had arrived. Two and a half days of damp and drizzle. If that wasn't bad enough, the Paris metro workers were on strike, so instead of zipping from one locale to the next on fast, *dry*, subway trains, they had sloshed through the streets or, as they were waiting to do now, had taken the much slower and very crowded busses. Because of the strike, Parisians had been about as welcoming as the weather.

"What's wrong, Kurt?" Jessica Randall asked. She was the other student billeted in Germany – a blond pixie from Oklahoma, always intent on spreading her cheer among the group.

"Nothing," Kurt replied. "I love being soaking wet in the rain."

"Hey, Jess!" Tyler Green called. "What's up with Sour Kraut this time?"

Kurt gritted his teeth. Tyler had started calling him that name yesterday, after Kurt had made a comment in the Louvre about the famous *Mona Lisa* being so small it was hardly worth the fuss, or the long line of tourists streaming constantly past the Da Vinci painting. Kurt narrowed his eyes. "This bus goes all the way to Gare d'Austerlitz, Green. I'm sure there's a train leaving for Spain that has an empty seat you could claim."

Jessica lowered her umbrella and stepped under Kurt's. She faced Tyler. "Y'all are both going to get in trouble if you pick a fight. Kurt didn't hassle you in London, Ty, when you could never remember to look right before crossing the street. He even pulled you back once." When Tyler shrugged, Jessica turned to face Kurt. "And you've been horrible all weekend, Kurt. Whatever's bothering you back in Berlin isn't here, so just...cheer up."

A bus pulled up. The driver opened the door, yelled something in French, then drove away. Half the students had collapsed their umbrellas expecting to get on. They reopened them.

"What did he say?" Tyler yelled. His Spanish gave him a better chance of understanding French than Kurt's German did, but everyone in Paris seemed to speak in fast forward.

Rhonda Michalchuk from Ontario replied, "His bus is full. Another's coming in ten minutes."

The group groaned like a single gigantic beast roused unexpectedly from sleep.

Kurt made his way to a burly, dark-haired supervisor. "Jim? Mind if I go see if that bistro down the street has a washroom?"

"Go ahead, but get back before that next bus or this bunch might hang you from a lamppost with that umbrella of yours."

"You're a funny guy, Jim."

"I wasn't joking. Do you want one of the French-speaking students to go with you?"

"I'll be fine."

Wet socks squished between Kurt's toes as he made his way down the street. A bell tinkled over the door when he opened it. Entering the yellow and blue café was like stepping into a patch of sunshine. Kurt collapsed his umbrella, grimaced at the lake forming around his feet, and avoided the scornful regard of two elderly women seated by the window as he headed for the serving counter.

His runners squeaked across the blue tile floor. A waiter hunched behind the counter with his back to Kurt, polishing a glass. The man's ring of hair was as white as his shirt. Kurt cleared his throat. The waiter kept breathing on the glass and rubbing it. Perhaps he was hard of hearing.

"Excuse me?" Kurt said in English.

The waiter straightened, as if doing so took great effort. He pivoted on his high stool and studied Kurt with watery yellowed eyes set in a face mapped with wrinkles. The man had to be at least as old as Kurt's grandfather, if not older.

Kurt said, "Do you speak English or...or German maybe?"

The wrinkles on the waiter's forehead deepened to crevasses.

"Ah, I just need to use your washroom." Kurt trailed off under the harsh stare. He quietly added, "My bus will be here in a few minutes."

"*Votre nom?*" The old man's voice creaked.

"*Nom?* My...name? What's that got...? I just need to use your washroom. Toilet?"

The waiter's withering gaze bored into Kurt's composure.

Kurt blew out his breath. "Sorry. Kurt. Kurt Schreiber. And your...*nom?*" He extended his hand, wondering why the introductions were necessary.

Lifting his chin, the waiter said, "*La toilette pour la cliéntele. Aller.* Cash yur buss." As the old man turned away, he spat and muttered, "*Sale Boche.*"

Kurt gaped at the waiter's bald head. He recognized *Boche* as an insulting name the French had called Germans during the two world wars. Abruptly, he spun away to see the two women eyeing him with greater disdain that before. He resisted the urge to give them a Nazi salute. Instead, he stomped back into the rain and snapped his umbrella open with a *whap*.

Returning to the bus stop, Kurt hovered near the back of the group and got Rhonda Michalchuk's attention. When she joined him, he whispered, "What does *sale* mean?"

Rhonda glanced down at Kurt's muddy pant legs. "It means 'dirty.' Did a waitress give you a hard time about messing up her floors?"

"Something like that."

She smiled and returned to helping the French-speaking students teach the group a children's song, "*Sur la pont d'avignon, l'on y danse tout en ronde.*" Kurt wanted to yell at them to shut up, that he was sick of hearing French.

Jessica appeared at Kurt's side and ducked under his umbrella, as she had been doing every chance she got all weekend. She smiled up at him. "Feel better?"

"Loads. Learned lots, too." Kurt peered through the drizzle and non-stop traffic, to the red *Metro* sign across the street. The entrance to the subway.

"Oh? What did you learn?"

Kurt shrugged. "Never ask an old Frenchman if he can speak German."

Jessica was even cute and spritelike when she frowned. Under her short bangs, her forehead puckered into even waves. "Why not?"

Kurt dropped his chin to his chest and arched his eyebrows to stare into Jessica's blue eyes. Summer blue, like the floor tiles in the bistro. "Think about it, Jess. If he's old, he was probably alive during World War Two."

"So...?"

How could someone so smart be so dumb?

"Tell me, Kurt. I really want to know."

"Haven't you studied World War Two?" When Jessica shook her head, Kurt sighed. She would bug him until he explained. "The Germans occupied Paris during World War Two. For all we know, German soldiers might've killed that man's wife, or brother, maybe his whole family."

"But...but that was so long ago. What does that have to do with you?"

"Yeah, well, not everyone is as forgiving as you, Jess. Here's the bus." Kurt gave her a gentle push, glad to end the conversation.

There was no room to sit, so Kurt stood at the back of the bus, three rows behind Jessica. Tyler wedged between two men to face Kurt. "You're looking more ticked off than before your potty break. What's your problem, Sour Kraut?"

Kurt glared. "Why don't you try it in French? It's *Boche*, so the waiter back in that café informed me. Can't help you with how to say sour, though. You'll have to ask one of the French students."

"Boche, huh? So racism is alive and well in gay Pair-ee." Tyler snorted. "I'll stick with Kraut. It's closer to crap, which is what you're dishing out if you expect me to feel sorry for you."

"I don't want your sympathy, Green. I don't want anything from you. What would you know about it?" Kurt tilted his head to peer out the window, hoping Tyler would leave.

"A whole lot more than you ever will."

Straightening, Kurt eyed Tyler's brown hair and fair skin with puzzlement. "Meaning what?"

"Meaning I've lived with taunts like, 'Run home to your mama, Jew-boy,' all my life. Meaning some jerks think I make an easy mark just because I'm Jewish. Meaning you know nothing about being a target, so quit whining." He paused. "Come to think of it, I was being a jerk, calling you that. I should've known better."

Kurt shrugged his acceptance of the near apology. He hadn't known Tyler was Jewish. He narrowed one eye. "So...when you get hassled, what do you do?"

Tyler grinned. "Offer to introduce them to the sidewalk. A face-to-face meeting. Though, no one has taken me up on it since I did a tae kwan do demonstration for the school with some other guys from my dojo."

"Ty? Did..." Kurt met Tyler's curious gaze for a second then looked away. "Did you have family in the war?"

"The war? Oh, you mean the Second World War? No family that fought. My great-grandparents came to America in the 1920s and both my grandfathers were too young to fight. They both had family back here in Europe that, you know, got caught."

"Death camps?" Kurt winced at the way he had blurted it out.

Tyler just nodded. "Some. How about your family?"

"I'm not sure. Grandfather won't talk about it. I found out that I might've had a great-uncle in the military, but..."

"But what?"

"If he was, he would've been...on the wrong side."

Tyler's brows rose. "You mean...a Nazi?"

Heat flared over Kurt's cheeks. He opened his mouth to reply, but Tyler's grin stopped him. It said, "I don't care." Kurt shook his head and chuckled, admiring Ty's cocky attitude.

Jim's voice rang down the length of the bus. "See Troop. Next stop!"

Kurt and Tyler both groaned. Kurt said, "I hate it when he does that."

"Yeah. Me, too." Tyler whispered, "Try not to goose-step off the bus, Schreiber."

"Shut up, Green."

The next stop for See Troop was the catacombs. Kurt was looking forward to a change from the endless parade of museums, monuments and cathedrals.

Kurt noticed the excited looks on the girls' faces as they filed under the sign that read, "*Entrée des Catacombs.*" Each trip, the girls got to pick one site no matter what the guys thought, and the guys got to do likewise. This site had been the guys' choice and the girls didn't seem to know what was coming, or he was pretty sure some of them would have complained. Kurt shared a grin with Tyler; neither of them was about to ruin the surprise.

Not wanting to miss the girls' reactions, Kurt made sure he was at the front of the line. They headed, single file, down a narrow staircase that seemed to go on forever. As they descended, the air cooled. A chill seeped through the stone steps and enveloped Kurt's wet feet.

The stairs gave way to a long poorly lit corridor. Wet gravel crunched underfoot. Everyone kept silent as they hiked down the stone tunnel.

At last, the *real* entrance. Square pillars painted with white silhouettes of castle turrets guarded a doorway with a sign above it that declared: "ARRÊTE! C'EST ICI L'EMPIRE DE LA MORT." From reading about it, Kurt knew the sign translated "Stop! This is the empire of the dead." Behind him, a few mutters rippled through the group.

Kurt entered the hallway and stepped aside to watch the girls. He wasn't disappointed. Upon seeing the first pile of skulls and bones, variations of disgust appeared on their faces. One girl, Charmaine, shrank back, only advancing when the lone female supervisor braced her arm across Charmaine's shoulders and whispered something to her.

Under faint overhead lighting, hundreds of shadowed, sightless eyes stared at them. Empty eye sockets that had witnessed centuries of history and countless thousands of tourists. Kurt was impressed. This topped a fusty museum filled with artwork any day.

Rhonda Michalchuk nudged Kurt with her shoulder and whispered, "I couldn't believe that the other girls didn't seem to know what the catacombs are."

Kurt eyed her with surprise. "You did?"

"Sure. I'm billeted less than an hour outside Paris. This is my third visit. It's a pretty amazing place, don't you think?"

"Ah...yeah." Kurt smiled. "Thanks for not saying anything."

Rhonda returned the smile and shook her head as she walked away.

Jim struck out, warning everyone to watch their steps in the sometimes slippery passages, and not to touch anything. Kurt waved his small flashlight's beam over brown skulls and pale yellow walls as Jim read from his booklet how the remains of six million bodies had been moved down here in the 1800s to make room in the overcrowded cemeteries. One of the girls whimpered. Charmaine, probably.

Kurt turned toward Tyler, hesitating when he saw that Ty looked almost...haunted. As Kurt watched, Tyler shook himself and leaned down to listen to something Jessica was saying. Wes, from Kansas City, kept looking at the ceiling as if he was afraid it was going to collapse on him. Kurt wondered how they saw the place; there was so much history down here that, like Rhonda, he found it fascinating.

The walls of human remains consisted primarily of what appeared to be leg bones, with regular patterns of skulls wedged into the surface: one row of skulls less than a metre from the floor, scattered skulls in the middle and another row of skulls along the top. See Troop halted in a large chamber that held an altar so everyone could get a good look and take pictures.

Jessica waylaid Kurt and whispered, "Y'all tricked us, telling us these were just underground tunnels, nothing but old quarries." She tended to say *y'all* when she was upset.

Kurt held up his hands in mock surrender. "They were...before the skeletons moved in."

"Ha. Ha."

"You could've read the tour info."

"I trusted you." Jessica swept past him, like a southern belle snubbing a scoundrel. Scarlett O'Hara, Kurt thought, to his Rhett Butler, as in *Gone With the Wind*.

Everyone else had drifted to the other side of the chamber, and suddenly Kurt wanted to be alone. He glanced around, then slipped under an archway into the tunnel beyond. He would take a look and be back before anyone noticed he was gone. The sounds behind Kurt faded, absorbed by the stone, or perhaps bone. He walked softly to prevent his footsteps from echoing. Kurt kept his flashlight aimed at the rough floor to

27

avoid puddles and protruding rocks. When he entered the next chamber he was surprised to find it empty of tourists.

Kurt shined his light over the walls of skulls and bones. A steady *drip, drip* broke the silence. Occasional drops landed on his shoulders and head. The chamber seemed to breathe the remembered breaths of all the former lives it stored. Hollow gazes pinned Kurt into immobility.

Did they resent his intrusion, like that old waiter in the bistro? Maybe these skulls had been silent conspirators with the old man, back in the war when the old man had been young and these catacombs had been headquarters for the French Resistance. The Nazis had never discovered these secret passageways. Did these skulls know more about Kurt's past than he did? Did they sense Nazi blood in his veins and despise his presence? *Sale Boche*.

The thought was more frightening than staring down a room full of skulls. If his grandfather had been a Nazi, he hadn't been a coward – he had been a monster. If a monster's blood ran through his veins, was it corrupting him until, like a werewolf under a full moon, he would become a creature of evil? Kurt tried to laugh at the thought. The sound came out as a strangled gasp.

"Kurt!"

Flashlight and umbrella both dropped. Heart drumming in his ears, Kurt spun and squinted against the glare of Jim's flashlight shining in his face.

"You're supposed to stay with the group." Kurt heard the anger in Jim's voice, though he couldn't see the supervisor's face. "There are miles of tunnels down here. Do you have any idea how easy it would be to get lost?"

"Sorry," Kurt muttered, though he was sure the catacomb tunnels were blocked off from the rest. He decided it was wiser not to point that out to Jim. He shaded his eyes and bent to retrieve his flashlight and umbrella as Jim barked at him to follow.

Kurt gave the chamber a final look before he headed down the tunnel to rejoin the others. He had once read a quote that said if you didn't know history, you were doomed to repeat it. Except for two small newspaper articles, Kurt didn't know anything about his own family's history – a fact that bothered him more each day. The need to know was beginning to burn inside, scorching his gut.

Because, he decided as he turned away, there were worse fates than being a coward.

Chapter Four

The closer the train got to Berlin, the harder it became to sleep. Kurt gave up and peered at the dark countryside. The sky was fading to a blue grey wash, so they had to be getting close. He rubbed his aching neck, unable to shift to a more comfortable position without waking Jessica, who was using his left arm as a pillow.

Jessica's host family lived in Dresden, a few hours south of Berlin. They were meeting her at *Ostbahnhof*, which was also Kurt's stop, to spend the day shopping in the city. Kurt would be heading from the train station almost straight to school.

He stifled a groan and closed his eyes. He was too tired to deal with Peter Neumeyer today. Then he must have dozed: when he opened his eyes, the train was slowing down for the massive main train station – *Hauptbahnhof.* To the right, the tall gilded Victory Column, called "Golden Elsie" by the locals, marked the centre of the Tiergarten. He stood, waking Jessica as he did so, and caught a glimpse of the top of the Brandenburg Gate before the train entered the station. After World War Two, Berlin, like Germany itself, had been divided into American and Soviet sectors – and when the Russians had built the Berlin wall to better control their area, the

Brandenburg Gate had stood just inside the Soviet side. Kurt was glad he was here in a time when the wall no longer existed and he could walk under his favourite monument without fear.

As usual, *Hauptbahnhof* was a chrome and glass hive of activity. People rushed off the train; others waited for their connections. A kaleidoscope of swirling colours that was more fun to watch than to move through. Despite the crowds, Kurt and Jessica managed to get to their next train, a local one, with a few minutes to spare.

The train pulled out, heading to the southeast station where Herr Klassen was probably already waiting for Kurt. The Klassens were never on time – if they could be early. They were nice people and he was glad the second billet hadn't worked out, allowing him to remain with them instead of switching in February as he was supposed to have done.

Jessica's host family was waiting on the platform. They hugged her and took her luggage. Before she followed them, she stepped close to Kurt and smiled up at him. She was so short and slight that he always felt very protective of her.

"Email and tell me what has you upset," Jessica said. Before Kurt could say it wasn't that bad, her finger pressed against his lips. "And promise I'll see you in two weeks."

Kurt could feel heat creeping up his neck. "I...I'll try."

"You'll have to do better than that, especially after y'all tricked me about those awful skulls." Jessica stood on tiptoe and framed Kurt's face with both hands. "I'll forgive you this time because I know you really are a Sweet Kraut." She pulled Kurt's head down and kissed him. Kurt was so shocked he couldn't move. She flounced away, paused in a beam of sunlight and twirled to give Kurt one last wave. He still didn't move, just watched her until she left the platform, bewilderment blanking his thoughts. Where had that come from? She had flirted with him before...but she flirted with all the guys in See Troop, even the supervisors.

"Who vas that? Tinklebell?"

Marta's voice, in softly accented English, startled Kurt. She stepped into his line of vision, her serious expression hinting of disapproval. Heat flamed up his neck.

"What are you doing here?" he blurted in English, then backtracked. "Tinklebell?"

"You know, from the child's fideo."

"Peter Pot?"

"Yes. No, dat...*th*at sounds not quite right." Marta planted her hands on her hips and switched to German. "Are you teasing me, Kurt Schreiber?"

Also in German, Kurt replied, "I wouldn't dare." He fought the smile trying to break free.

Marta pinned him with a shrewd look. "So who is she?"

"One of the other exchange students. Jess. I'm sure I've mentioned her."

"That's Jess? I thought Jess was a guy. A...Jessie."

"No. Think Jessica, like the old actress, Jessica Tandy, or −"

"Right. I understand." Marta's look turned suspicious. "Why will you see her in two weeks?"

"It's her birthday. She wants our exchange group to come, but Dresden isn't very central, so the only ones who'll likely make it are me and Sam, as in Samantha. She's billeted in Vienna."

"I'm sure your Jess will be quite disappointed if Sam is able to make it." Marta picked up Kurt's bag. "We should go."

Kurt stared after Marta for a few seconds, puzzling over her comment and her attitude, then jogged to catch up. He snatched his bag. "*My* Jess. What do you mean by that?"

"You're quite smart, Kurt. Acting thick-headed doesn't suit you."

"I'm not –" Kurt snapped his mouth shut. Girls were so frustrating sometimes. Maybe he should change the subject. He glanced around the station. "Where is Herr Klassen?"

"It's almost 8:30. He had to take his car to the garage before work. I asked if I could meet you. If we catch the next train we'll get to school partway through our first class."

Kurt rubbed the back of his neck. "I can't face school right now. I'm so tired I feel sick. It rained all weekend and I think my jeans are mouldy. I need to walk, loosen up. Wake up."

"Can't face school, or can't face Peter?" Halting suddenly, Marta faced Kurt. "Did you really run away from him on Thursday?"

"How'd you know about *that*?"

"Peter's been working hard while you were gone, making sure everyone knows – whether it's true or not."

Kurt searched her face for judgment but found only compassion. Marta smiled. Not an easy smile like Jessica tended to bestow on everyone, but a tentative one that said, "you have been judged and found worthy of friendship."

They wandered towards Muhlenstrasse and the East Side Gallery, a stretch of the old Berlin wall with murals painted on it. Kurt gave them only fleeting glances. The first time he'd seen them, he'd been fascinated by this broken reminder of two Berlins, two Germanys – East and West. The wall had been part of the "iron curtain" that stood between the democratic

West and the socialist East. Zethen had also been behind that curtain – until the wall fell and the country was reunited.

"How was Paris?" Marta said.

"Don't ask."

"Okay." She stuffed her hands in her pockets. "I rescued a wounded hedgehog while you were gone. I named him Rick, like in your *Casablanca* movie."

"Fits. In the movie, Rick was prickly."

"You have been, too, lately."

Kurt halted before a mural with "Dancing to Freedom" written across the top. "Sorry, Marta. This whole thing has messed with my mind. I want to find out about Grandfather, but...what if I don't like what I find? Why can't life ever be simple?"

She placed a hand on his arm. "I have no answers, but I'll help you look for them."

He gazed into brown eyes warm with concern. Pretty eyes in a pretty face. The unexpected desire to kiss her made his cheeks warm. What was he thinking? This was his friend, Marta, not –. He spun around and waved at the wall. "What was it like in East Germany before the wall came down?"

She looked puzzled by the change in topic, but said, "That was in 1989, before I was born. My parents talk about it sometimes. There were bad things, like lineups and shortages, and wondering if your neighbour was spying on you, but there were good things, too, like almost no unemployment, good child care and social security. They know some people who wish reunification hadn't happened. No one our age says that, though." She pulled out her cellphone and checked the time. "Are you awake now? Should we try to catch the next train?"

"Yeah. Let's go make Peter's day."

She elbowed him gently and smothered a laugh.

School was an endurance test. Snickers followed Kurt down the halls. Scornful looks warmed his neck. And another name joined his growing list: Coward Canuck. At least it had a ring to it. Kurt found himself doodling interlocking Cs in the margins of his notebooks.

The third bell rang. His next class was Sports and Peter was in it. Kurt had the urge to hit his head against a hard surface, preferably hard enough to knock himself unconscious.

Instead of veering toward a wall, Kurt grabbed his gear from his locker and headed to the change room. He didn't want to run away again, even if Peter knocked him out, which, considering the guy's gorilla hands, was a definite possibility. Kurt was a few minutes late getting to the change room. He took his time changing into his shorts and T-shirt. He was bent over one running shoe when someone called his name.

Victor Liebermann, who had never been more than polite to Kurt, stood at the door that led outside. The light behind gave Victor's shaggy blond hair a halo and darkened his amber eyes. He motioned for Kurt to come. "Peter can't do much with the teacher on the field. Hiding will only prove what he's been telling everyone."

While Kurt agreed with the futility of hiding, he wasn't so sure about the teacher's ability to protect him. He followed Victor out the door, but halted on the sidelines of the soccer pitch. Laps had been run, teams chosen. The teacher presided over the kickoff. Kurt knelt on the grass to retie his left shoe. Black cleats appeared by the toe he was so intent upon.

"Schreiber, are you ill?"

Kurt looked up at his teacher. "No, Herr Instruktor."

The ruddy-faced teacher threw a sash in Kurt's face. "Get out there. Your team needs a fast winger."

Kurt drew the mustard-coloured sash over his head so it stretched diagonally across his chest like a beauty contestant's, conscious of his teacher's sharp regard. Had the teachers heard the rumours, too? He trotted onto the field, thankful he had been assigned to a wing, and not put in the position of striker. He would rather feed the goal scorer than be it – especially with Peter in goal for blue.

The first time halfbacks squeezed him out of the play and left him eating grass, Kurt thought it was part of the game. The third time it happened he knew it had been planned. Both half-backs were Peter's friends. Kurt got to his feet slowly, rubbed his aching grass-stained knees, and with a glance at the teacher, who had his attention fixed on the ball, rejoined the game.

Late in the second half, Kurt's abilities as a runner came into play. Other players began to tire; Kurt kept running. He found himself alone in front of the goal. He kicked the ball ahead and charged forward. From the corner of his eye he saw Peter racing to cut him off.

They reached the ball at the same instant. Peter slid, feet first, kicking the ball away and sweeping Kurt off his feet. A classic tackle. Kurt twisted and landed on his back with a thud that slammed the air from his lungs.

Wheezing, Kurt pushed to his knees. A running shoe sank into his gut and folded him over. He lay on his side, fighting for air, unable to defend against the next kick that he knew was coming. Through the ringing in his ears, he heard a shrill whistle. The teacher yelled, "Showers!"

"You'll never beat me at my own game, Schreiber."

Eyes only open to slits, Kurt saw Peter's leg drawing back as he prepared to give a parting kick. *What game?* Kurt wondered as he waited for the blow. *Soccer or intimidation?*

"Neumeyer! Walk away unless you want to clean the equipment room," the teacher yelled.

Peter said, "What is it about you, Schreiber? Teachers and girls always want to protect you. Are all pretty boys such cowards? I bet your grandfather was a pretty boy, too."

Air rattled down Kurt's throat as Peter spun and jogged away. Kurt flopped onto his back and took deep breaths as he willed his stomach to stop roiling. A shadow fell across his face. He squinted up at Victor, who extended one of the long arms that helped make him a good goalie. Kurt took his hand and pulled himself to his feet.

"Thanks." Kurt cleared his throat. "You probably shouldn't get too close. You don't want Neumeyer deciding that you're a good target, too." He held his hand against his side.

"I was one already," Victor said. "Two years ago. Peter likes to pick on a different student each year. Being a foreigner made you a novelty."

"Maybe at first, but there's more to his dislike than that." Kurt caught Victor's puzzled glance as he pulled the yellow sash over his head. Kurt shrugged. "My grandfather grew up in this town. Maybe the two families didn't get along. I don't know."

"Couldn't tell you. We moved here when I was three. I don't know the town's history."

Kurt spent the afternoon in the school library, catching up on work he had missed while in Paris. It was after five o'clock when he packed up. Outside, heavy clouds hovered over the town. The quiet streets waited for the rain. Kurt walked quickly, head down, thankful that Frau Klassen had picked up his suitcase and umbrella from school earlier. At the second intersection he eyed the glowering sky, then the street sign.

Friedenstrasse. Peace Street. The cemetery (*der Friedhof*) was on this road. Kurt turned onto the street. Frau Klassen didn't serve supper until seven o'clock and she wouldn't begin to wonder about his whereabouts until after six. That gave him time to check out his great-grandparents' graves. He cast another wary glance at the steel grey sky.

Kurt passed a thuja hedge with finches huddled in its branches. A row of weary houses squatted in small yards. Yellowing masonry and crooked shutters framed the windows with gloom, and they stared at Kurt as if blaming him for their sorry state. He was relieved when he reached a two-metre-high wall that stretched for two blocks, its tan surface cracked and dotted with faded graffiti that had resisted a scrub brush. Halfway down, the wall angled in to iron gates and a one-lane road.

Kurt halted under a towering linden tree that guarded the gates. A fine drizzle began. He peered up at the heart-shaped leaves keeping him dry, then beyond black bars to rows of tombstones. Reluctance made him pause. This is what he had come for, wasn't it? But Frau Klassen would be worrying now that it was raining. Kurt left his shelter intending to head to the Klassens'. His feet betrayed him and carried him through the half-open gates into the cemetery.

The map was still in Kurt's pocket, barely readable after getting wet in Paris. He didn't need it; he had memorized the path. He followed the road for a short distance, then swung left and strode between moss-trimmed tombstones streaked with rain – brooding granite markers, some erect, some showing their age as they leaned against their neighbours.

Shade trees helped the overcast sky shroud the cemetery in greyness. The place looked deserted, but Kurt felt as if he was being watched. He paused at a grave marker topped with a stone angel and searched its eyes for signs of life. Blank grey orbs returned his stare. Shivering, he turned up his collar and jammed his hands into his jacket pockets.

The clouds dropped lower as they threatened to swallow the treetops. The rain soaked Kurt's hair and trickled down his neck. The smell of damp earth and wet stone filled his nostrils. This was the right row. Three spaces down, he crouched before a low wide tombstone.

JACOB ERNST SCHREIBER   ELSE GERTRUD RICHMANN SCHREIBER
1899–1943   1904–1943

Now he knew his great-grandparents' birth years and his great-grandmother's maiden name. So what? Kurt traced 1943, the carved edges rough against his finger. What did he expect? A list of their children, their occupations? Still, he had hoped for more than dates and a name.

A movement caught Kurt's attention. He popped to his feet as an old man stepped around a linden tree two metres away. Thin as a flagpole and just as straight, the man wore a brown trench coat and held a tapered dark cane. The old man stared, his face white. His mouth opened, closed, opened again. The sound that escaped was a heavy rasp.

"Jäger?"

From under a brown fedora, the old man's light eyes fixed Kurt like a collector's needle pinning a butterfly. Kurt held his breath, unable to look away or move. The man lifted his cane and grasped it below the handle. A carved wolf's head nodded at Kurt. The man stepped closer.

"Jäger? How can it be? Is it you?"

The name meant *hunter*. In fourth grade Kurt had known a boy named Hunter who had died in a car crash. Kurt shook his head, unable to make his feet obey his silent plea to move. Leave. Run.

The old man's voice grew stronger. "Kurt Schreiber?"

Hearing his own name spurred Kurt into action. He backpedaled a half dozen steps, wheeled and ran. Into another tombstone. His thigh slapped against it as he grabbed its top edge to steady himself. He cut around the granite slab and took off like a sprinter out of the starting block.

Behind him, the old man called, "Wait!"

Kurt didn't wait. He didn't look back. He didn't slow down.

Chapter Five

Kurt kept his voice low and tilted his head toward Marta as they walked. "I tell you, that old man was creepy. Dressed like someone out of a 1940s movie. Like Rick in *Casablanca*. But the way he stared at me reminded me more of...Dracula getting ready to attack his next victim."

Marta smothered a giggle. "Maybe you were just frightened by being in the cemetery. I'm sure he was harmless."

Casting an injured look at his friend, Kurt said, "The Paris catacombs didn't scare me, so why would a few tombstones? It was his eyes. And the way he just seemed to appear. Maybe he was a ghost. He was white enough to be one."

"Well, if he was a ghost, at least you had good reason to run away."

Kurt rolled his eyes and fell silent. He exhaled slowly. He was tired of running away. With a glance over his shoulder at the schoolyard, he said, "Yesterday, I faced off against Peter during a football match."

"I know. I'm sorry I wasn't able to watch it. I had a lab report to finish. I heard he tackled you, then kicked you in the stomach before you could get up."

"Who told you that?"

"Rebekka Waring. She was watching from the sidelines. She's dating Victor Liebermann and loves to watch him play."

"He's a good goalie."

"Yes. Rebekka said you were the fastest winger on the pitch, that you run like a deer."

"I'm a great runner. Lots of practice." Kurt heard the bitterness in his words and wished he could take them back.

Marta stopped on the street corner. The look she gave Kurt was a mixture of concern and confusion. "I wish I didn't have to work again today. Are you sure you don't want to walk to the apothecary with me?"

"No." Kurt glanced at the street sign – Friedenstrasse – and the cottonball clouds in the sky. No rain today. "I want to go back to the cemetery and see if there are other Schreiber graves near my great-grandparents'. Maybe that son mentioned in the obituary was buried there."

"What will that tell you? The newspaper archive is a better place to find information."

Kurt shrugged. "I know. I'm just curious. I'd rather go through the archives with you...if you're still willing to help."

"Of course I'm still willing." Marta's smile threw gold sparkles into her brown eyes. "Does that mean you like my company?"

"It means that place is so boring I need someone to keep me awake."

"So, I'm just a human alarm clock? Maybe I'll rethink whether I want to help."

"I was teasing, Marta."

"Oh?" She raised her eyebrows. "I've been hanging around you too long then. Your teasing isn't funny any more. I'll give you the same advice my grandfather gives me: you catch more flies with honey than with vinegar." She spun and crossed the street.

Kurt scowled. Would he ever understand girls? His teasing was vinegar? She used to laugh, or at least smile, at his comments. Did she want sweet, empty flattery? Batting eyelashes and fishing for compliments wasn't her style. That was something he would expect from Jessica, who never let him forget she was a girl. Marta...was just Marta. She'd rather hike up a hill than go dancing. She liked walking, history and animals. She was a great friend.

"Hey, Schreiber!"

Kurt turned and waved hello to Victor. "How's it going?"

"Good. Was that Marta Fischer you were talking to?" Kurt nodded and Victor said, "Rebekka tells me you two spend a lot of time together. The four of us should go to the cinema some night."

"But we aren't −"

"It would be fun. Movie, ice cream, a walk in the park." Victor grinned. "We have to keep our women happy." He glanced at his watch. "I'm late. I'd better run."

"But −"

"I'll call you to arrange a date."

"I...ah...I'd have to... I mean, I might..."

"Good. It's settled." Victor waved and jogged across the street.

Kurt snapped his gaping mouth shut. It was settled? He started down Friedenstrasse puzzling over Victor thinking of him and Marta...as a couple. That was ridiculous. Well, not ridiculous. Marta was pretty, and it was normal to think she would have a boyfriend. Why didn't she? Probably because she was too busy coddling her biggest stray, Coward Canuck.

A thuja hedge loomed on his right. Kurt swiped at the branches, sending a scattering of leaves across the sidewalk. Ahead, an angry voice interrupted the stillness. Kurt drifted past the roughly trimmed bushes and halted. His eyes widened.

A large man in a thin sleeveless undershirt — muscles and stomach sagging — stood by the front door of an old house that also drooped. He used a beer bottle to point at an aging car in the driveway and yelled, "Hurry up! If your mother gets a chill, you'll both wear my boot prints."

Kurt's attention swung to the broad back of someone lifting a frail woman out of the car. A wheelchair waited for her, held by...Stephan Neumeyer. Kurt watched the younger boy shift from foot to foot as he cast nervous glances at the man who had to be his father.

The man continued to yell a combination of insults, directions and threats. He made no move to help. His mother deposited in the wheelchair, Peter Neumeyer straightened. Stephan nodded toward the street. Kurt retreated a step as Peter turned and glared at him. Heat flashed across Kurt's cheeks, as if he had been caught shoplifting. He hadn't meant to violate their privacy; he hadn't even known that this was the Neumeyers' house.

"Move your lazy carcass and help your brother with these stairs!"

Peter's eyes narrowed. He turned away and Kurt hurried down the street, happy to get away from the fear in Stephan's face and the stony anger in Peter's. Their father's bellowing could be heard halfway down the block and only stopped when a door slammed.

Kurt halted outside the cemetery gates, under the shelter of the linden tree. He glanced over his shoulder, feeling pursued by Peter's glare. Goosebumps skittered down Kurt's arms. He rubbed them. It looked like Peter had it rough at home. That should inspire sympathy, not fear, though Kurt had the feeling if he said anything smacking of sympathy, he'd come away with a lot more than a bruise on his stomach.

About to enter the cemetery, Kurt noticed a figure and retreated back under the linden's shadows. The old man. His fedora, trench coat and cane made him instantly recognizable. While Kurt watched, the old man wound his way between tombstones at a stately pace. Someone tending a grave called out to him. The old man saluted with his cane and continued on. Not a ghost then, if other people greeted him so cheerfully.

Curiosity surfaced. Who was this old man? More importantly, if he knew Kurt's name, had he known his grandfather? Kurt slipped through the gates and dodged toward the nearest tree. He peered around the trunk at the old man's back, then dashed to the next tree and hid. Three trees later, he stopped his advance across the cemetery when the old man stood before a low tombstone and bowed his head. Kurt frowned. That looked like his great-grandparents' grave.

The man seemed to lean heavily on his cane for a moment. Then he stepped forward, set something on the granite marker and turned away. Kurt ducked behind the tree, unease clutching his throat, heart thumping. He kept the trunk between him and the old man, not leaving his shelter until the brown figure exited the cemetery and turned right.

Kurt jogged to the tombstone. He stared at the carved names of Jakob and Else Schreiber, wondering how the old man knew his family. He examined what the man had left behind.

A silver medal, round with a stylized helmet where it attached to a red ribbon with a white-banded blue stripe. It read: *WinterSchlacht im Osten, 1941/42*. Winter battle in the east. The Russian front in World War Two? Why would the old man leave his medal behind?

Kurt saw the caretaker leaning on a hoe, watching him. He jogged over to the man, who straightened and brushed his dirty hands on equally dirty green overalls.

"Hello, Herr Hausmeister." Kurt referred to the man's position as caretaker since he didn't know his name. Politeness was important to most Germans. "Do you know who that man was who you said hello to earlier?" Kurt clutched the medal in his fist, unwilling to show it to the man.

"Ah. You refer to Herr Brandt." The caretaker lifted his cap and scratched his forehead, leaving a black smudge. "Brandt like the famous West German chancellor, yes? But he is no relation that I know of. But a politician, yes. Wolfgang Brandt was our mayor for more years than I can remember, back when we were made to swear allegiance to Moscow instead of Berlin. A hard position to be in. But a good man, Herr Brandt."

The caretaker looked as if he was about to settle into a long account of what made Herr Brandt such a good man. Kurt walked backwards as he said, "Thank you very much." He pivoted and jogged away before the man could respond.

At the gates, Kurt looked both ways, then remembered the old man had turned right. No trench-coated figure was in sight. Kurt headed right anyway. He walked quickly, conscious of the medal imprinting his palm. Curiosity outweighed any previous unease. Wolfgang Brandt. A good man. Then he wouldn't mind telling Kurt why he had left his campaign medal – a Nazi medal – on a Schreiber tombstone.

Kurt paused at the first intersection past the cemetery. Which way? No brown fedora could be seen in any direction. It was as if the man had disappeared. Frustrated, Kurt broke into a jog, straight ahead toward the lake. His bookbag slapped against his back. When he arrived at the park that edged the lake, he stopped and spun around, still searching.

The old man sat on a bench five metres away, staring at Kurt as if he had been expecting him. Both hands were capped on that cane – a carved wolf's head for a real Wolf – and his fedora lay on the bench beside him.

Kurt closed the distance between them. He nodded. "Wolfgang Brandt." It was rude not to refer to an older man as Herr, but right now he didn't care.

The old man nodded in return. "Kurt Schreiber."

"How do you know my name?"

"How do you know mine?"

"I asked the caretaker in the cemetery."

Something – disappointment? – flickered through pale blue grey eyes. Wolfgang Brandt indicated the bench, inviting Kurt to sit. "I knew your grandfather."

Kurt's heart leapt. He clamped his jaw on the surprised gasp wanting to escape. This was what he wanted, wasn't it? A person, not newspaper clippings. A person who could tell him the truth. *Coward*. Not an accusation, but the truth. The medal's edges dug into Kurt's palm. Still standing, he extended his hand and uncurled his fingers.

"You left your war medal on that tombstone. Why?"

"I wanted you to have it."

"Why? It's yours. It's probably pretty valuable being that it's...so old."

"Yes, yes." The old man nodded, his gaze drifting away. He blinked and met Kurt's gaze again. "It is old. But it is not mine."

"Not yours?" Kurt immediately thought of the son mentioned in the newspaper report of his great-grandparents' accident. The son killed by anarchists who had actually been resistance fighters. But that had been in Holland, not in Russia. "Whose then?"

"Your grandfather's, of course."

Kurt's fingers closed over the medal. A soldier got something like this for fighting in a battle. If this was his grandfather's, that meant he had been a soldier. A Nazi soldier. The accusing eyes of the old man in the Paris bistro returned to Kurt's mind. *Sale Boche.* Uncertainty churned Kurt's stomach as he gaped at the old man sitting so calmly, waiting for him to continue. *There are worse fates than being a coward.* Kurt shook his head. He stepped back, holding out the medal as if warding off a curse. "My grandfather was no *Nazi.*"

Wolfgang Brandt eyed him for a moment, his gaze icy. He picked up his fedora and leaned on the cane as he stood. He donned his hat and gripped the cane's shaft, so that the wolf's head glared at Kurt. "I hear the hatred in your words, but you do not know what you are saying, young Schreiber. For the sake of a dear friend, I will forgive your rudeness." The cane struck the sidewalk. "This time."

The old man walked away, his spine stiff and straight. Like an old soldier.

Lowering his gaze, Kurt studied the medal. A Nazi honour, awarded to a Nazi soldier. His grandfather, Kurt Schreiber senior. A Nazi. He spun and hauled his arm back, ready to throw the medal as far as he could.

It couldn't be. The quiet, gentle man who was his grandfather, a Nazi? There had to be an explanation. The lake glistened blue and clear – the colour Wolfgang Brandt's eyes had probably been when he had been much younger. When he had known Kurt's grandfather.

Kurt dropped his arm and stuffed the medal into his jeans pocket.

Chapter Six

Three nights running Kurt had the same dream. By the third night he was determined not to sleep. He fought it as long as possible. But still sleep came, and with it, the dream.

His grandfather is helping to round up Jews. Kurt recognizes the street scene from the movie, *Schindler's List*. His grandfather catches sight of a reflection staring back at him from a shard of glass. The face is Kurt's.

Kurt looks down, shocked to see a *Mauser* in his grasp, more shocked at how comfortable the rifle feels. The people he is guarding stink with fear. They cry and cling to each other. He jostles a man into line and sees a little girl in a red coat slip into a building. No one else spots her. Bile rises in his throat because he knows what's coming. *Don't hide, little girl. Run.*

He blinks and it's dark; the street is empty except for a squad of soldiers. The *Kommandant* orders the house-to-house search to begin. Kurt's legs obey, carrying him into the first building. He clumps through the rooms in heavy boots, kicks open doors, knocks over furniture. He hears other soldiers above him and moves to the next building. And the next.

When he enters the last building in the street, Kurt pauses and shouts, *"Juden! Raus!"* Jews! Out! His words echo down wooden hallways. He bypasses the main floor and thumps up the stairs. The corridor is lit by a single dangling bulb that does little to drive back the darkness. He kicks open the first door and enters, swinging the *Mauser* back and forth. Hungry for a target. *No!* Tattered curtains flutter in a broken window. The only sound in the room is his breathing.

Retreating to the hall, he approaches the next door, his gaze flicking to the last door on the left. He'll leave it this time. He won't look. He searches each room, his breathing growing louder. Sweat plasters his helmet to his head and trickles into his eyes.

Suddenly he is standing before the last door. He doesn't want to go inside. He tries to turn away, but reaches for the doorknob instead. He enters and stands in the middle of a shabby room. The shouts and gunshots from outside fade to an eager hush. Even his breathing quiets.

And then he hears it: a muffled sob.

The sound draws him to the doorway of a narrow bedroom. The only furniture is a simple wooden bed with a straw mattress. A suitcase and other belongings are scattered on the floor.

Kurt crouches down. Round eyes stare back at him. Brown eyes, dark brown curls – how Marta might have looked as a child. Sweet and innocent.

And terrified.

Resolving to let her win this deadly game of hide-and-seek, Kurt tries to stand. *Please let her win.* Against his will, he stretches out his arm and beckons with his black-gloved hand. "*Kom, bitte. Raus.*" His voice is deceptively soft. Come, please. Out.

Solemn brown eyes regard him for a moment. Kurt wants to shout at her to run. Run and never stop running. *I'm a monster. Don't trust me.*

The little girl in the red coat crawls out from under the bed. Kurt stands and smiles. She smiles back. Kurt raises the *Mauser* so its muzzle is almost touching her forehead. Her eyes grow round again.

Kurt woke up bathed in sweat, the rifle shot ringing in his ears.

Chapter Seven

Knocking woke Kurt up. The clock on his bedside table read 9:30. He moaned and threw back the covers. Late for school. Wait, it was Saturday. No school.

Another knock was followed by Frau Klassen poking her head inside Kurt's room. He pulled the sheet back over his boxers. "Kurt? Why are you still in bed? Herr Klassen is almost ready to go." She stepped into the room and studied Kurt's face. "You look terrible. Are you ill?"

Only sick of dreaming, Kurt wanted to say. Three dreams in one night. No. The same dream three times. "I'm all right. Just tired." He had only dozed after the last dream.

She tsked. "You look like you are becoming ill. You need to rest. I will tell Herr Klassen we will have to save our outing for another day."

Kurt rolled onto his side. He heard the door whisper shut and closed his eyes. They sprang back open. He reached over, pulled on the blind's strap so it rolled upward. Morning light poured into the room, driving away the pieces of dreams clinging to corners like cobwebs.

Saturday. Now he remembered. The Klassens were going to take him to see Sachsenhausen, a World War Two prison camp near Berlin, now a museum. A Nazi concentration camp. Kurt squeezed his eyes shut at the word, *Nazi.*

He never told Dad. He never told me. He's lived a lie for over fifty-five years. No, he just didn't tell anyone. Kurt remembered the ethics unit from English class. Keeping quiet about something important was a lie of omission. His grandfather had lied. Why? Because he had been a Nazi, that's why. A monster.

Kurt could have asked his grandmother, Oma, but she had died two years earlier. He had brought it up a few times, but even Oma had been silent on the subject of the past – perhaps on Grandfather's orders. She had taught him some German, though. Their secret language, Oma had called it. Grandfather hadn't allowed his only son to learn German, and he didn't like his grandson learning it, either. They lived in Canada; they should speak English.

So Kurt had never spoken a word of it to Grandfather, especially after the argument he had heard between his father and grandfather when he was in the eighth grade and his father had defended his right to take German classes. Kurt had never believed his father's explanation for the fight – that Grandfather wasn't himself since Oma had become ill.

Grandfather had wanted to leave everything about his past back in Germany, including the language. Now Kurt knew why. He couldn't decide why it mattered – maybe to end a lie told by a man who had always said truth was the path of honour – but he wanted to hear the truth from his grandfather. One time, no matter how ugly.

Stumbling into the washroom, Kurt grimaced at the face in the mirror. Not just pale. The bags under his eyes resembled the black paint North American football players smeared under their eyes. His hair stuck out in spikes, the cooled sweat acting like gel. If Neumeyer saw Kurt like this, he'd have to eat his words about Kurt being a pretty boy. Kurt turned away from the mirror and twisted the shower handle wide open so the water hissed and belched steam.

He entered the kitchen ten minutes later. Frau Klassen patted a wad of cookie dough, laid it on the pan and smiled. "I heard the shower. You look better, but still tired. You should return to bed." Kurt reached for a dough patty; she slapped his fingers. "If you are not sick, eating raw dough will make you so."

Kurt grinned. "I sneak cookie dough from Mom a lot. I've never gotten sick."

"You steal from your mother, do you?" Kurt saw the twinkle in Frau Klassen's eyes. "No doubt she lets you, young man, hoping you *will* get sick and learn a lesson."

"You could teach me a lesson." Kurt stretched out his arm, fingers wiggling like pincers.

She laughed as she snatched the baking sheet and removed it from his reach. "You cannot be very ill if you are acting so foolish. Do you want to go to Sachsenhausen after all?"

"Ah... No, thanks. I want to rest later. Maybe some other day." Or maybe not. He might be interested in history, but his dreams had soured him on visiting a concentration camp any time soon. The last thing he wanted was to start dreaming about being a guard at one of those places. He leaned against the counter and hoped his voice was as casual as his pose. "I met someone the other day who said he knew my grandfather when they were young."

Frau Klassen deposited the baking sheet in the oven and set a small timer on the back of the stove. "Who would that be?"

"His name is Wolfgang Brandt."

Frau Klassen presented her back to Kurt as she washed some utensils. "Ahh. Herr Brandt. A fine man. And very important to our town. He acted as a buffer between us and our Russian masters for many years. I think he saved us from more pain than we will ever know."

A really great guy. A bit touchy about having been a Nazi, though. Kurt kept that observation to himself as he eyed the bowl of cookie dough. "I...need to use the phone."

Frau Klassen turned just as Kurt scooped a clump of dough out of the bowl with his index finger. She gave him one of her exaggerated scowls. "Out of my kitchen, young man. Go make your phone call and keep away from my dough."

In Herr Klassen's den, Kurt sat in the leather chair and dialed, glad for the Klassens' permission to phone home any time he wished.

"Hello?" The phone must have woken up the old man. He sounded frail and far away, even though the connection was good. Kurt winced at his idiocy – Calgary was eight hours behind Berlin so it was only quarter after two in the morning there.

"Hello? Hello?" Grandfather was waking up, sounding angry.

Since he had already goofed, Kurt plunged ahead. *"Guten Tag, Grossvater. Es ist Kurt."* (Good day, Grandfather. It's Kurt.)

A long pause. Finally, the reply came, in English. "Have you forgotten how to speak your mother tongue? English, if you please."

"Danke, nein. Deutsch, bitte." (Thank you, no. German, please.) Kurt held his breath. Was he crazy? He just felt he had

a better chance of getting to the truth if he stuck to German. After an even longer pause, Kurt said, *"Grossvater? Bitte?"* (Grandfather? Please?)

The clock ticked off thirty seconds before his grandfather spoke again, this time in German. "So, you have called to show off how well you speak *my* mother tongue?"

"No, Grandfather. I want..." Kurt took a calming breath. "I want to ask you some questions about the war. What you did. Where you —"

"Leave the past in the past."

How many times had Kurt heard that, growing up? "I need to know, Grandfather. I met a man —"

"You would believe a stranger's lies over your own flesh and blood?"

"My flesh and blood won't tell me anything. Besides, he —"

"You will not talk to anyone about my past. It is my story to tell."

"Then tell it."

Another silence. "You are too young."

"Right. And so is Dad, since you've never told him anything, either. I'm seventeen, Grandfather. When you were seventeen you were probably already killing Russians." Kurt squeezed his eyes shut. What a stupid thing to say.

Grandfather's voice was strained. "Since you know so much, you hardly need an old man to tell you anything." The line went dead.

Kurt stared at the buzzing handset, frustration bubbling like a pot of his mother's chili. *I don't know anything,* he wanted to say. *Only that you got a stupid medal. I want to know about you. I want to know how much of you is in me.* Frustration gave way to disappointment. With a sigh, Kurt laid the handset in its cradle and retreated to his room. He changed into shorts and a T-shirt. One runner lace snapped when he yanked it. He tied the pieces together, his fingers trembling.

When he jogged down the stairs, Frau Klassen called from the kitchen, "The cookies are still hot, how you like them."

"Later. I'm going for a run." Kurt winced when the front door banged behind him.

The conversation replayed through Kurt's mind for a kilometre. Down to the lakeshore, then left to circle the lake. Whether in English or German, he was still a klutz. Grandfather would never talk to him now.

After three kilometres of silently berating himself, Kurt gave himself over to the run. The rhythm pulsed through his muscles and pushed all thoughts out of his head, replacing them with sensations. The runners slapped the road. The breeze ruffled his hair. The air filled his lungs. The smell of sweat stung his nostrils. It was like meditating for Kurt.

He slowed to a fast walk for the last half kilometre to cool off and gather his thoughts. His grandfather deserved an apology. Would Grandfather ever forgive him? Kurt wasn't so sure, because he already knew he was going to disobey his grandfather. He *was* going to talk to someone – if that someone would talk to him.

After Kurt ate lunch and a pile of cookies, he sat through a gentle lecture from Frau Klassen on the dangers of exercising too vigorously when on the verge of being sick. He promised to lie down for a rest as soon as he got back, then left the house, armed with directions on how to find Herr Brandt's house. Like the Klassens' home, it was in an older part of town.

Ten minutes later Kurt stood before an old two-storey house surrounded by a high hedge and guarded by a wrought iron gate. It was small but neat, the masonry freshly painted. Rows of tulips lined the walk. Two children played in the front yard. Herr Brandt had company.

Shoulders hunched, hands in pockets, Kurt headed for home. He thought of going to see Marta but remembered she had family stuff happening all weekend. By the time he got to the Klassens, his lack of sleep had caught up with him. He retreated to his room, pulled down the blind to shut out the afternoon sun and flopped across his bed.

He didn't dream. Two hours of wonderful nothingness.

After an evening spent helping the Klassens in the garden, Kurt was certain he was so weary that nothing could disturb him that night. But the dream returned. Everything was the same, except for the last moments. As always, he walks into the bedroom, following the whimpers. He crouches down and beckons to the little girl in the red coat. As in the earlier dreams, her glistening brown eyes pierce his soul, and he silently pleads for her not to come out even as he tells her to. She doesn't. The person who crawls from under the bed is not the girl. It is Kurt's grandfather, old and weary. They both stand. Kurt raises the *Mauser*.

Kurt woke up before the rifle shot. His feet hit the floor before he was completely aware. He stood beside his bed, legs quivering, gulping in air. When his surroundings sank in – his bedroom, not a shabby 1940s apartment – he sat on the edge of the bed and glanced at the clock. 3:00 a.m. Elbows on knees, he buried his face in his hands. No way was he going back to sleep.

Still shaking, Kurt dressed in the dark. Jeans, shirt, runners. No socks. He stole out of his room. At the outside door, he retrieved his jacket and slipped into the night. He sat on the steps for a few minutes, letting that middle of the night chill clear his mind.

Reluctant to return inside, Kurt walked. He paid little attention to his direction as he paced the streets through pools of yellow light. The night breeze nipped at his cheeks. Twice, dogs alerted the neighbourhood to Kurt's presence. He wound up at Herr Brandt's house. He leaned against the elm tree across the road from the old man's gate and studied the dark building.

Herr Brandt had said "for the sake of a dear friend." Kurt knew he had meant his grandfather. The thought that the two old men had once been friends was enough to encourage Kurt to trust Herr Brandt. His grandfather had always valued honour and loyalty and honesty.

That was a laugh. Honesty. *Leave the past in the past.* His grandfather had stuffed his past into a strongbox. Kurt's gut told him Herr Brandt held the key – if he was willing to use it. He had to be willing. Why else would he have given Kurt that medal? His grandfather's medal. A Nazi medal. It could be a hard truth Kurt was asking to hear. Did he really want to know what his grandfather had done during the war? The truth couldn't be worse than his dreams.

A light came on in Herr Brandt's house. Kurt straightened. His heart began to tap dance. This was not the time, Kurt told himself. He peered at his watch. 4:30. Definitely not the time. He left the shelter of the elm, headed for the lake, a block away, and followed the shore until he was only four blocks from the

Klassens'. Settling on a bench in one of the small parks dotting the lakeside, he waited for the sunrise and wondered how his grandfather could have been a coward and a Nazi. Was it too much to wish he had been neither? The medal didn't allow for that choice. It condemned him more loudly than any words. And Grandfather hadn't denied it.

Maybe his grandfather had been...a nice Nazi. Kurt snorted. Those were two words that didn't belong together. But that guy from the movie, *Schindler's List*, had been good. He had hung out with his Nazi pals at the same time he was saving Jews. And the movie had been about a real man. Grandfather could have been the kind of Nazi that secretly worked to save people. Or he could have been the kind that aimed his *Mauser* at five-year-old girls and pulled the trigger without a second thought.

Frustrated by the way his thoughts were running in circles, Kurt stretched and walked back to the Klassens'. The neighbourhood was waking up. Birds chirped. A car door slammed. A sprinkler started up. Rubbing his neck, Kurt headed up the sidewalk to the Klassens' front door. As he reached for the handle, the door flew open. Startled, he stepped back.

Frau Klassen, still in her bathrobe, hair askew, grabbed his arm and pulled him into the house. "Oh, Kurt. Thank God. You gave me such a fright. I woke in the early hours. Too much tea, you know. When I turned on the washroom light, I noticed your door was ajar. You always sleep with your door closed. Your bed was empty. Your coat was gone." Barely taking a breath, she led Kurt into the living room. "I've been watching for you, wondering if you had run off or gotten into trouble or were hurt. But why would you even go out in the middle —"

"Enough," Herr Klassen's deep voiced boomed, silencing his wife as if he had turned a switch. "Let the boy breathe, if you haven't used up all the oxygen in the room. Let him explain."

Kurt perched on the edge of a rocking chair. The Klassens sat across from him on the sofa. Herr Klassen was dressed, coat on, keys in hand. Kurt dropped his gaze. His host had been preparing to search for him. After a moment's silence, Kurt said, "I had a weird dream and couldn't sleep. I went for a walk and wound up by the lake. I didn't think..." Kurt shrugged. "I just didn't think. I'm sorry I worried you."

Herr Klassen stood and gave his wife a knowing look. "See? Didn't I tell you it was nothing to get upset about?" He turned to Kurt, his expression solemn. "But please do not do it again. If you must prowl the streets in the middle of the night, at least leave us a note."

"Yes, sir."

Herr Klassen gave Kurt a nod; his beard rubbed his chest. "Since I am dressed, and since my mother bakes buns every Saturday evening, I am going to beg some fresh buns for breakfast."

After her husband closed the door behind him, Frau Klassen tsked. "I do tend to think the very worst when someone is even a few minutes late. Hans is so patient with me. He never gets upset." She paused and eyed Kurt speculatively. "You were upset yesterday. Now you are waking from bad dreams. Is this something you want to talk about?"

Kurt shook his head.

"This has to do with your phone call to your grandfather yesterday, yes?"

Kurt nodded. "It's nothing for you to worry about. I'll be fine."

"Yes, I think you will be. And what are you planning on doing this fine Sunday? A little nap to start the day, perhaps? I know that is what I plan to do as soon as Hans returns from his errand and we eat breakfast."

Kurt closed his eyes as he slowly inhaled. "No. I think I will go to the Pergamon."

"Ahh. You do love that museum. And will you take a friend? Marta, perhaps?"

She's busy." Kurt paused. Being alone would be asking for his thoughts to drive him crazy today. "I'll phone Victor and see if he can come."

"Is this a boy from school?"

"Yes. He's in a couple of my classes."

Frau Klassen smiled. "So, I am very glad. You have made friends."

And enemies, thought Kurt, though he would never worry Frau Klassen by saying it.

Kurt waited until eight o'clock, but he still woke Victor up with his call. Victor offered a trade. He would go with Kurt to the museum until early afternoon, then Kurt could join his family on an outing to the Spreewald. Kurt agreed.

Frau Klassen sent Kurt out the door, a third breakfast roll, stuffed with cheese and salami, in hand and a lunch in his backpack big enough to feed him, Victor and a small troupe of street performers, should one happen by. They took the train into Berlin and got off at Hackescher Markt, only a short walk from *Museumsinsel* (Museum Island) and the Pergamon.

Victor hadn't been to the museum for years. It was filled with architecture and antiquities, and Kurt had been there several times over the last eight months. His favourite exhibit was the Gate of Ishtar with its blue glazed bricks and parade of lions.

"This gate was built over 2500 years ago, around 550 B.C.," Kurt said. "That blows me away. Everything in Calgary is so new and we seem to tear down anything old. Did you know King Nebuchadnezzar walked through this gate? He's the guy in the Bible that my Oma told me about. Threw three guys into a furnace because they wouldn't worship some statue he made."

Victor laughed and sat on a bench. "You should hire on as a tour guide. English tourists would love you. And you sure make history more interesting than our teachers."

"How difficult is that?" They shared a grin. Kurt declared, "Time to eat. It was nice of your parents to say they'd pick us up. When will they be here?"

"They were so amazed I was going to a museum that they were happy to make the trip into Berlin." Victor glanced at his watch. "We have twenty minutes."

"Thanks for coming with me, since it isn't your usual thing. Let's head outside and see if we can find an army to share this lunch with."

"Not so fast, Schreiber. You said Frau Klassen packed cookies?"

"Lots of cookies. And the thickest ham sandwiches you've ever seen."

Victor licked his lips. "You don't want to give that away. We might get hungry later."

"Good point."

They shared another grin.

Kurt dozed during the ninety-minute car ride south to the town of Lübbenau. No dreams, but he jerked awake at any loud sound. When they arrived, Victor commented on Kurt's tiredness but didn't ask for details, which was good. How could Kurt explain it? *I keep dreaming I'm in a Steven Spielberg movie, only it's real and I'm a killer – of little girls and grandfathers.*

Kurt shut the thought out of his mind and focused on the coming boat ride.

The Spreewald was like another world. The Spree River split into countless branches and canals, becoming a watery maze like something out of a Tolkien story. Kurt could imagine Gollum lying on a log, paddling his way through the confusion of streams, searching for Frodo and the Ring.

While Victor's parents opted to ride on one of the sightseeing punts with a tour guide poling them through the waterways, Victor and Kurt rented a two-man kayak.

Although it wasn't even May, the lush greenness struck Kurt. He was surprised that houses and farms dotted the banks, many only accessible by water. No motorboats broke the silence. Victor told him only farmers transporting goods to market and emergency vehicles used motors. Even mail delivery was done by a flat-bottomed punting boat. Thatch-roofed houses with carved snakes' heads on the gables and cone-shaped haystacks made by hand added to the sense that the place was a medieval realm rather than a slice of modern-day Germany.

When they entered a narrow canal with trees bending over to form a canopy, Kurt lifted his paddle and arched his neck to stare at the dappled blue and green.

"The girls would love this place," Victor said.

"Hmm?" Kurt kept his gaze skyward until they floated into a patch of sunlight. He gave Victor a puzzled look over his shoulder. "Who?"

"The girls. Rebekka and Marta. This is just the kind of romantic place girls would love."

Kurt studied the stream ahead. "I suppose." There didn't seem to be many hiking trails. Marta would rather go someplace where she could walk.

"So when should we set up that double date?"

Kurt winced inwardly. He had forgotten that Victor thought he and Marta were a couple. "We're not...you know...dating."

"No? You might as well start. You spend so much time together. So we'll make this your first date." Victor grinned. "You can't say you've never wanted to kiss her, even once? She's pretty. I know a few guys who'd ask her out but, like me, they figured she was taken."

"I'm just happy she adopted me as a friend." Kurt rubbed his neck, trying not to think about kissing Marta. "I could ask her. We could go with you, even if we're just friends."

Victor snorted. "Right, Schreiber. Keep telling yourself that. Friends. How about Friday?"

"I'm going to Dresden. Wait, that's Saturday morning. Sure. Friday sounds good. I'll ask Marta and let you know tomorrow." Kurt sank lower in his seat. What was he getting into?

"What's in Dresden?" Victor asked.

"A girl from my exchange group. It's her birthday."

"Whatever you do, don't tell Marta about *her*."

"Too late."

"Bad move, Schreiber, going from one girl's arms into another's in less than a day."

"I'm not going into anyone's arms, Liebermann. I'm just..."

Kurt thought about the way Jessica fluttered around him, always smiling, staring into his eyes. And she had kissed him. He groaned. Marta was right. He was thick-headed. Dresden suddenly looked like a bad idea.

"Just what? Getting into trouble with Marta before your first date?"

"Something like that. And don't call it a date. We're friends. Why mess that up?"

"Keep talking like that and I'll start believing the rumours Neumeyer is spreading."

Kurt shrugged. "They're true. I ran away from him and his gang. If that makes me a coward, so be it. At least I'm not a thug, picking a new victim every year."

"The guy who runs away lives to run another day."

Kurt half turned in his seat and narrowed his eyes. "You ran from Neumeyer?"

"Do I look stupid? He's twice my size. Of course I ran from Neumeyer, when he didn't corner me. Running isn't always cowardice. Sometimes it's self-preservation."

"I guess. But it feels like cowardice."

"No. It feels like cookies. Running always makes me hungry."

Smiling, Kurt dug the bag of cookies from his backpack and tossed it to Victor. "Help yourself." Victor returned it with only two cookies left. As Kurt bit into one, he wondered what Marta would think if he asked her out on a date – a real date. He wasn't sure he wanted to. Being friends was easier. He would be leaving in less than three months anyway.

When the Liebermanns dropped Kurt off, he leaned through the open back window. "If you ever want to run around the lake with me, let me know. I try to do it at least twice a week."

Victor winced. "Around the whole lake? You're crazy. That must be six kilometres."

"Eight, though there's a detour I like to take that makes it ten."

"I'll do 1.5 with you and turn back."

"Deal." Kurt stepped back from the car. "Thank you, Herr and Frau Liebermann."

"You are very welcome," Frau Liebermann replied. "It is so nice to see Victor doing something other than kicking a ball around."

Victor rolled his eyes. Kurt laughed as the car pulled away.

Frau Klassen fed Kurt a late supper. He managed to make a plate of food disappear, despite his claim that he wasn't hungry, but refused Frau Klassen's offer of seconds.

"Marta called twenty minutes before you arrived," Frau Klassen said.

"I think I'll walk over there instead of phoning."

"So long as your homework is done."

Kurt gave her a wry look. His mother couldn't have imagined a better substitute. "You know I did it on Friday afternoon." He stood and rubbed his neck.

"You are still very tired. Maybe you should call her and then go to bed early."

"I'll be fine." *I want to be exhausted before I fall into bed. Too exhausted to dream.*

Kurt changed out of his sweaty shirt. As he was buttoning his blue shirt, he noticed the drawer on his bedside table was open a crack. He slid the drawer open. The medal winked up at him. He took it out and ran his thumb over the words. *WinterSchlacht im Osten, 1941/42.* He folded the red ribbon over the silver medallion and tucked it in his shirt pocket, planning to show Marta and tell her everything.

His traitor feet led him to the elm tree across from Herr Brandt's house. He eyed the gate and front door. From where he was standing that path looked longer than a run around the lake.

A throat cleared.

Kurt spun around, almost tripping over his own feet.

Wolfgang Brandt peered at Kurt from under his brown fedora. "Knocking is more polite than spying." He stepped into the road and walked toward his gate without looking back.

Kurt stared at that board-stiff spine until Herr Brandt disappeared inside his house. It was creepy the way he could appear by your side without a sound. Old men were supposed to wheeze, or their bones were supposed to creak, or something.

The gate squealed as a gust of wind blew it open. Herr Brandt had forgotten to latch it; most people kept their gates locked. Was it an invitation? Kurt crossed the street. He grabbed the curved upper bar. It was cool under his sweaty palm. He considered the tree behind him and the door in front of him. He was halfway there. No point in turning back now.

Taking care to latch the gate, Kurt pivoted and strolled up the sidewalk, pretending a calm he didn't feel. On either side, the rows of red and yellow tulips nodded in the breeze.

Kurt hesitated with one foot on the bottom step. He was supposed to be at Marta's. If she called back for him, Frau Klassen would worry again. The board groaned as he stepped up. He stood before the dark brown door, looked for a doorbell but saw only a brass knocker hanging in the middle of the door, at chin level. A wolf's head with a ring hanging from its mouth.

He could still walk away. Run, if it came to that. Kurt looked over his shoulder toward the beckoning freedom of the street. But then he might never know the truth.

Kurt grabbed the brass ring and banged it against its plate.

Chapter Eight

Kurt released the brass ring and stared at the wolf's head that held it. What was he doing knocking on Wolfgang Brandt's door when he was supposed to be at Marta's?

He rubbed his neck. He was beyond tired; his eyes stung with the effort of staying open. He leaned right and tried to peer beyond the window's reflection. What was taking so long? Had he misunderstood Herr Brandt's comment about knocking instead of spying? Blowing out his breath, Kurt shoved his hands in his jeans pockets and turned to go. A cavity settled in his gut.

A click spun Kurt back around. Herr Brandt held the door half open. "Yes, yes. Young Schreiber, you decided to stop lurking. But were you leaving? You need to learn patience when knocking at an old man's door. My legs will not carry me as fast as I would like." He opened the door wide. "Come in. I was making myself some tea. Would you like a cup?"

Kurt disliked the bitter aftertaste of many teas, but he said, "Thank you."

The narrow hall faced a stairway and opened to a cramped dining room on the left. A bouquet of daisies gleamed on a round cherrywood table, white on black.

Herr Brandt indicated the small living room on the right. "Make yourself comfortable. I will bring the tea." He cut through the dining room toward a door in its back corner.

Kurt sat in one of two plaid, wingback chairs. He fingered the arm's woven material. A pole lamp behind the other chair acted like a spotlight, throwing the rest of the room into shadow. Dark gold curtains were drawn against the evening sun. The colour was repeated in light gold walls and warm wood floor. Dark moldings and trim, a brown leather loveseat, an old-styled heater between the chairs, all made Kurt feel as if he had stepped into a different time. Except for the book on the round pedestal table under the lamp. *The Falls* by Ian Rankin. Kurt's mother liked that author. He hadn't expected Herr Brandt to read something so current, or so English.

"Here we are."

Kurt jumped to his feet.

"Sit down." Herr Brandt set a tray on the side table at Kurt's elbow. "I took the liberty of adding a little lemon for you."

"Ah...thanks." The pale liquid almost glowed in the white cup. "Could I use your phone?"

"Yes, yes." Herr Brandt waved at the corner by the loveseat. "I do not own one of those fancy cordless things, but I am certain you will manage."

Kurt slipped across the room and dialed Marta's number. She answered on the second ring. Kurt smiled at the sound of her brisk greeting. "Hi. Frau Klassen told me you called."

"Yes. My family party ended after supper. How was Spreewald?"

"Great. I'm not at home, so I can't talk. Could we walk to school together tomorrow?"

"Yes. I'll come by your house."

"Good. See you then. Bye." Kurt placed the black handset back in its cradle.

Halfway between the loveseat and chair, Kurt hesitated. Herr Brandt sat studying Kurt as if he were a new species of insect. Which was how Kurt felt. He almost wished he could scurry out of sight, under the loveseat, or better yet, out of the house. He cleared his throat. "If this is a bad time, I could come back..." He edged toward the door.

"You are here. I invited you in. So, sit. Despite my name, I rarely bite."

A faint smile tugged at Kurt's mouth. He returned to the chair and sipped the tea, so weak it was almost like drinking hot lemon juice. It was worse than overly strong tea – at least that had some flavour. He set the cup down with a rattle. Why was he here?

"So why are you here, Kurt? May I call you Kurt?"

Startled by the echo of his own thoughts, Kurt jerked his gaze to the old man's face. It was quite smooth for someone who had to be well over eighty. Fine lines framed his eyes and mouth. The skin along his jaw only sagged a bit. A silver crewcut topped his high forehead.

"Kurt is fine, sir." He looked away. The old man's grey blue eyes were like steel traps – not letting you go, probing under your skin. Kurt rubbed his neck. He usually found it easy to talk to adults; it must be his tiredness that was making him feel awkward. "I'm here...to find out about my grandfather, I guess. I want to know what he was like when he was young."

"He is...alive?" An odd tightness filled the old man's voice.

Kurt nodded.

"So ask him."

With a sigh, Kurt said, "I did. He doesn't want to talk about it."

"What makes you think I would speak of things he will not?"

Kurt pressed his fingers against his burning eyes. He stood, took three steps, spun around. "I need to know. I can't even –" He pulled the medal from his shirt pocket and held it out. "Why did you leave this on the tombstone? You knew I would find it, didn't you?"

The old man nodded. "I did. I was hoping you would return – if you were not a ghost. I saw you coming down the street before I entered the cemetery. I even saw you trying to hide behind that tree." He leaned forward. "I have good eyes. I also see that you are tired. Your eyes are bloodshot, did you know that? What is keeping you awake, Kurt Schreiber? That medal?"

Kurt shrugged and looked away.

"If you want honesty from me, young Schreiber, then you will have to give it."

Kurt stuffed his hands in his pockets. "I've been... dreaming."

"Not pleasant dreams if they keep you from sleep. Dreams about the medal?"

Kurt shook his head. He exhaled slowly. "About being a N–, a soldier and shooting –" He squeezed his eyes shut. He hadn't intended to say anything about the dream to anyone, but Herr Brandt's smooth voice was so insistent.

"I see."

What did he see? The medal dug into Kurt's hand as his fingers wrapped around it. "I need to know if Grandfather really was a... And what he did. If I have –"

"You leave many blanks. Shall I fill them in? You want to know if your grandfather really was a Nazi. And if you have... What? Tainted blood?"

Kurt looked up sharply.

The old man nodded. "Nazis were always very concerned about such things."

"I'm no Nazi."

"I did not say you were. Are you afraid you might become one?"

Kurt retreated to the chair and sat, shoulders hunched. He muttered, "Blood will tell."

Herr Brandt cupped his hand around his ear. "Blood will...tell? Who told you that?"

"Oma used to say it. I think she was trying to...warn me."

"Nonsense." Herr Brandt sipped his tea. "Has your grandfather told you nothing at all?"

"No. He hasn't told Dad, either. This medal..." Kurt pulled it from his pocket and laid it on his thigh. "...is the first I've ever known about anything in Grandfather's past. I mean, he talked about his early days in Canada, but never anything before that."

Herr Brandt raised one bushy grey eyebrow. "And if I choose to tell you what you want to know, do you think you will be able to sleep?"

"I...hope so. The truth can hardly be worse than what I've been imagining."

"Do not be too sure about that, young man. Those were terrible times." Herr Brandt pushed to his feet. "I am not so sure I want to speak of them, not even for the sake of an old friend's grandson." He held out his hand and Kurt gave him the medal. He stared at it.

Quiet ticking floated from the dining room. Kurt stifled a yawn.

The old man's eyes had a faraway look in them. Suddenly, they cleared. "Perhaps I will help you. But I want something from you in return."

Kurt stood. "What?"

"Your grandfather's telephone number. I lost contact with him five years ago."

Kurt thought back to when he had been twelve. "That was the year Oma got sick and they moved into Calgary to be closer to us. Do you have a pen?"

Herr Brandt pointed to the table with the telephone. Kurt spotted the pad and pen. He sat down. Pen poised above the paper, Kurt looked up. "You were friends, right?"

With a curt nod, Herr Brandt said, "Closer than brothers."

"Why did you have his medal?"

"When I tell a story, I tell it from the beginning. You are asking about the last chapter."

"But he gave it to you?" Kurt winced. "I mean, I don't think..."

Herr Brandt chuckled. "Your rudeness is forgiven. You are trying to protect your grandfather." He tossed the medal; it bounced on the sofa and landed by Kurt's leg. "He left it on the tombstone, just as I did."

Kurt wrote down the telephone number.

"Thank you," Herr Brandt whispered. "We only ever wrote letters. The telephone was so expensive, and who knew if unfriendly ears were listening. It will be good to hear his voice."

Kurt started to pocket the medal, hesitated, then did so after Herr Brandt nodded. "I'd like to hear everything right now, but...it is getting late. Could I come back one day this week?"

"Thank you. That might be best. My children and grand-children overran my house this weekend. They celebrate my birthday by wearing me out." Herr Brandt's smile was thin.

"Oh. Happy birthday. I saw your grandchildren playing in the yard yesterday."

"Yes, yes, thank you. My great-grandchildren, more likely. They are three and four years old. And what did you see in my yard at 4:30 in the morning?"

Kurt flushed. "I...didn't think you had seen me. I left right after the light went on."

"I have lived in this house since 1946. I can move around without lights." The old man winked. "I am glad you admitted it was you. My eyesight is not that good. I turned on the light because I feared the spy might be a burglar."

"Sorry. That was dumb of me. I couldn't sleep so I went for a walk." Kurt hesitated. "Could you answer one question before I go?"

"If I can."

"Were you and Grandfather real Nazis?"

"Real?"

Kurt shrugged. "I guess I hoped...that Grandfather had been some kind of resistance fighter, working undercover, get-ting information to the Allies."

Herr Brandt laid his hand on Kurt's shoulder. "I am afraid neither of us can make such a claim. As for being Nazis, it depends on how you define the word. What does it mean to you?"

"I..."

"You think it is another word for monster."

Kurt's gut wrenched. He scuffed the floor with his toe, unable to respond as he worked a lump in his throat. Unable to deny the pressing weight of that word. *Monster.*

"You will find, as you age, that things are never so black and white as we would like. We live in a grey world, young man, and the lines between good and bad often blur or disappear." Herr Brandt gave Kurt's shoulder a squeeze. "Will it help your sleep to know that we were both *Wehrmacht*? Regular soldiers, not the dreaded ss. We never got around to actually joining the Nazi party, but I cannot deny that the army served the Nazi government. I have a medal like your grandfather's. We got them fighting a battle that the Führer himself ordered."

The Führer. Hitler. Kurt stared at the old man's chin, not wanting to see what memories lurked in his eyes.

"You are making me get ahead of myself," Herr Brandt said. "Go home. Know that your grandfather was not a monster. Sleep."

Kurt raised his eyes. "Thank you. I'll try."

The old man opened the front door. As Kurt's shoe hit the sidewalk, he thought he heard a whisper: *"Guten Abend, Jäger."* He looked over his shoulder, but the door was closed.

Chapter Nine

"**Y**ou wanted to talk, but you haven't said a word in three blocks." Marta swung her bookbag forward and back as she walked. "Where were you last night?"

"Remember I told you about that man in the cemetery? I was at his house."

"The *creepy* old man? Was that smart? Maybe he invites young men into his house and poisons them."

"*Arsenic and Old Lace.*"

"What?"

"It's an old movie starring Cary Grant, about two wacky old ladies who poison men and stash the corpses in the basement."

"Oh! You and your old movies." Marta rammed her shoulder against Kurt's arm, almost sending him into the street. He grabbed a lamppost and swung around it.

"Hey! Maybe you should try out for the Calgary Flames." At her blank look Kurt added, "Hockey team. They need good defencemen and you have a vicious bodycheck." Kurt grinned. He felt good this morning. For one thing, he had slept. Maybe having the medal under his pillow had kept the dream away. Or maybe it was knowing he was going to find out the truth.

"So what did the old man tell you?"

"He and Grandfather were both soldiers. *Wehrmacht*, not ss." Kurt wasn't sure what the difference was, but he hoped that Herr Brandt would explain. "They weren't party members, though."

"They were unusual, then, even if they were in the army. Most jobs in Germany back then required people to be party members. Only fools are proud of that awful time in our history, but we can't change it; we can only make sure it doesn't happen again. But why should it matter so much to you?"

"It's hard to explain. Canadians fought against the Nazis, so to have a Nazi in the family feels... Never mind. Anyway, he told me I could return and he'd tell me about when he and Grandfather were friends and what they did."

"That's good, right?"

"Yes." Definitely. Goodbye dream.

"So that's what you wanted to tell me?"

Kurt watched a Mercedes convertible cruise past. He craned his neck when it disappeared behind a row of parked cars. Marta elbowed him. "What did you want to tell me?"

Massaging his ribs, Kurt said, "You'll laugh."

They rounded a corner. The school came into view. A stream of students, on bicycles and on foot, poured toward the main doors from every direction.

"I will not laugh. I promise."

"Well..." Kurt blew out his breath. Talking to an old man was much easier than talking to a pretty girl. Not that he had any trouble talking to Marta. He didn't. But he usually talked to her as a friend, not as...a what? A possible girlfriend? He started to walk faster. "Forget it."

"No." Marta caught up with him, grabbed his arm and yanked him to a standstill. "This doesn't have anything to do with that coward stuff, does it?"

"In a way." Victor would think he was a coward if he didn't ask. "No, it doesn't."

"You are confusing me. Just...tell me. I'm not letting go until you do."

A pair of girls walked by them. Heat brushed Kurt's cheeks when he heard them giggle. "Fine. Victor thinks..."

"Go on."

"He thinks we're...a couple."

A laugh erupted from Marta. She clamped her hand over her mouth. "Sorry." The word was muffled. Her eyes sparkled amusement.

"I told him you'd laugh."

Marta dropped her hand from her mouth and released Kurt. "You surprised me, that's all. Why did you need to tell me what Victor thinks?"

A trickle of sweat ran down his neck. "He thinks... He and Rebekka are going to a movie on Friday night and he asked if we wanted to go with them." There. He had said it.

"*He* wants to know if *we* want to go? Like a double date?"

Kurt shrugged. "I told him we're not dating. We could go anyway. Friends go to movies."

"We have gone to movies before."

"Right. We would just be going with a couple of other friends, that's all."

Marta nodded. Kurt couldn't tell what she was thinking behind her solemn mask. "So what do you think? Do you want to go?"

"Do you?"

"I... Sure. Why not?"

"No. I mean do you want to go *with me*?"

Kurt's gaze dropped to her mouth. He had never noticed the curve of her bottom lip before, how it was full but not too full. Inviting. Tension coiled in his stomach. He swallowed hard and blinked. "Of course I want to go with you. What kind of a question is that?"

She sighed. "A foolish one. Come. The bell is going to ring in a minute."

As they climbed the school's four steps, a voice on their left called, "It's the coward. Where's he been hiding all weekend?"

A round of laughter followed. Kurt paused. Peter Neumeyer and his friends sat on a low wall, slapped their legs and pointed at Kurt. Marta tugged on his arm. Peter sneered and Kurt could almost hear the comment about letting girls protect him. He shook free of Marta's grip and took a step toward the group of young men, who fell silent. "I've been around, Neumeyer."

"I know. Stephan saw you running on Saturday." Kurt had seen Stephan, too, south of town, horsing around with a boat near the lakeshore. He had thought Stephan hadn't noticed him. Peter added, "How far does a coward run to keep in shape?"

"Eight, sometimes ten, kilometres. But I don't even need half a kilometre to outrun you." Several of Peter's friends snickered. Kurt headed into the school. Behind him, Peter yelled at someone to shut up.

As the bell rang, Marta said, "He will hurt you for that."

"He has to catch me first."

Marta elbowed him. "You promised me a movie on Friday. That doesn't mean a movie on a thirty centimetre hospital TV."

Kurt cast Marta a sidelong glance. "Does that mean you'll go with me?"

"Yes, but you're paying, even if we are just friends."

"Deal."

The morning flew by. During Sports class, they ran hurdles. Kurt and Victor offered to help the teacher put them away. As they loaded the flexible hurdle stands onto a trolley, the teacher commented on Kurt's ability. "Too bad you don't qualify to join the track team."

Kurt recalled Peter tripping over a hurdle and falling onto his hands and knees, then getting up, red faced and furious. He set another hurdle on the trolley and smiled. "It's just a matter of finding your rhythm. Like breathing when you run."

The teacher nodded. "Only a runner understands that. I mention *rhythm* to soccer players and they laugh and ask if they were accidentally enrolled in dance class."

Victor grimaced behind the teacher's back. Kurt grinned. "That sounds like what a hockey player would say. I saw a bumper sticker once that read 'Be kind to animals. Hug a hockey player.'"

The teacher laughed and said, "The showers are waiting. Thanks for your help."

Kurt and Victor jogged toward the school, slowing a half dozen metres before the door.

"Hug a hockey player?" Victor rolled his eyes.

"Sure. Though here in Europe you could probably say soccer player."

"Hah. Soccer fan, maybe. We players are very civilized."

Kurt threw his arm across Victor's shoulders and squeezed. Victor pulled away and gave Kurt a dark look. "What are you doing, Schreiber?"

"Being kind to animals."

"So funny. Save your hugging for Marta. Are you two coming Friday?"

Kurt nodded and tried not to look pleased. But Victor's grin made his break loose. "We're going as friends. Okay?"

Victor shrugged. "Your loss, Schreiber."

He pushed the change room door open and headed for his locker. Kurt swung around to the second row to get his towel. He froze. Peter was leaning against his locker, arms crossed, muscles bulging under his black T-shirt. Kurt stepped back and bumped into a wall of flesh. He sidestepped so he could see both Peter and his friend, Wil.

"Make sure Herr Instruktor stays out, Wil." The friend nodded. He was almost as big as Peter, but not so muscled. Peter said, "And Liebermann?"

"Steiger is keeping him quiet," Wil said.

"Good. Schreiber, you and I are going to have a talk." Peter indicated the shower room.

Kurt glanced at Wil, who glared back. "Leave Victor out of this."

Peter sneered. "Funny how cowards band together. Steiger won't hurt your pal unless he gets noisy." He turned and sauntered toward the showers, as if confident Kurt would follow.

Kurt closed his eyes for a second. It would be easy to bolt into the safety of the school hallway. Would Peter punish Victor for it? He couldn't take that chance. It was a win-win situation for Peter. If Kurt ran, his cowardice was confirmed. If he didn't run, Peter caught him.

After kicking the bench in the center of the aisle, Kurt marched into the shower room. As he stepped inside, Peter's long arm snaked out and grabbed Kurt's wrist. A fist glanced off Kurt's cheek as he was turning, but still felt like a hammer blow. He staggered to the side.

Peter jerked Kurt back and twisted thick fingers into the front of his T-shirt. "Now we talk." His grip tightened; his knuckles pressed against Kurt's throat. "I've never liked you, Schreiber."

"I think I noticed," Kurt rasped. His cheek throbbed and his eye was swelling shut.

"You have a smart mouth."

"Can't seem to help it."

"You'd better learn how." Peter shoved.

Kurt slammed against the wall, grazing a shower tap. He sank to the floor, holding his ribs and biting his lip. Peter booted Kurt's thigh. And again. Kurt grunted and tried to press himself against the wall to escape the mini-explosions of pain.

"Listen closely, Schreiber." Peter hovered over him like a giant vulture seeking a sign that the victim was dead so the feast could begin. "I'm going easy on you because I think you're a quick learner. Embarrass me in front of my friends again and I'll take a crowbar to this leg. Then we'll see how far and how fast you can run."

Peter's shoe sank into Kurt's thigh again, drawing a gasp as agony flashed outward. Peter stepped aside and cranked on the cold water. Then he walked out.

The cool tile soothed Kurt's cheek. Icy water sprayed down, soaking him in seconds. He sat with eyes closed and let the water numb his leg. He heard a shout. A door banged. Footsteps drew near. The water stopped.

Kurt opened the one eye that he still could and squinted up at Victor, who stood shaking his head. "Didn't you hear what I said about self-preservation yesterday?"

Victor hooked his hand under Kurt's arm to help him up. Kurt couldn't raise his voice above a whisper. "And let you have all the fun? Besides, I think he's starting to like me. He thinks I'm a quick learner." He groaned when he tried to put weight on his pulsing right leg.

"Lucky you." Victor frowned. "You're bleeding. Look at your T-shirt."

Kurt peered down at his left side, at the growing pink spot under his hand. He let Victor roll up the white T-shirt and they both examined a wide scrape. Kurt touched a finger to the raw skin and grimaced. "I'm going to have a bruise. Nothing feels broken, though."

"You know what broken ribs feel like?"

"Yes. A cross-country run when I was fifteen. Took a tumble, landed on some rocks."

"Broken ribs from slipping on a few rocks?"

"It was the two-metre fall to the rocks that did it. Doctor said I was lucky that was all I broke. I didn't feel lucky." Kurt took a hissing breath and pressed his back against the wall. "I couldn't breathe for the first week without it hurting, could barely move for two weeks. This...is nothing." Kurt winced anyway, as he tugged his T-shirt over his head and dropped it on the floor.

"You're going to have a black eye, too." Victor picked up the shirt.

"No kidding? That would explain why it feels like a grenade went off by my face."

"Yes, that's what I remember Peter's fist feeling like."

"What about his kicks? Did he wear steel-toed boots back then, too?" Kurt grimaced as he tried again to put weight on his right leg. He leaned back against the wall, wishing he could borrow Herr Brandt's cane.

"How many times did he kick you?"

Kurt leaned on Victor and hobbled toward his locker. "Three, I think."

"Did he say why?"

"He doesn't want me to be able to run so fast. I made some stupid comment this morning about being able to outrun him easily."

"You're right. Sounds stupid. You need to learn to keep your mouth shut around Peter."

"He said the same thing." Kurt sat on the bench, glad that his locker was low. He toweled his chest dry, shrugged into his grey and green shirt and buttoned it, his fingers fumbling over the simple task.

"As soon as we're changed, we'll go to the office," Victor said.

"No chance, Liebermann."

"This is more than a little bullying, Schreiber. The head-master might want to call the police."

"No headmaster. No police. I'll handle it."

"Yes. We've seen how well you can handle it."

Kurt exploded. "I'll handle it!" He held his splayed hand up. "I'm sorry. I'm sorry. I just...need to get home and rest. Okay? No police. My parents would flip. They'd have me on the first plane heading to Canada. I can't go back. Not yet."

Victor ran fingers through his wavy hair. "If that's the way you want it."

"It is." Kurt added, "I didn't mean to yell. Thanks...for all your help."

"Sure. It's what friends do."

"Are we friends?"

"I thought so."

Kurt's smile was twisted by pain. "Good."

Victor indicated Kurt's leg. "How are you going to get home if you can barely walk?"

"Very slowly. Hopefully I'll be there for supper."

"I'll call my mother to give us a ride. She always has a late lunch."

"Thanks."

"She'll want to know what happened."

"I'll tell her I fell in the shower."

"You think she will believe that?"

"Sure. Parents like to believe the simple explanation. And it's true...in a way. My real problem will be explaining this to Marta. She will grill me until she knows every last detail." What would he tell her? *I cowered and let Peter beat me.*

He thought of a little girl, eyes wide with fear as she crawled out from under a bed, himself standing over her with a gun. *Better a coward than a Nazi*, he thought.

Chapter Ten

Kurt gripped Herr Brandt's gate and shifted his weight to the left leg. He waited for the ache in his right leg to fade. Peter had left a big three-leaf-clover bruise of angry purple and, from years of running, Kurt knew his thigh muscles were hurt. He forced himself to walk, to keep limber, though it woke the pain. It had only been twenty-six hours. In a few days the pain would disappear and he could start running again. In the meantime he would continue avoiding Peter.

The afternoon stretched before Kurt, empty and boring. No homework. Marta was running errands for her mother. Victor was at his father's garage, filling in for a sick employee. And Kurt couldn't endure another afternoon of being clucked over by Frau Klassen.

The wolf's head knocker gleamed against the dark door and beckoned Kurt. He had no idea whether Herr Brandt was home. He should have called. He unlatched the gate but didn't move.

Kurt closed his eyes. The dream had returned just before dawn. The same start; a different ending again. As he was searching the houses, looking for hiding Jews, knowing he would find the girl, he realized he was being followed. Hunted.

He fled through empty apartments, catching glimpses of a black uniform, black boots, a pistol. No face. He ran, clutching his rifle like a shield. Onto a rooftop. The dark figure followed. He charged a gap between two buildings and jumped. A shot rang out. And that's when he had awakened, cold with sweat, his grandfather's medal clutched tight, fingers numb.

Kurt's hands throbbed. He forced his white-knuckle grip to relax. Taking a breath, he pushed the gate open and strolled down the sidewalk. Tried to stroll. He rolled out each step so he didn't limp. Up the three steps to the dark brown door.

The knocker had a tinny echo as Kurt banged it against the small plate under the ring. The brass wolf's head stared at him with knowing eyes. Kurt heard a muffled, "Yes, yes," through the thick wood. The door swung open. Surprise filled Herr Brandt's eyes. "Ja–. Kurt! I was not sure when to expect you again." He stepped outside and closed the door.

"I'm sorry I didn't call ahead, sir. I hope it's all right, dropping by like this."

"Old men love company." Herr Brandt paused. "Your dreams are becoming more violent."

Kurt touched his tender left cheekbone. "No. I'm just becoming more clumsy."

"Ah, you fell against someone's fist, did you?"

"Something like that." Kurt had no trouble admitting the truth to Herr Brandt, who didn't treat him like a child as so many adults did. "The class bully decided I needed a lesson."

"Did you learn one?"

"Stay out of his reach."

"Not always possible, I fear." Herr Brandt laid his hand on

Kurt's shoulder and guided him down the steps. "It is too nice to sit in the house. We will try the garden."

Kurt let Herr Brandt lead the way. He didn't want the old man to notice his limp. A shed sat in one corner of the garden. Fruit trees ready to blossom were scattered around the yard. Herr Brandt settled in a wicker chair by two apple trees and waved at the matching white loveseat. Kurt sat with his right leg outstretched. The uneven surface irritated the scrape on his ribs. He tried not to wince as he shifted to the right. The old man watched him but said nothing.

"So, you are anxious to hear about the past are you?"

"Yes." Kurt peered over Herr Brandt's shoulder to a canopied patio swing near steps that lead down to the back door in the cellar. His mother had a similar swing on their deck. If Frau Klassen told his mother about the beating, she would make him come home and he would never know the truth. The cellar door squeaked as someone opened it. Kurt eyed legs gracefully ascending the stairs, long legs accented by a slim green skirt ending above the knees. The skirt was familiar. His gaze flew up.

Marta's attention was on the tray in her hands, its pitcher and two glasses. "Opa, you disappeared on me. Why didn't you say –" She gaped at Kurt. "What are you doing here?"

"I..." Heat crept up Kurt's neck. "I'm visiting Herr Brandt. What are you...?" Kurt trailed off. She had said "Opa"; Herr Brandt was her grandfather. Oh, great.

Marta's eyes widened, then narrowed as a frown dropped down over her forehead. "Opa is your 'creepy old man'? You think my grandfather is creepy?"

Kurt felt Herr Brandt's regard. He peered sideways, but saw only curious amusement. "That first day when you appeared out of nowhere, looking so white, it was weird." He shrugged in apology.

"For me, as well," Herr Brandt replied. "So you know my granddaughter. No introductions are necessary, then." He raised both brows, pinning Kurt with his blue gaze. "It is polite for a gentleman to assist a lady."

"Oh. Right." Kurt had hoped Marta wouldn't see him walk until his limp was gone. He stood, flinching when his right leg protested. Herr Brandt nodded encouragement. Kurt's attempt at a casual saunter failed. His leg muscles clenched and he ended up limping across the grass. He took the tray from Marta, whose frown had grown fiercer.

"Why are you limping?"

"It's a prerun stretching exercise."

Marta pursed her lips. "I'll get another glass for the lemonade." She spun and marched down the stairs into the house, arms swinging.

Kurt hobbled back to Herr Brandt and set the tray on a small table between the chair and loveseat. He sank down with a sigh.

"Lying is never good for a friendship," Herr Brandt observed.

"That wasn't lying. It was sarcasm." Kurt gently massaged his thigh.

"I see. So that makes it acceptable?"

"As acceptable as lying by saying nothing. Maybe lying in its many forms is something else I inherited from my grandfather."

"You will not speak with disrespect when you speak of my old friend." Before Kurt could speak, Herr Brandt held up his hand. "You should know that I spoke with your grandfather yesterday morning. Well, in the new hours of the morning. It was still Sunday in Calgary, around five o'clock, I believe. After you left, I could not sleep. So I called him."

Marta came out of the house, carrying a plate of cookies and a glass. Kurt only spared her a glance. A band around his chest tightened. "And?"

"We had a very long visit. A good visit. We should have done so years ago."

Kurt leaned left to see past Marta as she poured herself a glass of lemonade. "Did you mention...?" He searched the old man's face for a clue to what he was thinking. Now he knew where Marta got her ability to hide her thoughts.

"Yes, yes. We spoke of my giving you the campaign medal. And of your dream trouble."

"What dream?" Marta asked as she sat down on the loveseat.

Kurt ignored the question. Would Herr Brandt refuse to talk now that he had spoken to Grandfather? Why couldn't he have waited? Tension snaked from Kurt's belly into his throat.

Herr Brandt bit an oatmeal cookie and chewed thoughtfully. "After a long talk, your grandfather decided..." He tilted his head. "That I should tell you what you wish to know."

The breath Kurt had been holding whooshed out; he sagged against the wicker back.

"You should have more faith in your grandfather, young man. When I explained how earnestly you needed to know, he agreed. Kurt Schreiber the elder is a man of integrity. I see hints that perhaps his grandson has also inherited *that* trait."

"Thank you," Kurt whispered. He was more relieved than he had expected that Grandfather had given his blessing.

"Do you know why he has never spoken of his past?" Herr Brandt asked.

"Not really. Was it because he didn't want anyone to know he was a Nazi?"

"Nonsense." Herr Brandt scowled. "He was afraid. You know what that's like, don't you, young Schreiber?"

Kurt shrugged and looked away. He wasn't sure he wanted to know this particular detail, but after a moment he asked, "Why?"

"Because he lied to get into Canada. He claimed he had spent the last few months of the war resting from injuries suffered on the western front and that he came from a town in the west. There was no way to confirm the story. He had good reason to lie. Many who had fought on the Russian front and surrendered to Americans or British were then handed over to the Russians. As a result, he never wished to speak of it, for fear the Canadian government would find out he had lied and would send him back to Germany."

"But Germany is a beautiful country," Kurt said.

"Germany in 1945 was a pile of rubble. Every major city except Heidelberg had been almost leveled. Even seeing the pictures you cannot imagine... Everything was in short supply: food, shelter, pride." Herr Brandt closed his eyes. "We were a beaten people. Even in West Germany, where the Allied countries poured money into reconstruction, it took years for life to return to normal. Here in what was East Germany, it took much longer. Compared to Germany, Canada was a land of milk and honey. Your grandfather was right to want to stay there."

"It's good he left then. He missed all that," Marta said.

Kurt frowned. "But Grandfather said he came to Canada late in 1946."

"Yes, yes," Herr Brandt said. "He tasted the devastation of our homeland for over a year before he escaped. No government moves fast in such matters, though eighteen months was quick, I think. A newspaper friend of his father's who had moved to Canada before the war sponsored him. While he waited for his papers he worked for a farmer at Braunschweig."

Brunswick on an English map. "But that's a long ways west. Why wasn't he here?"

Herr Brandt shook his head. "*Ach!* Do you think the Russians would have let a German soldier who had fought on the eastern front just leave? Never!" A heavy scowl drew his brows together. "You are making me get ahead of myself again. I told you that if you heard the story, it would be from the beginning."

Marta said, "Opa has been writing his memoirs. He keeps telling us that he must write it down, from the beginning. And we cannot read it until he has reached the end." She rolled her eyes. "Now you get to hear the beginning before any of us. It's not fair." She slid sideways, bumping Kurt's shoulder and thigh. Pain erupted.

Kurt yelled and twisted away. Marta jumped up. "What! What's wrong with your leg?"

Eyes squeezed shut, Kurt whispered, "Bruised."

"Oh, no. It takes more than a little bruise to make you yell like that."

"Did I say little?" He squinted up, saw the concern darkening her chocolate eyes and was slapped by guilt for not having told her what had happened.

Marta sat back down. "How did you get hurt? You told me the black eye was from slipping in the shower at school. Is that true?"

"Sort of." Kurt glanced at Herr Brandt, who nodded. He turned back to Marta. "I did fall in the shower, but...I had some help."

"Help?" Shock crept over Marta's face, rounding her eyes and arching her eyebrows.

"Why are you so surprised? You're the one who told me Peter was going to hurt me for mouthing off at him. It turns out I was easier to catch than I thought."

Marta sprang to her feet again and began pacing. "Peter Neumeyer did this to you? Your eye, your leg." She halted and glared at Kurt. "Any other injuries I should know about?"

"A scrape on my ribs." Kurt shrugged. "I'll be all right. Don't make a big deal about this."

"Don't make –" She resumed pacing. "He ambushed you in the shower room after class, didn't he? Were you even dressed? No! Don't answer that. I don't want to know."

Marta blushed, a rosy hue that matched her lips. Kurt was transfixed; he had never seen her embarrassed before. It made her even prettier. She continued; six steps, spin, six steps back, spin. Both men, old and young, watched her as if she were a ball in a tennis match.

She halted in front of Kurt and planted her fists on her hips. "Did you already go to the police? If not, we need to go today."

"No, and no."

"No?"

Kurt started to stand, then thought better of it. "Letting anyone – police, headmaster, parents – know I've been in a fight could get me sent home, Marta. We had to sign agreements, including rules of conduct, to come on the exchange. Fighting was very high on the forbidden list. If my mom knew, she'd come over here and drag me home." He shot a worried glance at Herr Brandt.

"I believe you should tell the authorities – not doing so only gives the bully power over you he should not have," the old man said, "but I will say nothing if you wish it."

"Thank you, sir." Kurt held Marta's gaze. "I don't want to go home, Marta. I want to hear my grandfather's story. I want..." *To kiss you, just once.* Where had that thought come from? Victor, of course. From Sunday. He released his breath. "I like it here, Marta." He searched her face, hoping she would understand. He could hardly say "I like you" in front of her grandfather.

"You...like it here?" Marta whispered. An unreadable look shuttered her eyes.

"Very much."

"Yes, yes. So we know Kurt wants to stay, and we will keep our silence so he can."

Herr Brandt's voice snipped the thread that had connected their gazes. When Marta sank to the loveseat, Kurt stood. He limped around the loveseat and braced himself against a tree branch.

"But now that Peter has hurt Kurt once, he will enjoy doing it again," Marta said.

"Then Kurt will have to find some other way to deal with this bully."

Simple. Grow eight centimetres and put on fifteen kilograms, preferably by tomorrow morning. Kurt avoided Marta's scrutiny and inhaled the sappy sweet smell of the leaves. Time to change the subject. "When did you and Grandfather join the army?"

"That is also getting ahead of the story. I think this story must start earlier than that, if you wish to understand the boy your grandfather was, and the man he became. Are you sure you want me to begin today? Perhaps you should go home and rest your leg."

"No. Today is good." Kurt returned to the loveseat. He lowered himself to the ground and leaned against the seat to stretch out his leg. Marta's finger brushed the back of his head, then she flicked him. He threw her a scowl; she wrinkled her nose.

"And do you wish Marta to stay or go?" Herr Brandt asked.

Behind him, Marta huffed. Kurt could imagine the look she was giving her grandfather. A half smile escaped. "Well... If you have no objections, I guess she can stay."

Marta flicked him again. Kurt ducked his head and chuckled.

Amusement twinkled in the old man's eyes. He gave Marta a small nod. "*Leibchen*, I have told you these stories a thousand times in my mind. It is good you will hear some of them aloud." Marta's smile made Kurt's heart lurch. Herr Brandt said, "So, where to start... You know about the Nazi rise to power, yes?"

"Sure," Kurt replied. "I did a lot of reading before I came over."

"Yes, yes. Then you know that Germany was crushed by the Allies after the Great War and suffered many hardships through the 1920s and into the 1930s. One of the reasons the people liked the Führer was because he restored our pride. And with it, jobs. My father was in business. I recall him having doubts about some Nazi ideas, but his business prospered, even grew, under the Nazi regime, so he was happy. Jäger and I were ten years old when Hitler took control of the government."

"1933," Kurt said. "But who was Jäger?"

"That was your grandfather's nickname, though he had not earned it yet. But it is the name I still call him in my mind."

"Do you have pictures? My grandparents didn't own a camera until Dad was born, and then only because Oma insisted upon it. Grandfather was in his late thirties then. I'd like to know what he looked like when he was young." Kurt snapped his mouth shut. He was babbling.

Herr Brandt stared at him for a moment. "No pictures, except those in my head. I am certain some existed once..." A faraway look entered his eyes, as it had a few times before.

Kurt knew the old man had to be seeing the past. He held his breath, waiting for Herr Brandt to speak. The old man hummed a catchy tune. He began to sing, so quietly Kurt had to lean forward to hear. Marta laid her hand on Kurt's shoulder as she also strained to catch the words.

"Our flag flutters before us. Our flag represents the new era." Herr Brandt hummed another line, then sang, "Yes, the flag is greater than death!"

The hairs on Kurt's arm stood at attention. He shared a puzzled look with Marta, who only shrugged. Whatever stories she had heard growing up, none had included this song. Kurt shivered. *Ja, die Fahne ist mehr als der Tod!* Yes, the flag is greater than death! A Nazi song. Even though Herr Brandt had fallen silent, the melody dipped and danced through Kurt's mind, whistling a tune as merry as the Pied Piper's. *Come follow me. Follow me...*

Kurt tried to block the song from his mind. It faded only when Herr Brandt began to speak in a voice that sounded much younger than his eighty years. The voice of his youth.

Blood and honour. That is where it began. Blood and honour. Jäger and I were ten years old in 1933 and so excited. All we could think of was joining the DJ – *Deutsche Jungvolk* – which was the younger section of the HJ – *Hitlerjugend.* We nagged our parents until they let us. We loved our uniforms. Light brown shirt, black shorts and a shoulder strap. We pretended we were real soldiers. We marched in parades, with drums pounding and bugles trumpeting. We learned to ignore the pain our leaders put us through and laughed at those fools who did not join.

Even at ten years old, we could sense the excitement. It sang through our veins. We were part of something special, something big. We were rebuilding Germany into the greatest of nations. It was intoxicating. We were drunk with the thrill of it all.

We lived and breathed the DJ and longed for the day when we would take the next step toward manhood. The HJ. Those boys were so big. Powerful. Fearless. It was all we talked about, Jäger and I. The day we would join them.

He was already Jäger by then, having earned his nickname in the DJ. We would go on camp-outs with other DJ squads and have contests to capture the other's flag. Brutal affairs, fought in forests and fields. I often came away with bloody noses and bruises. Even then, Jäger could find safe paths through enemy territory or locate the enemy. He had a bloodhound's nose. He was Jäger, our hunter. The team that underestimated him did so at its own peril.

The day we had prayed for came in the spring of 1936. We were only thirteen years old. You were supposed to be fourteen to join the HJ, but our town was little and they needed the numbers to fill out our Schar – our squad. Jäger was still small, but very fast. He could outrun many of the older boys. And, of course, he could hunt. The ScharFührer – leader of the troop – specifically requested Jäger. At thirteen, I was already growing, my muscles hardening. So we were both chosen, along with Dietrich Nagel, to advance with the fourteen-year-olds.

When we marched into that school auditorium and down that centre aisle, our chests were swollen with pride. Townsfolk filled the chairs on either side. The swastika decorated the podium, a portrait of our beloved Führer hung behind it, flags decorated the walls.

At the end of the aisle we halted, our feet striking the hardwood floor like a single rifle crack. We shot our arms into the air and shouted, *"Heil Hitler!"*

Dignitaries on the stage saluted back, then the audience saluted and shouted, *"Heil Hitler!"* The sound pealed through the building like a cathedral bell and I thought my buttons would burst. We marched past our troop in the front rows, onto the stage and took our positions. Speeches followed. Local Nazi leaders, even a real major from the *Wehrmacht* with his gleaming boots, polished leather shoulder strap and a Walther pistol strapped to his belt. He was tall and lean and everything we wanted to be. When he told us to stand firm for the Führer and the Fatherland, the joy I saw in Jäger's eyes echoed what I felt in my heart.

One by one we stepped forward and made our pledge. Jäger's voice was strong and clear as he said, "I promise to do my duty in love and loyalty to the Führer and our flag."

After the ceremony, our parents congratulated us. My parents were both solemn. Jäger's two younger brothers, both in the DJ, were beaming. He was embarrassed because his mother was crying. Maybe she saw the paths her boys would walk. Or maybe she was proud. All I know is that Jäger escaped as soon as possible.

The HJ had a huge bonfire down by the lake that night to welcome us into the squad. We sang marching songs and drank malt brew and laughed at the rough jokes of the older boys. Then two of the oldest decided to leap the bonfire. They did it!

The ScharFührer dared us newcomers to do the same, to prove we were men, not boys.

Silence fell over the group. Jäger and I exchanged looks of fear and excitement. The other boys appeared just as uncertain. In a tight whisper, Jäger said, "We can do this, Wolf." When I started to shake my head, he said, "We must."

Jäger was never one to refuse a dare. He took a step toward the fire. The flames lit his dark brown hair with gold. He simply said, "I'll do it."

Some of the older boys laughed. Here was the smallest of them all, saying he would do what only the largest had attempted. We had been friends all our lives. I could not let him do this thing alone. So I stepped up beside him. The ScharFührer grinned and nodded.

Jäger and I jogged down the shore a good eight metres to get a run at it. When we turned and faced the bonfire, I was quivering. Not Jäger. He was tense, limbs coiled like springs, eyes focused on the fire. He leaned into a runner's stance and whispered, "On three, Wolf. We shout and run. Yes?"

My mouth was filled with cotton. I could only nod. Jäger counted; I took a shaky breath. We both shouted, *"Heil Hitler!"* and dashed toward the flames.

Neither of us took the center. Jäger outran me and was over the fire when my feet left the ground. I passed through a wall of heat and landed with a grunt, barely clearing the hot rocks encircling the bonfire. The boys surrounded Jäger and me. We shared grins as a shout split the night and set every dog in the nearby yards barking.

Jäger pointed at my feet and laughed. A flame must have licked my heel and melted a hole in the back of my sock. I was too excited to feel anything. The next morning, when my mother applied a salve to the burn, I still refused to admit it had been a foolish thing to do.

Six months later we faced our *Mutprobe* – our test of courage. We had to swim from the middle of the lake to shore when the wind was rising. It was hard, fighting the waves, seeing the shore as you topped one crest, with it not looking a metre closer when you topped the next. It was October and the water was cold. I thought my arms were going to fall off. I couldn't feel my legs. By the time I reached shore, I could only crawl from the water to the bonfire waiting to warm us. Someone gave me a wool blanket and put a mug of hot chocolate in my hands. I spilled some, my hands were shaking so much. Jäger didn't look any better. I swear his lips were blue. But he was grinning.

We had made it. Not so Dietrich Nagel. He had to be pulled into the boat. Even over the wind we could hear him begging to be put back into the water, that he could do it. No one would look at him as he was carried from the boat. He had failed. He would have to work twice as hard, face twice the punishment to be accepted now. I felt sorry for him. I could tell by the way Jäger stared into his cup that he felt the same way. But neither of us said anything.

Our sorrow didn't last. So much backslapping and laughter, it was impossible not to be happy. We were now official members of the proud and strong Hitlerjugend.

The Führer himself had declared he wanted his young men to be swift as greyhounds, tough as leather, hard as Krupp's steel. That is why the HJ was so hard – weakness was hammered out of us.

Jäger and I were proud. And we were strong. And we had passed the *Mutprobe*. In all my thirteen years, I was never so close to being overwhelmed by emotion as I was the day our ScharFührer placed my very own HJ dagger in my hands. This was not the short-bladed travelling knife we all wore on our belts, but a ceremonial dagger, inscribed with the HJ motto: "Blood and Honour."

That night I wrapped my right hand around my dagger's blade so it cut my palm. Jäger did the same. We clasped hands to let our blood mingle and swore we would always be blood brothers, that we would always be together. We swore it upon our honour as Hitlerjugend.

"Blood and Honour."

Chapter Eleven

The dream snaked its misty tentacles around Kurt and wouldn't release him, though his mind cried, No! It dragged him into that familiar, vivid world of hatred and violence. Why couldn't it be in black and white like the Spielberg movie? Why did it have to show him the colour of fear? Its sour stink was bad enough.

The beginning never changes. The rounding up of Jews. *"Juden! Raus!"* Seeing the little girl in the red coat running away. The room to room search through the tenements. Entering the bedroom where Kurt knows he will find her hiding. No hunter stalks him this time.

He crouches down and sees the little girl under the bed. He beckons her to come out. When she does and they both stand up, Kurt finds himself staring at Marta.

"Don't stand there," he shouts. "Run!"

"No," Marta replies, her brown eyes warm with friendship. "I trust you."

Kurt snaps his *Mauser* into firing position and sights along the barrel. "Run! I will kill my own grandfather if I'm ordered to do it."

She doesn't move. "I trust you, Kurt."

"I'm not Kurt! I can't be Kurt!" His vision blurs as he pulls the trigger.

Kurt's eyes sprang open. He rolled onto his back, gasping. His thigh pulsed with welcome pain, proof he was awake. He must have been sleeping on his sore right side.

Groaning, Kurt swung his feet to the floor. Clad only in boxers, he stumbled to the washroom and returned with a cold cloth. He lay down and draped the icy wetness over the bruises. Air hissed between his teeth. The clock said 5:00 a.m. – he knew he wouldn't even try to go back to sleep.

By late morning Kurt was dragging. The smell of the dream lingered and his brain kept replaying Herr Brandt's story. The limp was better, though, and he'd only suffered one insult from Peter. He should be happy; instead he felt like an abandoned towel on the shower room floor.

Since he wasn't attending Sports class, Kurt left school early. The last thing he expected was for Marta to appear at his side. He gave her a quick glance but said nothing.

"Hello, Marta," she said. "Hello to you, Kurt. You didn't say hello in History class. I'm sorry, Marta. My mind was on other things. Oh? What other things, Kurt? I'd really like to know."

Kurt walked slowly, afraid if he looked at Marta he would see her eyes with the muzzle of a rifle pointed between them.

"What other things, Kurt?"

Kurt shrugged. "Why aren't you in Chemistry class?"

"I saw you leaving and told the teacher I had an appointment. Since my lab report is done, he let me go." They walked in silence until Marta said, "Why are you angry at me?"

Kurt halted and turned toward her. He almost winced. She looked just as she had in the dream: full of trust. "Don't –" Kurt clamped his mouth shut. He had almost said, *Don't trust me.* He lurched into motion again. "I don't think I'm angry. I don't know what I'm feeling."

Another silence, this one broken by Marta's intake of breath. "You're upset over what Opa told us. That's why you were so quiet afterwards. That's why you left suddenly, saying you had History homework. I *knew* you didn't have any homework, because *I* didn't have any."

"You're a regular Sam Spade."

"Who? Oh, let me guess. An old movie, right? What was a Sam Spade?"

"A detective in *The Maltese Falcon.*"

"But I'm a terrible detective. I can't think why you're upset. You wanted to know the truth."

"Right." Some truth. *Blood and honour.*

They stopped at an intersection. Marta pursed her lips as she studied Kurt. He stared at her forehead and the tiny wisps of hair fringing it.

"I thought you'd be glad," Marta said. "You already know your grandfather wasn't a coward."

Not when he was thirteen, anyway. Kurt still avoided Marta's gaze. "He was a real hero. He could leap over bonfires in a single bound."

"Oh, you're just being stubborn. Nothing is going to cheer you up. If you want to be miserable, you can do it by yourself."

"Good. I wouldn't want you to be late for your *appointment.*"

Marta sniffed. "You were my appointment and you know it. I see now that expressing concern was a waste of my time." Marta spun away, then turned back. "What about Friday?"

Kurt frowned and pushed his fists deeper into his pockets. "What about it?"

"Do you still want to go?"

"Do you?"

"I asked you first."

Kurt hesitated. He was going to ruin everything if he kept it up. He sighed. "Yes."

"You don't have to sound so miserable about *that*, too."

When she started to leave, Kurt grabbed her wrist. "Marta, please. I want to go. Don't be angry. I'm sorry I'm being a jerk."

Softness smoothed Marta's forehead and relaxed her mouth. "Do you promise you won't be a...jerk...on Friday night?"

Kurt's gaze dropped to her lips then away. He nodded. "Do *you* still want to go?"

"Of course. I just didn't want you to feel you had to go even though you didn't want to."

"Oh." How was he supposed to tell if she was doing something because she liked him or because she felt sorry for him? The heat tingling in his fingertips reminded him he still held her wrist. Kurt released it. "If you decide you don't want to go, call me. It's okay." He turned right and started down the sidewalk.

"Where are you going?" Marta called.

"For a walk."

Kurt listened for Marta's footsteps, but they didn't follow. He didn't look back. Running away at a slow walk.

When Kurt looked up he was passing Peter Neumeyer's house. His stomach clenched. He hadn't realized he was on Friedenstrasse. At the cemetery gates, he leaned against the linden tree and studied the grey tombstones beyond the iron gates. Grey like his thoughts.

He continued down the street to the lake, to the bench where Herr Brandt had been waiting for him that second day. Had it only been a week ago? Kurt sat, not wanting to walk. Not wanting anything – except to escape from his thoughts and dreams. The wind ruffled the water's surface. The lake was small, barely over a kilometre wide and not quite three kilometres long, connected with another by canal. Even half a kilometre in cold choppy water would be a hard swim. Possibly dangerous. Kurt tried not to think about it.

An hour later, someone sat beside him. From the corner of his eye, Kurt saw a cane with a wolf's head. He rested his forearms against his knees and stared at his upturned palms.

Herr Brandt said, "Marta came for lunch. A pleasant surprise, but a rare one. Between seeing you together yesterday and talking to her today, I can tell the two of you are good friends. Fate is strange. I was in Greece over the winter, at a friend's villa. On the phone, Marta said she had a friend who was a Canadian exchange student. I don't recall her giving a name. I pictured a skinny blonde girl. Imagine my surprise when her friend turned out to be the grandson of my best friend. I saw you on Saturday. You run like him, you know. Like a greyhound."

Kurt's churning stomach twisted into a knot. *Like a greyhound*. That's what Herr Brandt had said the day before, that Hitler had wanted his young men to be swift as greyhounds.

He rubbed his face and rested his forehead on the heels of his hands, his fingers tangled in his hair.

"Marta thinks you are upset about what I told you yesterday," Herr Brandt continued. "I assured her that could not be. You were eager to know the truth. When she said you had walked down Friedenstrasse, I knew where to find you. Now, seeing you, I think Marta may be right. What is disturbing you, Kurt? Was it something I said?"

Was it something he had said? Kurt almost laughed, but he could barely breathe. The strain (*Blood and Honour*) of trying to accept, (*loyalty to the Führer and our flag*) wanting to deny, (*Heil Hitler!*) but needing to understand, was swelling like a flooding river behind an earthen dam. How could the man who had taken him fly-fishing in the mountains and taught him to fillet fish, but refused to take him hunting because he disliked firearms, be the same man who sang that a flag was greater than death and loved the most evil mass murderer in history?

"Kurt?" Herr Brandt touched his shoulder.

Kurt bolted to his feet and pointed at the surprised old man. "You lied to me!"

Herr Brandt's eyes turned to steel. "I do not lie. I am a man of honour —"

"Honour and blood, you mean. You said he wasn't a monster. But yesterday..." Kurt shook his head, still wanting to deny what he had heard. "What you told us, how Hitler took you and Grandfather and...and millions of others and turned you all into monsters."

Herr Brandt pushed to his feet. He clasped his cane with both hands; the dark wood quivered. "You are right that Hitler captured our hearts and minds and held them with an iron fist.

He could stir the souls of men with his words. How easy it was for him to draw children under his spell. Children, Kurt. We were children. Do you understand that?"

"I –"

The cane cracked against the bench. "We were *not* monsters. Some in the Hitler Youth learned to love dealing death, but our leaders were not creating monsters. They were creating soldiers. Completely loyal, completely obedient soldiers."

"Killing machines. Monsters whose only purpose was to kill."

"Soldiers, Kurt. *That* is what your grandfather and I were. *Not* monsters."

"That's your defence? We were soldiers. We only did what we were told to do."

The old man lifted his chin. "And what did we do, Kurt? I thought that is what you wanted to know. Instead, you assume the worst. Do you think Jäger and I were responsible for running the death camps? That is what I am hearing. You have taken a brush labeled *monster* and have painted us with it before you hear the whole story. I thought you were a fair-minded young man. I would never have agreed to this if I had realized that you are as full of hate as any of the death camp guards ever were."

Kurt gaped at Herr Brandt. The old man straightened his fedora, turned up the collar of his trench coat, then pivoted and walked away.

For the second time Herr Brandt had accused him of hatred – both times at this very spot. Only this time there was no forgiveness offered. The old man's ramrod figure turned a corner and disappeared. Kurt sank onto the bench, more confused than ever. He hadn't meant to explode like that. When feelings were messed up, why did anger seem to surface so easily?

He had always thought of himself as accepting of others. He never had problems at school with students from other backgrounds or races. They were just students like him. He wasn't like a death camp guard, or any Nazi. They were masters of hate –

Did he hate his grandfather? No! Not who he is; who he was. A Nazi, one of the bad guys. Kurt hunched forward and stared at his hands again. Any war history book he had ever read had confirmed it. The bad guys. Did any movie show the Nazis to be anything other than monsters? They were always depicted as they were in the *Indiana Jones* movies. Pure evil. Cruel and barbaric. *They were children.* The back of Kurt's eyes stung.

How could his grandfather have been a child of hate? All Kurt knew was the stern old man who expressed his love by squeezing Kurt's shoulder and winking at him. He always knew when Grandfather was teasing or approved of something he had done – because of the wink. Kurt doubted his grandfather would be winking today.

On Thursday afternoon, Marta was working again, so Kurt decided to run around the lake. He jogged less than two kilometres when the growing ache in his thigh forced him to turn and walk back. The run hadn't been long enough to clear his thoughts and they were still as tangled as yesterday.

Kurt flopped onto the grassy bank and stared at the lake. Jewels of sunlight danced on the water. *Come follow me.* The *Hitlerjugend* anthem crooned through his thoughts, as it had so often since Herr Brandt had sung a few lines. Kurt had looked it up on the Internet. The site he found said the song had been called, *"Vorwärts! Vorwärts!"* ("Forwards! Forwards!"). It sang of youth being future soldiers, who marched for Hitler through night and hardship, but it was that one line that haunted Kurt. *Yes, the flag is greater than death.*

Thirteen years old and willing to die for a man so evil the brightest light couldn't penetrate his darkness. Kurt understood that the youth of that day had seen Hitler as a hero, but he couldn't seem to get his heart to believe it of his grandfather. It left him feeling hollow, confused, even a little afraid.

Lord of the Flies. Kurt startled, as if yelled at. He plucked a long blade of grass and began to shred it. In grade eleven, they had studied the book, *Lord of the Flies.* He had liked the story and still remembered it. A group of boys had been stranded on an island. No adults. Every child's dream – like Peter Pan and Never-Never Land. Without rules, or adults to enforce them, the boys had turned into savages. Kurt recalled the teacher saying that the author believed it was society's rules that kept people from giving in to their most basic, evil instincts.

What happened when society's rules encouraged those instincts? Survival of the fittest. Strength is everything.

The pieces of Kurt's thoughts snapped together. Herr Brandt and his grandfather had been like those savage boys. The Hitler Youth had taken them from their parents, the people who had taught them the rules of decent behaviour. And then they had learned new rules. Hitler's rules. Kurt's heart finally agreed: they *had* been children. Too young to control their own fates.

He rose and jogged along the lakeside, speeding up as his thoughts raced. His thigh pulsed but he ignored it, intent only on his realization. Herr Brandt had firmly stated they had not been monsters, which told Kurt that somehow, through it all – the Hitler Youth, the war and who knows what – his grandfather might have held onto a thread of goodness.

The gloomy clouds that had clung to his mind began to blow away. With rising hope came a new realization: Kurt had to find a way to apologize to Herr Brandt.

Chapter Twelve

"**H**err Brandt agreed to tell you about the war years?" Frau Klassen plucked a weed from her flower bed, her expression thoughtful. She sat back on her heels, knees indenting a foam pad. "It is unusual to find a veteran of World War Two willing to speak about his experiences. He is extending a very special gift to you."

"Because of his friendship with Grandfather, I think." Kurt blew out his breath and tugged at a weed growing up through a crack in the walk. "I really messed up. I'll be lucky if he agrees to give me the time of day now."

"Do you still wish to know more, even though you have not liked what you have heard?"

"More than ever."

"And how can I help?" Frau Klassen attacked the flower bed with her miniature shovel, turning the dirt over, breaking up clumps.

"I need to know how I can apologize to him. Just saying 'Sorry' doesn't feel like enough."

"Your instincts are good, Kurt. Herr Brandt is part of an older generation. More than most, those people value politeness and formal behaviour appropriate to the situation. A formal apology means a *handwritten* one. You need to give him the apology note, and perhaps a gift, if you wish to stress your sincerity, then wait for him to decide if he will accept the apology."

Kurt rubbed his neck. This was going to be tougher than he thought. He'd rather write a ten-page essay than something personal. Worse, it would have to be readable. His mother always hassled him about his handwriting – *You were born to be a doctor. I can't read a single word you write.* He was used to working on the computer; handwriting was so old-fashioned.

But so was Herr Brandt. Kurt sighed. He stood and massaged his thigh, suddenly conscious of his running shorts and the way they exposed his bruises.

"When does your train leave for Dresden?"

Kurt had almost forgotten about this weekend; he wished there was a way to back out of going without insulting Jessica – other than Peter Neumeyer landing him in the hospital. "Early Saturday. I was going to stay until Sunday evening. Is it all right if I come back early Sunday?"

"Of course. Let us know the time and Herr Klassen will be there to pick you up."

"Thanks." He started to turn away, then stopped. "I almost forgot. I'm going into Berlin tomorrow night with a few friends to see a movie."

"How nice. Who all is going?"

"Victor and his girlfriend." Kurt stared at his running shoes. "And Marta."

"Ahh. Four of you. Is this a double date?"

"No," Kurt blurted. He cleared his throat. "Marta and I are just friends, you know that."

"She is a very nice girl."

"I know that." Kurt's hands itched to hide in pockets his shorts didn't have. "I need to have a shower and change." Under her measured gaze, Kurt felt like a fruit being inspected for blemishes. "And...I need to do a load of laundry, too." He made good his escape.

Kurt laboured over the apology note all Thursday evening, crumpling up at least twenty bad starts. He showed his final copy to Frau Klassen.

"Good, Kurt. Now put it on nice stationery and, this time, try to write a little more neatly."

Kurt scowled. "All I have is computer paper."

"I have stationery that will be suitable."

"How about some lessons to fix my handwriting?" Kurt was half kidding, half hopeful.

Her smile was kind. "Only if you wish to delay the apology for several weeks."

Kurt muttered, "I'm running out of weeks."

"Yes, it is hard to believe you only have two months left with us. I will miss you when you leave." Frau Klassen crossed to her small desk in one corner of the kitchen, obviously not expecting an answer. She handed Kurt two pieces of sand-coloured paper with a simple brown line border, and a matching envelope.

"Thanks, and...I'll miss you, too."

When her expression turned soft, Kurt beat a swift retreat.

Friday afternoon, Kurt haunted the stores, searching for a small gift Herr Brandt might like and finally found an ornament carved out of grey stone. He set the small wolf on the palm of his hand and held it at eye level. Perfect. A few more euro than he had wanted to spend, but it couldn't be helped. He was out of time. Marta, Victor and Rebekka were meeting him at the train station in little more than an hour.

His stomach flipped. He had been so busy with this apology thing, he hadn't thought to be nervous. *Don't be stupid*, he told himself. *It's not like it's a real date.*

Kurt paid for the wolf and had it boxed. He hurried home, changed into his black jeans and grey shirt. After scowling at his fading black eye, he ran a comb through his hair. The front lock flopped down, refusing to be tamed. His scowl deepened. He stuffed his wallet in his pocket, grabbed the letter and gift box, and headed downstairs.

Now to face Herr Brandt. Kurt walked from the house as if heading to his own execution. At Herr Brandt's house, Kurt entered the yard without hesitating, but stood at the door for a full minute before he could lift his hand to knock. Another minute passed before he heard noise behind the door. He stepped back, fighting the urge to turn and run.

The door opened. Herr Brandt stood tall and forbidding, his face in shadow. His voice was flat, giving no hint of his thoughts. "Young Schreiber."

Kurt nodded. "Herr Brandt. Good day. I..." He held out the box and letter. "I apologize for my rudeness." When Herr Brandt took the offering, but said nothing, Kurt cleared his throat. "Right. I have a train to catch. Thank you, sir." He nodded again and paced down the sidewalk.

When he paused at the gate and looked back, Herr Brandt still stood in the doorway. Kurt lifted his hand; no salute was returned. He turned and hurried toward the train station.

Adate with Marta. Not a date. A...something. The train ride into Berlin was the longest forty minutes of Kurt's life. He didn't know what to say. He forced a smile whenever Victor glanced his way and avoided looking at Marta, though he studied her from the corner of his eye. She looked great in her slim green skirt and pale yellow blouse. Her hair hung in loose dark curls, something he had never seen. She usually tied it back. The curls seemed to darken her brown eyes and made her appear...way too much like a pretty young woman. Not at all like his friend. By the time the train pulled into Bahnhof Zoolischer Garten, the train station near the Tiergarten, Kurt's palms were sweaty.

They had time for a snack before the movie, so they bought some *Currywurst* from the takeout counter of a busy café on the Ku'damm. The sausage discs with spiced ketchup on them were a favourite of Kurt's. They sat on plaza steps near the ruined church that was a war memorial. *Gedächtniskirche.* Victor kept the girls laughing while Kurt grew more nervous.

Victor said, "Rumour has it Marta gave you that black eye when you tried to kiss her."

Kurt frowned. "Who has been saying that?"

"I have." Victor grinned.

Marta laughed, clear as a chime. The sound shattered his anxiety – it was the sound of a friend he had known for months. A smile tugged at Kurt's mouth. His friend still lurked within the shell of this beautiful creature she had become. It was stupid to be nervous.

Victor led the way to *Zoo Palast*, the big cinema a block south of the rail station, his arm around Rebekka's waist, their blond heads tilted toward each other. Marta pointed out a man dressed in a gaudy outfit – the kind some dance clubbers liked.

Kurt said, "Someone let him out of his cage early. The clubs don't heat up for hours."

Marta burst out laughing and grabbed Kurt's hand. "That's terrible! But it's wonderful to hear your sarcasm. I was starting to think you had forgotten your promise to be cheerful."

Aware of the heat trickling up his arm, Kurt almost slipped his hand from her grip, then squeezed. "Who was being sarcastic?" She laughed again.

After the movie – a wannabe James Bond special that was so poorly dubbed all four wound up laughing and being shushed – they burst onto the street, still shaking with laughter.

When they quieted, Victor punched Kurt in the arm. "Come on, you have to admit he was a very manly man. And the lust of his life did have a few...assets."

"Yes." Kurt wiggled his eyebrows. "They almost fell out of her blouse a few times."

Victor slapped his thigh. They both roared.

Marta kicked Kurt's right ankle. "Ouch!" he cried. "Be careful! That's my injured leg."

"Don't look to me for sympathy if you are going to make such awful comments. Another and I might kick you right in your...bruises."

Victor and Kurt winced.

"She's heartless," Victor said.

"Her teasing had gone from terrible to vicious," Kurt commented.

Marta smiled. "Who was teasing?" She took Rebekka's arm and led her away.

The two guys trailed behind. Victor said, "What do you expect? We're guys."

"That doesn't mean you have to act like them."

Kurt snorted, then winked at Victor. "Should we act like girls, then?"

Marta released the giggling Rebekka and spun around. She planted her hand against her hip. "Don't you dare, Kurt Schreiber. You know what I mean."

Kurt's hand was halfway to his hip in imitation of Marta's stance. She narrowed her eyes. Kurt shrugged innocently and lowered his hand. Victor chuckled as he stepped past Kurt and took Rebekka's hand. "Let's take the train back to Friedrich-strasse and walk down Unter den Linden."

With a repentant grin, Kurt crooked his arm. "Shall we?"

Marta rolled her eyes and linked her arm through his. They strolled along the street, Kurt relishing how good it felt to be walking with Marta like this. The S-Bahn stop was way too close.

Kurt was silent during the train ride, and very conscious of the way Marta's thigh brushed his. When Victor and Rebekka shared a long kiss, Kurt flushed and peered out the window. To break the couple apart, he gave Victor a gentle slap on the back of his head. "This is our stop, Romeo."

Rebekka giggled. She didn't seem to say much, only giggled at whatever Victor said and smiled at him. As they got off the train, Kurt whispered to Marta, "Does she ever talk?"

"Yes, but she is a little shy around strangers."

Kurt thought about the kiss he had just witnessed. "Not that shy."

Marta gave him a wry look, as if she knew what Kurt was referring to.

They found an ice cream shop and stopped for cones before continuing down Unter den Linden. Kurt watched Marta take a bite of her orange mango frozen yogurt. A film of pale orange clung to her lips; Kurt had the urge to find out what it tasted like. He swallowed hard and looked away.

Unter den Linden was a broad avenue with a tree-lined boulevard in the centre where people could walk. Many of the old buildings had been rebuilt since World War Two and an air of bygone days clung to the street. The warm April night didn't require a jacket. Still, a chill prickled over Kurt's skin when Victor and Rebekka finished their cones and clasped hands, shoulders rubbing. This was to be the *romantic* part of the evening, according to Victor's plan, and Kurt found himself at a loss. Silence hovered between him and Marta, awkward, huge. He had never noticed how long Unter den Linden was. His thigh started to pulse quietly.

Ahead, the Brandenburg Gate glowed golden under flood-lights. The horse-drawn chariot seemed to be landing atop the high arches. As always, a mixture of awe and pride stirred in Kurt. And with it a surge of courage. He took Marta's hand.

She halted. Kurt faced her, preparing to be rejected. Marta's brown eyes were black in the evening shadows. Her expression remained solemn, unreadable. Kurt was about to release his grip when she turned and started walking again, without having said anything. Kurt jerked into motion to keep pace with her. He felt the warmth of their interlocking fingers and smiled.

When they stopped to admire the gate, Victor noticed the hand holding. He opened his mouth; Kurt shot him a dark look. Victor smiled and leaned down to whisper in Rebekka's ear, then kissed her and announced they should walk through the Tiergarten on their way back to the train station. As if a romantic stroll through a park hadn't been his plan all along.

Halfway through the park, Victor led them away from the main thoroughfare, down a path lit by circles of lamplight that didn't quite overlap. Three times, Victor halted in shadows to kiss Rebekka. Each time Kurt's mouth grew a little drier.

Victor veered toward a bench; Kurt gave Marta an embarrassed look. "They could be a while."

Marta pointed. "There's another bench. We'll wait for them."

They left Victor and Rebekka to their necking and sat on a bench under a lamppost. The silence stretched until Marta asked what had happened between him and her grandfather, then sighed. "Opa was grumpy Wednesday night. He came for supper and left right after."

Kurt began to explain about the argument and the apology. As he did, the tension leaked from his shoulders and the knot in his stomach loosened. He shifted to face Marta, watching for the slightest change in expression as he spoke. No judgment crept into her eyes or thinned her lips. He stared at them each time Marta asked a question.

When Kurt told about delivering the letter and gift, Marta nodded her approval. "Give him a few days. I've never known Opa to be angry for very long."

A hush settled between them, as comfortable as broken-in running shoes. The trees huddled around them, muffling the night sounds of Berlin. So long as he ignored Victor and Rebekka behind him, Kurt could almost imagine he and Marta were alone.

Off to the left, a nightingale warbled. A breeze rustled through the leaves.

Kurt studied Marta's features, as if seeing them in a new light. Her fine dark brows and high cheekbones. Her soft lips and firm chin. She smiled and his gaze jumped back to her lips. A new tension coiled in his gut. Warm, not cold.

"What is it, Kurt?" Marta's whispered question prodded him into motion.

Even as his mind told him to stop – *Run away!* – Kurt leaned forward, heart pounding. Marta's eyes grew round. Kurt closed his eyes to the sight.

And then they kissed.

Chapter Thirteen

Kurt looked up from his chair on the large patio belonging to Jessica Randall's wealthy host family. He smiled when Tyler Green strode around the corner. The sight of another male was sheer relief. Kurt jumped up and jogged to meet Tyler halfway. "John Wayne! Is it good to see you."

"John Wayne?" Tyler gave Kurt a puzzled frown, as if he had never heard of the old hero of western and war movies.

"You have *got* to save me, Ty. Jessica is trying to round me up and brand me."

Tyler burst out laughing. "You only just noticed? She's been chasing you for months."

Heat washed Kurt's face. His voice dropped. "Guess what she did in Berlin when we returned from Paris."

"She kissed you. Lucky guy."

Kurt stepped back. "How did you know?"

"She's been crying on my shoulder, in her emails that is, that *y'all* have been ignoring her, only replying to one of her messages in two weeks."

Great. "She emailed me every day. I was afraid she might...get the wrong idea if I replied. Besides, I was busy. What did you tell her?"

Tyler ginned. "That you were only playing hard to get."

Kurt scowled and punched Tyler's shoulder. Tyler jumped back and landed in a fighting stance, the grin still plastered on his face. "Hey. Watch it. You're messing with a red belt."

Blinking, Kurt tried to think what Tyler meant. Oh, right. Tae kwan do. A thought struck him. "Maybe you can help me out two ways."

"I live to serve." Tyler pressed his hands together, prayer style, and bowed.

Kurt chopped the air in a few mock martial arts moves. "Can you teach me to – how did you put it – introduce a guy, a bigger guy, to the sidewalk? Maybe a few flips?"

Tyler shook his head. "Wrong sport. You're thinking of judo. *This* is tae kwan do." He skipped in place, his right foot switching from front to back. As he landed, he yelled and snapped his right leg up. His foot flashed past Kurt's face.

Kurt staggered back a step. "Whoa! You almost creamed me."

Tyler smiled. "If I had actually been aiming for your head, I would have." With a mocking expression, he repeated his bow.

Kurt released a frustrated breath. "There's no way I can learn that in a day."

"Never fear." Tyler slapped his hand down on Kurt's shoulder and turned him toward the pool. "I'm guessing your shiner came from Mister Bigger and you don't want another. This is your lucky day. When my mom and sisters took self-defence classes, I was their punching and throwing bag. I perfected every move, practicing on my good buddy, Aaron."

Kurt gave Tyler a wry look. "Are you still good buddies?"

Tyler laughed. "Don't question the master. These are modified judo moves I'm offering to teach you. Are you willing or not?"

Kurt thought of Peter's boots sinking into his thigh. "Yeah. I'm willing."

Jessica floated out of the house carrying a drink tray. Why couldn't she ever look like she was simply walking? She spotted the two guys. "Ty! You're here! I'll get another glass." She flitted back into the house.

Kurt frowned. "What are you doing here, anyway? Spain is a long trek from Dresden. I mean, not that I'm not thrilled to see you..."

Tyler chuckled. "My grandparents padded my bank account again. I told my host family that Jess would be crushed to celebrate her birthday without her favourite American amigo – or her favourite Canadian one, it seems. So I flew. Much faster than a train."

Kurt stretched out on a lounge chair. Tyler took the one beside him and said, "Why do I need to *rescue* you from Jess? She's pretty sweet. It wouldn't be so bad to get caught by her."

With a shrug, Kurt replied, "She's not my type."

"Oh? Did a husky German Fräulein catch your eye?"

"She's not husky." Kurt clamped his mouth shut. She was tall and slender and strong, with chocolate eyes and brown silk hair and rose lips. Jessica was tiny and blond and reminded him of Dresden china – expensive and easy to break.

"Not husky, huh?" Tyler's musing interrupted Kurt's thoughts. "And how does *she* kiss?"

Kurt silently cursed the heat that enveloped his face. He had been trying not to think about how Marta kissed, which was... Wow. One kiss had not been enough. Tyler burst out laughing again, but avoided telling Jessica and Samantha what about when they returned to the patio.

When the girls went shopping for the "perfect birthday cake," Tyler and Kurt packed all the six lounge chair pads to the grass to create a mat for practicing self-defence moves. As Tyler lined up the pads, he asked, "What did you get Jess for her birthday?"

"A book on the history of German diplomacy and a brass bookmark."

Tyler's grin reappeared and he sat back on his heels. "Bad move, Schreiber. She was expecting something more personal from you. Diplomacy?" He grimaced.

"Well, she wants to be a diplomat."

"In a few years. Right now, she wants to be your girlfriend, though I can't think why. You might be good looking –" Tyler held up his hand. "Her words. I don't notice how *any* guy looks."

"So I messed up?"

"Big time. Unless you want her to think you don't care."

"I'd hate to see her upset, but... What did you get her?"

"A poster of a Spanish couple flamenco dancing and a pendant of the same thing."

Kurt whistled. That sounded expensive. "Better than a book?"

"Much better." Tyler stood.

Kurt shrugged. "We'll get her to open mine first, then she'll really love your gift."

"That *is* my hope. I'll comfort her however I can after you disappoint her."

"I owe you, Green."

"Hey. I never step between a couple, but since you're stepping aside for me, I'd say we're even." Tyler nodded at the makeshift mat. "Time to learn to fall."

"I thought I was going to learn to throw."

"First you learn to fall. It's the key to avoid getting hurt if Mister Bigger gets the upper hand."

A lesson Kurt could have used a week earlier. He grimaced and studied the row of pads. "Okay. How do I fall?"

Kurt's feet flew into the air, swept from under him. He landed on his back with a grunt. Grinning again, Tyler leaned over him. "Lesson one: never take your eyes off your opponent."

Chapter Fourteen

The early train back to Berlin wasn't crowded on a Sunday morning. Kurt sat in a back-facing chair, removed his shoes, and propped his feet on the seat across from his.

Jessica had pouted at him at lot, but Tyler had distracted her time after time, making her laugh, flirting outrageously with her. Kurt hoped that her half-hearted goodbye this morning meant Tyler had caught her interest.

Kurt reviewed the self-defence moves Tyler had taught him. Maybe Marta would practice with him. But he didn't want to throw Marta to the ground – lie beside her on the grass maybe... He dozed off imagining kissing Marta under a shady elm on a sunny day.

On the drive from the Ostbahnhof back to Zethen, Herr Klassen was quiet and Kurt kept nodding off. Frau Klassen greeted him with news that a letter had arrived for him the day before and was on her desk. Kurt retrieved an off-white envelope that looked like woven cloth. No stamp. No return address. He used Frau Klassen's letter opener to slice it open. "It's from Herr Brandt."

"Yes, I know. He hand delivered it. May I ask what it says?"

"He wants me to visit him tonight at seven o'clock." Air leaked between Kurt's lips. He felt as if he had been holding his breath for the last two days. The fresh air filling his lungs tasted sweet. Not quite like orange mango frozen yogurt, but good.

"So he accepted your apology?" Frau Klassen asked.

Kurt skimmed the letter again. "It doesn't say. But he wouldn't invite me to his house if he wasn't talking to me." Kurt hesitated. "Would he?"

Frau Klassen's smile was encouraging. "It would be very difficult to visit without talking."

Refolding the letter and returning it to its envelope, Kurt said, "I'm really tired. We didn't get much sleep last night."

"We?" Frau and Herr Klassen said together, both with that same "explain yourself" tone.

Kurt squeezed the back of his neck. "It's not what you think. Jess and I are *definitely* only friends. There were four of us. We watched movies and played video games for most of the night. Until 4:00 a.m., actually."

"Ahh." Frau Klassen nodded and smiled. Herr Klassen only nodded.

"I'm going to bed for the rest of the morning." Two hours sleep and a snooze on the train weren't nearly enough. At least so little sleep had stopped his dreams. Come to think of it, he hadn't dreamed on Friday night, either. Nothing unpleasant. Maybe that was the key to a good sleep: think about how soft Marta's lips had felt, how sweet they had tasted.

"Are you waiting for us to carry you up the stairs?"

Herr Klassen's voice pulled Kurt back to the present. He shook his head and turned toward the stairs before the Klassens noticed the warmth seeping up his neck. In his bedroom, he stretched out on his bed and interlocked his fingers behind his head. He felt good – a little stiff from Tyler's self-defence lessons, but good. He fell asleep thinking about kissing Marta.

The dream returned.

As Kurt walks down that final hallway, toward that last door that hides the girl in the red coat, panic begins to close off his throat. His breathing rasps. His footsteps echo loudly. His hand shakes as he grasps the door-knob. *I can't walk into that bedroom. What if Marta crawls out from under the bed? I can't aim my* Mauser *at her again. Can't pull the trigger...* Kurt yanks his hand back from the doorknob and spins away.

Kurt hit the floor with a thud. He rolled onto his back, his breath coming in puffs. A grin spread across his face. He woke up – before the end of the dream, before the gunshot. It felt like he had run, and won, a marathon. The bedside clock read 4:00 p.m. He would celebrate by actually going for a run. A short one. Four kilometres at the most.

In the end, Kurt ran around the whole lake. Eight kilometres was farther than his thigh wanted to go; it complained for the last two. Still, even limping, muscles stiff, Kurt felt refreshed as he walked the last block. By the time he had showered and eaten, it was time to go to Herr Brandt's.

The old man's gate stood like a barrier, a final chance to turn back before entering the wolf's den. Kurt hesitated, his hand on the latch. What was the problem? He had been invited. *Come into my parlour, said the spider to the fly.* Kurt chuckled at his nervousness and pushed past the gate. He paced up the walk, inspecting the tulips on parade, and clumped up the stairs.

The door swung open. Herr Brandt only held it half open. "Kurt, you are early. Go around back and say hello to Marta. I will join you in a few minutes." He closed the door.

Kurt stared at the wolf's head knocker. Its expression revealed nothing – like Herr Brandt's. The old man was acting oddly. Not that Kurt knew him well enough to know for sure. He headed around the house, his mind already on seeing Marta. She sat on the patio swing by the back stairwell, one foot tucked under her, the other giving little pushes to keep the swing moving. Her attention was focused on the book in her lap, so Kurt watched her for a moment. She looked up when the swing glided to a stop.

Marta's face lit up. "Kurt! When Opa told me you were coming over this evening, I asked if I could stay. I don't want him telling stories when I'm not here. Come see my baby pictures."

"Baby pictures?" Kurt strode to the swing, barely limping at all. The book in Marta's lap was a plain black photo album, styled to look old-fashioned, but with pockets to hold the pictures instead of corner tabs like his Oma had always used. He sat down and set the swing in motion. Leaning close to Marta, Kurt studied the photos. He laughed at one in which a toddler Marta stood by an open cupboard door with pots and pans scattered around her feet. He flipped back a page. A baby Marta was propped against a black dachshund, her eyes wide, as if she were about to tip over. The dog looked at her with mournful eyes.

"That explains it," Kurt said. "A faithful dachshund once saved you from bumping your head, so now you feel obligated to save every stray animal you find. Even chickens from Canada."

Marta sniffed. "You are not a chicken, Kurt Schreiber."

Kurt smiled at the strength of her response. "Look at those chubby cheeks. Beautiful." He studied Marta's face. Her brown eyes grew wide – as in the picture – when his index finger touched her jaw. "Your cheeks are still beautiful."

Pink tinted Marta's face. He stared, wondering why he had never noticed how pretty she was. Marta whispered, "What are you looking at?"

"A pretty girl."

The blush darkened. "Why?"

"I don't know why she's so pretty, and I don't know why I was so blind."

"No. Why are you looking?"

"Can't a guy look? It's better than doing what I want to do."

"Which is?"

"I want to kiss you." Kurt flinched inwardly. Had he really just said that?

Marta's tongue tip brushed along the underside of her top lip. Kurt followed its progress and swallowed. Her voice was soft. "Why is it better just to look?"

"Well...considering where we are..."

They both looked at the closed door at the bottom of the stairwell, then back at each other.

"What are we, Marta?" At her puzzled frown, Kurt said, "Are we still just friends?"

"Friends...who are thinking about being more, perhaps."

"More." Kurt's finger traced Marta's bottom lip. "I like the sound of that. All day Saturday I thought about our kiss on Friday night and that's what I wanted. More."

They both looked at the cellar door again. Kurt searched Marta's eyes for anything resembling a red light, but he only saw a green one. Or was that his own eyes reflected in hers?

Her mouth drew his like a powerful magnet. She tasted of cinnamon. As their lips moved in an uncertain dance, Kurt's hand drifted to her waist and slipped around to the small of her back. Marta's fingers skimmed up his arm to tickle the base of his neck. Electricity skittered down Kurt's spine. Their lips danced with more boldness.

A throat cleared.

Kurt leaped to his feet. He took in Marta's horrified expression and stared at the ground, unable to look at Herr Brandt. When had the photo album fallen off Marta's lap? Kurt scooped it up and held it out to Marta. She took it with trembling fingers.

Herr Brandt's voice beat the air like a rubber sole slapping pavement. "Inside, young Schreiber. Marta, give us a few moments alone."

Surrounded by gloom, Kurt followed Herr Brandt down into the cellar and up the stairs to halt in a back hall by a bathroom. Kurt turned toward a cheerful yellow and white kitchen on the left. Herr Brandt stopped him. Kurt inhaled and looked into eyes of grey slate. No trace of blue.

"I invited you here to accept your apology, young man."

"I...I'm sorry." Kurt nodded toward the back yard. "It won't happen again, sir."

One bushy eyebrow raised, its skeptical arch calling Kurt a liar. He flushed, hating how easily he blushed when it came to Marta. Herr Brandt cleared his throat and looked down his nose. "I will accept your apology on one condition."

Confusion jumbled Kurt's thoughts. Which apology? This one or the written one? "I... Of course. What condition?"

"That you allow me to show you what your grandfather looked like."

Kurt's jaw sagged. This *was* about the written apology; Herr Brandt was going to ignore the kiss. *What about Marta?* Kurt snapped his mouth closed before the question could escape, then said, "I thought you had no old pictures of Grandfather." Kurt thought of the photo album with Marta's baby pictures and smiled. "Did you find some after all?"

"Do you agree?"

"Sure. You know I want to know what he looked like."

"Follow me." Herr Brandt opened a door on the left and walked into a bedroom.

Kurt trailed behind and closed the door, taking in the carved headboard of golden oak, the matching dresser, the oval full-length mirror standing in the corner. He leaned against the door and almost grinned when he noticed the small carved wolf on the bedside table.

Herr Brandt motioned toward the bed. "I want you to try it on."

Atop a thick comforter of cream and pale green lay a grey tunic. Five round buttons down the front, two on chest pockets and two more fastening white-trimmed shoulder straps. Bars decorating a dark green collar. Over the right pocket, a straight-winged eagle with a wreathed swastika in its talons. A Nazi uniform.

Kurt eyed it as if it were going to jump up and attack him. He whispered, "Whose?" His breathing clogged his ears. He saw Herr Brandt's lips moving and said "What?"

The old man frowned. "I said, it was your grandfather's."

"But how –" The doorknob dug into Kurt's back.

"When Jäger took Hedda away at the end of the war, he left it with his father-in-law. Apparently he told Herr Brauer to burn it. Instead, Herr Brauer called me to his house. With the Russians approaching he was afraid to keep anything Nazi around, afraid even to burn it in case they searched the ashes. So I took it and hid it, along with my own uniform."

The air seemed to leak from the room, replaced by mothball stench. Kurt's throat tightened.

"Try it on." Herr Brandt's voice came from a distance.

Kurt shook his head.

"You agreed, young Schreiber."

"I... Not to this. I didn't know what I was agreeing to do. No. No way."

"You gave your word. A man of honour keeps his word, even when it takes him down a path he does not wish to travel."

Kurt scowled at the old man, who remained unmoved by his anger. "You tricked me."

"No. You believed what you wanted to believe. I simply let you do it. Now decide if you will be a man of honour." Herr Brandt paced to the window and stared into the backyard, his hands clasped behind his back.

Kurt glared at the uniform, at the old man's stiff back, at the uniform again. A man of honour. *Blood and honour.* His fingers groped behind him and wrapped around the doorknob. They twisted the glass orb until Kurt heard a quiet click.

Run!

Decide if you will be a man of honour.

An old black mantel clock on the dresser ticked the seconds away.

Kurt sighed and released the doorknob. Three steps carried him to the bed. The mothball stink rose to greet him. He wrinkled his nose and fingered a cuff, wondering at the seven centimetre split up the sleeve's seam.

Without turning, Herr Brandt said, "I suggest you keep your shirt on. There is enough wool in the tunic to make it slightly itchy. The trousers are not so bad."

Kurt spotted the trousers under the tunic. He pulled them out and held them against his waist, letting the legs hang down. "I thought you said Grandfather was short."

"By the time he wore that uniform he was your height and your build. It will fit."

The confidence in Herr Brandt's voice was unnerving. Kurt dropped the trousers on the bed and stood with his hands at his own waistband. Why was he even considering this? Because right from the start, Herr Brandt had treated Kurt as a man. Not a child. *Children, Kurt. We were children.*

Decide if you will be a man of honour.

Kurt kicked off his shoes and shed his blue jeans. Herr Brandt continued to stare out the window. Kurt slipped into the grey trousers, tucked in his shirt, fastened the button fly. The old man was right; they fit him almost as if they had been made for him. He unbuttoned the tunic, pulled it on, hesitated, then began buttoning it up. His fingers shook. Next came the belt, fine cracks marring the old leather. When he peered at the buckle, he noticed boots near his feet. High black leather ones. Kurt sat on the edge of the bed and pulled on the hobnailed boots. He stood and stared at the scuffed black toes. His grandfather had big feet.

"The boots are mine. Jäger was wearing his when he left."

Kurt looked up to see Herr Brandt with an odd glitter in his eyes. They were blue again. Blue and sharp. Kurt glanced at the door, wondering if he had made a mistake.

"Don't –" Kurt flinched and Herr Brandt continued, "Don't look in the mirror yet. You need one more thing." He pointed at a box on a chair behind Kurt. "Pick one."

Kurt opened the box. He pulled out a grey side cap made of the same material as the tunic, with a small version of the tunic's eagle on the front of the narrow wedge. He laid it aside and picked up a helmet. The distinctive helmet of the Nazi soldier – field green, bowl shaped and flared around the edges. It was heavily marked. Eyes on Herr Brandt, Kurt placed the helmet on his head.

"The strap," the old man whispered.

Kurt fastened the helmet strap on the second try. His fingers were trembling again.

Herr Brandt nodded and pointed toward the full-length mirror. As he approached it, Kurt eyed the mirror's stand. Anything rather than look at the reflection trying to get his attention. Kurt finally lifted his chin; Herr Brandt was standing behind him. Their gazes met in the mirror.

"Look closely, young Schreiber. That helmet hides the one feature that does not belong to your grandfather. His hair was darker than yours, more like Marta's. Look in the mirror and see what your grandfather looked like in 1941."

Kurt hesitated, then looked. A Nazi soldier stared back at him. White faced. Kurt reminded himself to breathe. He took a step back, lifted his foot, set it down. The quiet thunk made him wince.

"I called you 'Jäger' that first day in the cemetery. Can you see why?" Herr Brandt asked.

Kurt shook his head, keeping a wary eye on the soldier in the mirror. He had forgotten about Herr Brandt calling him that. The soldier returned his regard.

The old man pointed at Kurt's image. "This is why. I stepped around that tree and thought I saw Jäger kneeling at his parents' grave. Your hair was wet and looked dark. When you stood, I feared I had waited too long to keep my promise and that Jäger's ghost had come to bid me farewell."

Promise? Kurt frowned but couldn't open his mouth to speak; the soldier in the mirror also kept his silence.

"When you ran," Herr Brandt said, "I knew it was not the Jäger of my youth come to haunt me, but someone else. I was pleased when you returned the next day and admitted your name was Kurt Schreiber. What other name could you possibly have? Except, perhaps, Jäger?"

I'm not Jäger. I can't be Jäger. Hunting Jews in a tenement, night after night, dream after dream. Kurt's voice was little more than a croak. "Did he hunt Jews in this uniform?" The soldier in the mirror appeared insulted by the suggestion.

"No." The old man's voice turned shrewd. "Is that what you dream about?"

Kurt gave a short nod. Did the soldier appear almost cocky now? The reflection lifted his chin, drew back his shoulders, thinned his lips in an expression of... Pride? Arrogance? The uniform suited the soldier. Green eyes glittered under a green rim.

"It is very seductive, yes?" Herr Brandt asked, his eyes devouring the sight in the mirror.

"What is?" Kurt's voice had an edge to it. Or had the reflection spoken?

"The uniform. Almost any uniform will do that to a man. Have you never noticed?" Herr Brandt arched his brows in a knowing way. "He walks taller, stands straighter, borrows pride from the sharp creases and polished leather and shiny buttons and noble insignia." The old man leaned forward; his breath blew warm on Kurt's ear. "A uniform is almost as alluring as a young woman's lips, would you not agree?" His lips stretched in a thin smile; his eyes sharpened to steel grey. Krupp's steel.

Kurt paled. The soldier in the mirror recoiled.

The door swung open. Kurt spun on his heel, heart drumming.

"What are you two doing in here, Opa? It's been so long –" Marta's mouth fell open. Her eyes grew round as the buttons on the Nazi tunic that was suddenly trying to strangle Kurt. She stammered, "I...I... I'll put on the kettle." She slammed the door.

Kurt flinched. He tore at the chinstrap, then threw the green helmet onto the bed. It wobbled by Herr Brandt's pillow. "Why?" Kurt yanked off the belt, then fumbled with the tunic buttons. Mothball odour filled his nostrils, reminding Kurt of the smell from his dream. The smell of fear. His breathing rasped as he shrugged out of the tunic. More loudly, he repeated, "Why?"

"You wanted to see what your grandfather looked like. The resemblance is remarkable."

"You could have told me that without making me put *this* on." Kurt flung the tunic over the helmet. "What were you trying to prove? That any man can be fooled by a uniform?"

"Not fooled. Enticed. It draws you, sometimes blinds you to other truths."

"What truth?" Kurt balanced on one foot and yanked off a boot. "Blood and honour? Was that this uniform's truth? But somehow honour got lost in all the marches and 'Heil Hitlers'? " He dropped onto the bed, pulled off the other boot and hunched forward, fingers buried in his hair.

The dream. The dream had been right. His grandfather's face changed into his face...because they shared the same face. *I am not Jäger.*

Herr Brandt's voice was quiet but not soft. "Right or wrong, that uniform's truth was strength. To a nation that had been crushed for its sins in the Great War, humiliated, beaten into the ground and not allowed to rise, that uniform was strength and pride and honour reborn. It represented the phoenix rising from the ashes. Hitler rode on the back of the phoenix – on the back of Germany – and the men in uniform were the wings. *Every* child who looked at the magnificent creature rising to the sky and felt the breeze from the beat of its wings wanted to be one of the feathers."

Without looking up, Kurt said, "Didn't the phoenix burn and return to ashes?"

"Yes, yes, so we did. We burned to ashes in a horror of our own making. Only reunification, the wall falling, has allowed us to begin healing. A single nation once more."

Kurt stripped off the trousers. He tugged on his jeans and folded the trousers, then took the tunic and folded it as well, laying it atop the trousers. He set the helmet on the pile and stared at it. He felt hollow somehow, as if he had just discarded part of himself. *I am not Jäger.*

Herr Brandt said, "I sometimes marvel that I was allowed to live long enough to see Germany reunited. For many years I expected God to strike down our whole generation, like the rebellious Israelites in the wilderness, before he allowed us to pass into Canaan and be one people again."

Kurt peered at the old man, not sure what he was talking about. Something from the Bible. Oma had mentioned some guy named Caleb who had spied in Canaan – a land of giants that flowed with milk and honey. The soldier in the mirror had stared at him as if the soldier had been a giant. Kurt snatched his shoes and retreated to the door, eyes on the uniform.

The overwhelming size of the Brandenburg Gate came to mind. Everything in Berlin was big. He had always loved that about the city. But the Brandenburg Gate, in particular, always made Kurt think that maybe giants had once walked the earth.

Giants. Kurt paused at the door, his hand on the knob. The uniform still filled his vision. Almost to himself, he said, "A madman declared himself a god and men wore the god's uniform, believing they were giants." Like the soldier in the mirror.

"I could not have said it better myself, young Schreiber."

"I...I may have read that...somewhere."

The old man's eyes sparked blue. "Regardless, it is well said. It captures the *Zeitgeist* of Germany in the 1930s."

Zeitgeist. Spirit of the times.

Clear green eyes stared into faded blue ones. Kurt said, "Will you tell me more?"

"Another story?"

Kurt nodded.

"After I took advantage of you so I could catch a glimpse of a childhood friend?" Herr Brandt indicated the uniform. Kurt held the old man's gaze and nodded. He suspected Herr Brandt's motives had been far more complicated than that – and more generous.

"Very well. Under one condition."

Kurt cringed. "And that would be?"

Herr Brandt smiled. "Yes, yes. I knew you were quick. It is nothing terrible. I would like you to call me 'Wolf,' at least in this house and this yard."

The uniform whispered to Kurt. He spared it a glance. He would *not* become some ghost of his grandfather's past, no matter how much they looked alike. He said, "I am not Jäger."

"I *know* you are not my childhood friend and you cannot become him for me, Kurt. I will try, as I have had to try every day, *not* to call you 'Jäger.' I hope you will forgive me if I ever do. It would please me if you would call me by my name, especially if we are to be friends."

Friends? With his grandfather's best friend? A smile tugged at Kurt's mouth. He already spoke more openly with Herr Brandt than he did with many people. *Friends* sounded good.

"Before you agree, I should warn you..." Herr Brandt's tone made Kurt's smile disappear. "A friend would never, never hurt his friend's granddaughter."

"I...like Marta very much, sir." Kurt fought the blush heating his skin. "I would never do...anything...to hurt her."

"I am glad to hear it." Herr Brandt crossed the room and extended his hand. Kurt stared at it. "What do you say, Kurt? Friends? No blood will seal *this* friendship. Only honour."

"And truth?" Kurt asked.

"And truth. There is always truth between men of honour."

Truth and honour. That had a nice ring to it. Kurt clasped Herr Brandt's hand and was surprised by the powerful grip. He squeezed back, not wanting to seem weak or childish. "Friends it is...Wolf."

Chapter Fifteen

We were indeed giants, or so we felt. Perhaps that is how all sixteen-year-olds view life. For six years the HJ had been forging us into steel, telling us that we were the best, not just in Germany, but in all the world. So perhaps we can be forgiven our arrogance and cruel conceit. But in the harsh light of history, perhaps not. I cannot excuse what happened; I can only tell what I did.

The summer of 1939 was hot. The sun heated Berlin and made it glitter. Jäger and I went to the city every chance we got, drawn by a pulse in the streets. We saw it in the way uniformed men strode with purpose. We longed to be part of this new era, part of the power flowing through Berlin like the Spree in spring flood. But we were only sixteen, only Hitler Youth. We could only watch today's giants and long for the day when we would cast our own shadows.

Whatever was coming had to do with the Poles. They were mobilizing for war, refusing to acknowledge our Führer's just demands that the German lands in Poland be returned to us. We often discussed the situation within our HJ Schar. We were as outraged as any adults that the Poles were acting so unreasonable and warlike. We were confident that, as with the Czech Republic, our Führer would win the freedom of our German brothers in Poland without difficulty.

Thursday, August 31, dawned cloudless. My HJ ScharFührer knocked on the door during breakfast. He wanted Jäger and me to deliver important papers to an office in Berlin. They had to get there that day and he was tied up in district meetings. It was not the first time we had run errands for him, but to be singled out was always an honour. He gave me the papers and a few marks, and ordered us to take time to enjoy ourselves. I was out the door in moments.

Jäger was just as excited. He suggested we invite the girls to join us and go to the cinema later. That way, we would have an excuse to stay in Berlin all day. Whenever Jäger mentioned girls, he meant Hedda Brauer. He had been in love with her for six months, and though I teased him, he insisted she was the only girl he would ever love. I preferred to love whichever girl I happened to be with. That night it would be Hedda's friend, Katrina.

The train ride into the city was stifling, even though it was only morning. The open window let in blasts of steam along with the wind. The occasional whiff of pine broke through the constant odour of burning coal as the train chugged through the forest toward the city.

The Anhalter train station was buzzing, even more than usual. After agreeing upon a time to meet at Potsdamer Platz, the girls went to do some shopping while we set out to deliver our package. The traffic on Friedrichstrasse seemed to be mostly military.

Jäger walked with a bounce in his step. He asked, "Do you smell it, Wolf?"

I shook my head and watched a troop transport crawl by. Jäger was always smelling things. I craned my neck to catch a glimpse of the soldiers in the open back. Frames for canvas covers arched over their heads like exposed ribs.

Jäger said, "Something is about to happen."

I replied, "Yes. And we'll miss it." My HJ uniform, with its short-sleeved shirt and dark shorts, was welcome in this heat, but it marked me as a boy. I wanted to be seen as a man.

Jäger knew what I was thinking. He said, "Cheer up. The Reich is going to last a thousand years. In less than two of those years, it will be us riding in that truck."

I grinned and slapped Jäger's back. How could you argue with such logic?

We strutted down the sidewalk. Most of the people we met gave us encouraging smiles. A few looked away, and we repaid their ignorance with glares, rude comments and loud laughs.

Our errand took us to south-central Berlin. A long easy walk under a warm sun and jewel blue sky. When we arrived at the right address, we concealed our good moods beneath masks of seriousness. We handed over the envelope to a sour middle-aged Frau, her angles and creases sharper than anything on our uniforms. She nodded at our salutes and firm *"Heil Hitler!"* wrote a receipt and handed it to us without a word. We saluted again and left.

On the steps of the building, Jäger whispered, "She looked like a Doberman pinscher."

I said, "I'm glad she does not head up our HJ Schar." I growled and barked.

We walked away laughing. West to Wilhelmstrasse, then north. We approached an intersection as a black van tore around the corner in front of us. We glanced at each other and swung left – the direction the van had turned. It stopped in the middle of the long block. We suddenly realized where we were and what manner of van we were following. Prinz-Albrecht Strasse, home to the *Gestapo*.

Jäger and I halted when the back doors of the van opened. Two men hopped out, wearing trench coats on a hot day. I almost laughed, but did not dare. The two *Gestapo* agents hauled out a man who could barely stand. His head hung down as they dragged him into *Gestapo* headquarters. The question in my mind shone in Jäger's eyes. Would the man survive his interrogation? We had heard stories about *Gestapo* Headquarters. Everyone had.

"Poor fool," Jäger muttered.

"Fool is the right word," I replied. "Only a fool would do something to attract the attention of the secret police." The *Gestapo* might be necessary in the battle to rid Germany of its enemies, but no one liked it. Though if fear equaled respect, it was highly respected.

Jäger mentioned Herr Frankel and how he had never returned.

Herr Frankel had taught in our school. A year before, the *Gestapo* had raided his house and arrested him. I told Jäger to shut up, that the walls had ears, especially on this street.

I nudged him into motion and reminded him the girls were waiting. I spoke harshly, but a tremor rippled over my hot skin. The air felt muggy and damp with sweat. Herr Frankel had seemed a good man.

We turned north onto Stresemann toward Potsdamer Platz. The farther we got from Prinz-Albrecht Strasse, the clearer the air became. By the time we reached the plaza, the incident was behind us. We were giants, or soon to be, and no shadow – not even a *Gestapo* one – could darken our day or cast a bigger shadow than our own.

The girls were waiting for us in the lobby of the Fürstenhof. We hopped a streetcar, took them to the zoo and laughed at the animals, then strolled hand in hand through the Tiergarten and down the Unter den Linden. Our ScharFührer had been very generous.

Sunlight glinted off the insignia of officers' uniforms. We noted each rank, imitated each proud stride. Laughing, the girls linked their arms through ours and copied the haughty walk of a high-heeled Fräulein ahead of us. The line on her stockings was as straight as any HJ marching formation and led my eyes to slender ankles. Just before he took the Fräulein's arm, an *Oberst* – an actual colonel! – gave us a curt nod. In unison, Jäger and I snapped a salute, earning one in return. I was two centimetres taller when we escorted the girls into the cinema. Katrina gave me a look as warm and bright as the sun.

Inside the cinema, it was dark and cool. I paid little attention to the movie. My focus was on lovely Katrina. She had the long braids and modest uniform of a member of the League of German Maidens, but she filled out that uniform in all the right places. She leaned toward me when I draped my arm across the back of her seat, and tilted her head when I kissed her ear. She smelled of soap.

Jäger and Hedda were also ignoring the movie. They were busy kissing. Chaste kisses that satisfied the purity demanded by German Maiden teachings. Not what I had in mind at all.

Katrina was very accommodating and the back corner of the theatre was the perfect place to test the limits of her purity. Her mouth was willing, that much I quickly discovered. My hand had just established a beachhead inside her blouse when the rest of the audience groaned. Katrina shrank back. I looked up at the screen to see the picture disappearing as a circle of white burned toward the edges.

The lights came on. People began filing toward the exits. I slumped in my seat as Katrina tugged at her blouse and avoided looking my way. Such terrible timing. All I could think about was my desire to continue exploring the ample softness I had barely touched.

When it came to girls, Jäger knew I wanted nothing more than to take that all-important step in becoming a man. His warning look said, "Not with Hedda's friend." I was certain I could come close with Katrina but, for the sake of a blood brother, I would find a new target. I gave him a nod and took Katrina's hand to lead her out of the cinema.

Because the movie had ended abruptly, we had half an hour before Jäger's father was to meet us at the Brandenburg Gate. We strolled past a group of men outside the Adlon Hotel, civilians and soldiers, discussing a radio report. "How dare they cross the border!" a brown suit declared. Jäger and I halted, eyes on each other, ears on the conversation. The girls hovered beside us, their wary expressions revealing their uncertainty.

"They have gone too far, taking over a radio station like that," a blue pinstripe replied. He spat. "Dirty Poles."

The brown suit said, "You heard the report. The infiltrators were caught and shot."

The blue suit replied, "Not all of them. A few escaped."

An ss major pointed out that the Führer wouldn't let the Poles get away with such an insult.

Katrina yanked my hand and Hedda pulled on Jäger's arm. As we walked away, Hedda asked what the men had been talking about.

Jäger said, "It sounds like the Poles are looking for a fight."

Katrina's grip tightened. I squeezed back. Maybe I would have to test her defences one more time before I abandoned the field. She said, "Do you mean war?"

"I hope so," was my reply. My blood pumped at the very thought.

Jäger and I shared confident looks. We had no doubts who would win if Germans and Poles joined battle. We knew with equal certainty that the ss major was right: the Führer would not tolerate such an insult from the Poles. Our only regret was that we couldn't be part of it.

We woke the next morning to the news that our military had crossed into Poland, intent on securing peace in the neighbouring country. We were not surprised; the Poles had been asking for it.

Jäger and I had no time to listen to the radio broadcasts. School hadn't resumed so, though it was a Friday, we were scheduled for a full day of Hitler Youth training. The Schar was thrumming with excitement. The word hadn't been used yet, but this was war. I thought of my bravery during the live fire exercises we had undergone – creeping on our stomachs under real bullets, with real soldiers yelling at us to stay low and keep our heads down. I knew I was ready to face what our troops in Poland were facing. But the shooting would be long over before I got the chance to prove myself.

Though many of our parents were worried, the other older HJ members felt the same way I did. We released our frustrations in an extra-difficult training session, starting with the obstacle course and orders to run the whole way. No slacking. As usual, Jäger was the first one to finish the course. He laughed at the rest of us as we straggled onto the parade square. He pointed at me and said, "Bang! You're dead, Wolf. So slow, even a Pole could catch you!"

I bent over and braced my hands on my knees. "Not so!" I cried as I sucked in much-needed air. "I beat most of the others. They're the ones who are dead."

Jäger slapped my back and replied, "No Pole will get you on my watch, no matter how slowly you run."

I straightened and asked, "Does that mean your aim has improved?" We shared a grin.

When the whole Schar had completed the obstacle course, we practiced breaking down and re-assembling pistols. The younger boys were shaking so badly from the run, they could barely manage. Jäger and I took our pistols apart and put them together with no hesitation. We were both ready to join the regular forces; there was little else HJ could teach us. But an endless year loomed ahead of us, followed by at least six months in the Labour Service. Only then could we join the *Wehrmacht*.

Not the elite SS for us, though I had argued for it. Jäger had applied to the *Wehrmacht*, the regular forces, because that was the branch of the military his family had always served in. He wanted to be on the front lines, on the ground, in the trenches, battling it out hand to hand. Jäger, of course, could not imagine riding when you could run; I could not imagine service anywhere but at Jäger's side. We were a team. Blood brothers. I would join the *Wehrmacht* because Jäger was doing so. It did not matter to me, so long as I saw action.

Our HJ ScharFührer dismissed us in time to get home for *Abendbrot*. My mouth watered all the way, thinking about the bread and cheese and sausage waiting for me. After the evening meal I was tired, but restless. The radio reported the day's expected successes in Poland. Somewhere to the east battles were being fought, and I was stuck in Zethen.

I yelled to my parents that I was going over to Jäger's and let the door slam behind me. At Jäger's house, Herr and Frau Schreiber were on their way out. They sent me upstairs to Jäger's bedroom. It was one of two attic rooms, with short walls and sloping ceilings and a single window. His brothers shared the larger room at the front of the house. Jäger liked his room. It overlooked the garden which made it quiet; more importantly, it had a door.

A brief knock – our secret code – and I entered without waiting for a response. On the floor, Jäger was hunched over the radio he had repaired in the spring. He didn't look up. I don't think he even heard me, he was so intent, his left fingers poised on the dial.

A faint voice floated above the crackling. I closed the door quietly and strained to catch the words. It was a foreign language, though a few words sounded familiar. My heart stopped when I realized Jäger was listening to an English broadcast. The BBC.

He scribbled down something and turned his ear toward the speaker. He still hadn't noticed me. I prowled toward him, careful not to make the floorboards squeak. He wrote down something else. Jäger knew a little English, mostly because of his father, who read everything English he could get his hands on. Nothing much was available, but Herr Schreiber still managed to scrounge the odd newspaper – from where I never knew. A dangerous pastime, but I had never said anything because of my friendship with Jäger.

I halted behind Jäger, amazed I had been able to sneak up on him – something I had never done. The English words flowed from the battered radio in a garbled stream. The heat in the room pressed in as it tried to suffocate me. My heart hammered a wild beat.

I barked, "Attention!"

Jäger scrambled to his feet, his face white. He saw it was me and his breath whooshed out of him. His smile was shaky as he said, "You scared me half to death, Wolf."

My frown was fierce as I demanded to know what he was listening to.

He peered over my shoulder at the closed door and touched his finger to his lips.

I said, "It is the BBC, yes?"

He whispered, "Don't say that name. You were the one who said the walls have ears."

I replied, "And if they're listening, they know you're tuned to an English radio broadcast." I scowled down at him, though he wasn't much shorter than me any more, and ordered him to turn it off.

His look turned uncertain.

"Turn it off. Now. You know the law," I said as I pointed at the radio. "That could get your whole family arrested."

Jäger started to say, "But –"

I shoved him aside. He sprawled onto his bed. I kicked the radio as hard as I could. It flew against the wall with a thud. The front was indented, the speakers silent, but that wasn't enough. I ignored Jäger's shout and stomped on the radio. On the second strike it splintered.

"What did you do that for?" Jäger yelled as he jumped up.

"Why were you being so stupid?" I yelled back.

Jäger sagged onto the bed and said, "You're right. I don't know what got into me. I listened to the German broadcasts about Poland with my parents. I just wanted to hear...what other people were saying about our reaction to the Poles' attack."

I sat beside him. We were both quiet for a moment. Finally, curiosity demanded that I ask, "What did you hear?"

Jäger eyed the broken radio and said, "I couldn't understand everything. They talk too fast. The announcer said the invasion surprised the Poles, that they never received the Führer's settlement plan. In Warsaw they are saying the attack on the radio station in Gleiwitz was a lie."

"A lie?" I asked. "Who do they think attacked the radio station? Us?"

Jäger replied, "They're trying to make it look like they didn't start it, I guess, especially since they are already losing the battle after only a day."

I wanted to know what else they had said.

Jäger said, "They had just mentioned something about the first official German war communiqué when you tried to kill me with fright."

I replied, "I hope I scared the stupidity out of you."

"I guess you did," he said. Then he pointed at the shattered radio and complained he would never be able to fix it.

I was relieved. I forced him to promise never to touch the dial on his parents' radio. He did, noting that he didn't understand enough English to make it worth the risk anyway.

"Nothing is worth the risk," I said. "Remember those *Gestapo* we saw yesterday if you think about breaking a law again. We are Hitlerjugend. We don't break the law; we uphold it."

Jäger popped to his feet and snapped a straight-armed salute. *"Jawohl, mein Kommandant,"* he said as his usual grin returned.

I accepted the salute, smiled and said, "It's good to see you finally admitting who is in charge."

The silence in the living room was crammed with memories. Kurt pulled himself into the present. He smelled his own sweat and realized his heart was racing, as Wolf's had been in Jäger's bedroom on September 1, 1939. The first day of World War Two. Kurt slumped back. He felt wrung out, as if he had been there. After his pulse calmed again, Kurt turned to Marta, who was sitting on the loveseat beside him. She was staring at her grandfather as if he had grown a second head. "What's wrong, Marta?"

"I –" She broke off and continued to stare at her grandfather.

Herr Brandt chuckled. "I believe I know what the problem is, Kurt. I have shocked my granddaughter. She now knows that I was, shall we say, a Casanova in my youth." He leaned forward in his chair and whispered, "It is one of the reasons I married so late in life."

"Opa!" Marta flushed a deep crimson.

"Yes, yes, my dear. I apologize for shocking you. In truth, I forgot you were here. Sometimes, when I let myself remember, the past drags me into it and I forget where I am. I have always had a good memory. As I age it seems the memories from my youth are sharpening, not fading. Sometimes I remember those days better than I remember yesterday." Herr Brandt lifted a warning finger. "Do not think I am going senile. I remember yesterday just fine. Part of why I am writing my memoirs is to rid myself of those memories, or at least to soften them." He eyed Kurt. "You are not the only one who dreams, young Schreiber."

Kurt raised his brows but said nothing. He felt Marta's gaze. He hadn't told her the details of the dream and didn't intend to. Time to change the subject. "Will you tell us more?"

Herr Brandt sighed and relaxed into his wingback chair. "Not tonight. Even though I have rehearsed the stories so many times in my head, it is hard to speak of things I have been silent about. I never intended to speak about them at all, but expected my family to read my memoirs after I had died. If you were not Jäger's grandson..." The old man closed his eyes, his weariness visible in the sagging lines of his face.

You would not be telling me anything, Kurt finished silently. He studied Herr Brandt for a few seconds, then stood. After an awkward moment standing in the middle of the room, Kurt held his hand out and Marta took it. They headed to the front door.

"Kurt."

Herr Brandt's voice stopped the young people in the entry. Kurt peered at the old man, sitting under the light of the pole lamp like a prisoner in an interrogation cell. Except there was no fear in Herr Brandt's eyes – they were clear and blue, barely grey at all.

"Yes, sir?" Kurt said.

"Do not let my stories give you any ideas. You may walk Marta home. And I will allow you one kiss. A suitably modest kiss."

Heat surged over Kurt's cheeks. "Yes, sir."

Marta made a disgruntled sound.

"Not *sir*."

"Ah, right. I mean, Wolf."

The old man nodded. He closed his eyes again.

Kurt and Marta walked the first block in silence. Her palm was warm and dry where it pressed against his; her fingers rubbed his knuckles every few minutes. His enjoyment of the gentle touch evaporated when Marta said, "Why were you trying on that uniform? It was so eerie to walk in and —" She sighed. "I could almost convince myself Opa was just telling stories if I hadn't seen you. It makes it so real." She squeezed his hand. "Why, Kurt?"

"He wanted to show me what my grandfather looked like." Kurt frowned. "And he wanted to teach me a lesson."

"A lesson?"

"About the power a uniform has." *Come follow me.* The soldier from the mirror nodded in Kurt's mind's eye. "Never mind. You weren't supposed to see. It's...a man thing."

"A... Men are so childish sometimes. Why does Opa even have that uniform? I'm pretty sure it's against the law to own one."

"I don't think he has it because he still believes in Nazi ideas. He probably put it away and forgot about it...until I came along. After all, it was my grandfather's uniform, not his."

Suddenly she blurted, "I cannot believe my grandfather did that!"

Kurt looked at her. The way she was blushing, he knew her mind was no longer on the uniform. "Did what? Got fresh with a busty Fräulein in the back row of the cinema?" A grin tugged at his mouth.

Marta released Kurt's hand and elbowed him. "Don't you dare think it's funny."

Recapturing her hand, Kurt held tight. "Of course it's funny. While the German army was staging a fake attack on a radio station to start a war, sixteen-year-old Wolf Brandt was attempting his own...invasion." Kurt chuckled. When Marta flushed a deeper red than Kurt had ever seen, her lips thinned and her eyes glimmering suspiciously, Kurt cringed. "It's nothing to cry about, Marta. It just shows that he was a normal guy."

"Oh? Is that what you usually do in the cinema?"

"Well, ah...no." He rarely found the courage to ask a girl out.

"He's my grandfather, Kurt. It's not...proper."

They were on Marta's block. At the other end, Kurt noticed a group of three young men walking toward them, Peter Neumeyer in the middle. They were almost at Marta's house and she hadn't noticed them, so Kurt said nothing.

As Marta unlocked her front gate, Kurt asked, "Why does your grandfather always leave his gate unlocked? He's the only person in this town I know who does that."

She pocketed the key. "Every time Mom reminds him that he should lock it, he shrugs and says he would rather invite people in than lock them out. Mom thinks it's a habit from when he was mayor and liked to be thought of as someone you could come to with a problem." She paused. "What if...he used to leave it unlocked to...to make sure his lady friends could easily come and go?" She looked completely disgusted by the thought.

Kurt smirked as he ushered Marta into her yard. "Out of curiosity, did you hear anything your grandfather said after he told about his cinematic adventure?"

"Of course."

"Like what my great-grandfather liked to read?"

"I... No, I missed that." Marta sniffed.

Kurt glanced over his shoulder. No sign of Neumeyer. He followed Marta up the steps to her door. "Or how Wolf reacted to Jäger's choice of radio broadcasts?"

"No... Wait! Yes! He told Jäger to turn it off." Marta gave Kurt a smug look.

Kurt chuckled. "That picture of your grandfather with his hand down some girl's blouse really scrambled your brain, didn't it?"

The deep blush returned. "You ever try that with me in such a public place and I will cut off your hand."

"You'd have to stand in line behind your grandfather on that one. Do you think I'd even try? I didn't know I had the reputation of being a...Casanova." Kurt grinned. He cupped his hand along her jaw. "I am told, however, that I may kiss you. Only once, though."

"Oh? And what makes you think I'll let you kiss me at all?"

"I have permission." Kurt bent toward Marta, only a little, since she was almost his height. He whispered, "If I'm only allowed one kiss, we'd better make it a good one."

"But it has to be mod—"

Their lips meeting silenced Marta. Kurt lost himself in the kiss. Now she tasted like cinnamon and tea. She smelled of apples. When she would have stepped back, Kurt drew her closer and deepened the kiss. It was several moments before they broke apart.

Marta's eyes were dark, bottomless. Deep enough to drown in. Kurt couldn't look away. She licked her lips. "I don't think Opa would consider that kiss modest."

Kurt quietly replied, "But my hands behaved themselves."

Marta narrowed her eyes, opened her mouth, then closed it. "I'm going inside now. Good night, Kurt." She slipped inside and peered at him through a wide crack.

"Good night, Marta." Kurt smiled as she closed the door in his face.

Kurt spun and halted, his foot hovering above the second step. Peter Neumeyer stood at the gate, staring at him. How long had he been there? Kurt stared back, hoping his anxiety was hidden. With pretended casualness, Kurt sat on the step, as if waiting for Marta to return.

It was almost three minutes before Peter gave Kurt a sneer and continued down the street. Kurt waited another three for his pulse to return to normal.

Feigling. Coward.

Kurt rubbed his thigh, which had barely bothered him since his run around the lake. He waited a moment more, wondering what his grandfather would have done in a similar situation. But his grandfather had more likely been one of the bullies than one of the bullied. One of the Hitler Youth, harassing anyone who didn't fit in, punishing those who failed to pass the test.

We were children, Kurt.

Kurt rubbed his thigh again. Yes, but children could hit hard when they wanted to. They could even kill if they wanted to – as in *Lord of the Flies*. Kurt headed for home, after making sure Peter Neumeyer was nowhere to be seen.

Chapter Sixteen

"**I** should be angry at you," Kurt said.

Victor stopped and stared over his bicycle at his friend. "Why?"

Kurt kept walking and Victor joined him, still pushing his bicycle. Sometimes Kurt wished he had taken up Herr Klassen's offer to fix his old bicycle. It was how most people got around Zethen. With the patches of pine forest filling a block here, two blocks there, spreading the town into a crazy quilt of town and trees, cycling was easier than walking.

"Why?" Victor repeated.

"Because almost all I can think about is kissing Marta."

"Ha! And that's my fault?"

"Yes. You were the one who first suggested it."

"Otherwise you never would have kissed her on Friday night, I suppose. Okay. I'll take the blame for that. But why should one little kiss occupy your mind so much? It's not as if..."

Kurt studied the stand of trees they were passing, hating the heat colouring his cheeks.

"Wait." Victor grabbed Kurt's arm and they halted. "You've been holding out on me."

"I didn't know you expected to know every detail of every minute –"

"Just the interesting ones." Victor grinned. "Confess."

"What's to tell? We've kissed twice since Friday. No big deal." Kurt lurched into motion.

"Right. No big deal. You're the one mooning over three kisses." Victor snorted. "I saw the first one. It was pretty tame. The other two must have been something special."

"Shut up, Victor."

"You're the one who brought it up."

Kurt didn't answer. They turned onto Lindenstrasse, the main street in the old part of Zethen, where most of the businesses could be found. Two blocks down, Kurt saw the small round sign for *Gunter's Apotheke*, which brought Marta to mind again. Between thinking about her and his grandfather's past, it was hard to concentrate on anything else. He glanced at Victor, an unexpected friend – the one good thing to come out of Peter's bullying. The Liebermanns' garage was around the corner from the pharmacy and a block off Lindenstrasse. It was out of Kurt's way, but he enjoyed talking with Victor, even if he was too observant.

A block ahead, Kurt noticed a familiar brown trench coat and fedora. Herr Brandt strolled down the sidewalk, back straight, cane swinging in a lazy arc. Maybe age had slowed him, but he managed the change with the grace of a king, nodding to the subjects that he met. Because of his slow pace, they were gaining on him. They were half a block away when a trio burst out of the bakery onto the street and bumped into the old man. If it had not been for his cane, he would have fallen. Kurt's heart tripped when he realized the trio consisted of Peter and two friends. Kurt sprinted forward when Herr Brandt shook his cane at the young men. Peter stiffened and stuck out his chest. Still a few metres away, Kurt yelled, "Neumeyer!"

Fists balled, Peter turned his sneer toward Kurt, who skidded to a halt between the bully and the old man. Kurt said, "Back off, Neumeyer. Pick on someone your own age."

"You maybe?"

Kurt lifted his chin, trying to recall what Tyler had taught him about self-defence. "He's an old man. Even you can't be that much of an ass −" He cut off, inwardly cursing his mouth.

"What did you call me?" Peter seemed to grow in anger until he towered over Kurt, who just stared. Peter whispered, "You called me an ass."

"You kick like one. I have the bruises to prove it."

Peter's friends snickered. The bully looked around, as did Kurt, noting the bystanders. A pair of young boys stood by their bicycles, expressions eager. A middle-aged woman frowned at them. A policeman leaned against his green and white car. Flexing his fingers, Peter stepped away. "Watch your back, Schreiber. Not that it will do you any good."

"Do not threaten this young man simply because he chooses to act with honour," Herr Brandt said from behind Kurt.

"Stay out of this, old man. I said you can't beat me, Schreiber. I meant it. Your luck won't protect you forever." Peter glanced at the policeman and stalked away, his friends following.

Kurt let out a slow breath.

"Why did you have to let your mouth run away again?" Victor asked.

"Because I'm stupid."

"Can't argue with that." Victor gave Kurt a sympathetic look. "I have to get to the garage. Dad will be wondering where I am."

"I'll walk Herr Brandt home."

"Contrary to your belief, I do not need your protection, Kurt," Herr Brandt said.

"No, but I might need yours," Kurt said. Victor laughed and rode away on his bicycle.

"If you wish to walk with me, I need to stop at the pharmacy first."

"Sure. Do you like *Apfelstrudel?*" When Herr Brandt nodded, Kurt added, "I'll buy a few and we can eat them at your place, if that's okay." Kurt loved the delicious apple pastries and welcomed any excuse to buy some.

"That sounds fine, Kurt. Thank you." Herr Brandt headed toward the pharmacy.

When Kurt emerged from the bakery, the policeman was waiting on the sidewalk. He nodded at Kurt. "Thank you for stepping between Herr Brandt and young Neumeyer. That was brave. He would have hit you if he hadn't spotted me. Neumeyer and I have tangled before."

It wasn't brave, it was...what needed to be done. Kurt shrugged.

"Is there a problem, Herr Offizier?" Herr Brandt asked as he approached.

"No problem, Herr Brandt. I was just thanking the young man for what he did."

"Yes, yes. Brave, if a trifle foolish. But then the brave often are."

The policeman's brow wrinkled. "Are what?"

"Foolish. Rushing in where angels fear to tread." Herr Brandt tipped his fedora. "Good day, officer. Come along, Kurt."

Kurt matched his pace to the old man's slower one. "I'm not brave." *Just foolish.*

"So you say." Herr Brandt whistled a folk song and swung his cane as they walked. Kurt kept silent, wondering at the old man's confidence. Was it something that came with age? Kurt didn't want to wait that long.

At Herr Brandt's house, they settled in the kitchen since the clouds looked ready to release their loads. Herr Brandt filled the kettle and gave Kurt a plate for the *Apfelstrudel.*

The old man chuckled. "Six? Who is going to eat so many pastries?"

"They won't go to waste. I promise."

Reaching for some cups, Herr Brandt said, "Sit. You are hovering the way Marta does, as if I am going to collapse, exhausted from doing a few simple chores."

"Sorry." Kurt slid onto a chair and bit into an *Apfelstrudel.*

When the water boiled, Herr Brandt prepared the teapot and brought it to the table. He raised one eyebrow. "Only five pastries now? Your word is good, I see."

"Grandfather always says that a promise given should be a promise kept."

"True. Jäger's word was always good as well. I am the one who breaks promises."

Kurt waited for an explanation but it didn't come. The pair ate an *Apfelstrudel* each, then Herr Brandt leaned back to sip his tea. Kurt wrapped his hands around his cup and enjoyed the warmth. Impatience gnawed at him, but he strove to let Herr Brandt set the tone of the visit. They chatted about the places Kurt had visited with the other exchange students.

"The group's going to Amsterdam the first weekend in May. I'm not sure I want to go."

"That is this weekend."

Kurt glanced at the calendar by the refrigerator. He groaned. April had disappeared. He only had two months left in Germany.

"You should go. Amsterdam has many fine things to see."

"Yeah, I know. The canals, the museums. I'm not into art museums. I'll be stuck in the *Rijksmuseum* for hours with nothing but paintings to see. And I sure don't want to waste my time looking at sunflowers in the Van Gogh museum."

"The *Rijksmuseum* has some fine historical artifacts on the lower floor. Swords, armour, models of ships. I'm sure you can find something to interest you. As for Van Gogh, I do not care for his paintings much myself. But there are other museums in Amsterdam that might interest you. The maritime museum, for example."

"Maybe." Kurt shrugged. "It might be interesting to see the Anne Frank House." He sipped his tea, feeling suddenly awkward. Anne Frank had died in a Nazi concentration camp.

"Yes, yes. While you're at it, suggest to your leader that a visit to the *Verzetsmuseum* would be quite instructional."

"The what?"

"It is a museum commemorating the Dutch Resistance in World War Two."

Kurt blinked. "You've been there?"

"Is there a reason why I would not go to it?"

"Well...you're...you know..." Kurt averted his eyes and gulped down his tea.

"A former Nazi." Herr Brandt sighed. "That was a long time ago, Kurt. I cannot change the past. Believe it or not, I like to see people remembering so it does not happen again."

"But Sunday, when you were telling about being in the Hitler Youth, you sounded so...enthusiastic."

"So I was, back in the 1930s. I am trying to tell the story as it happened. To fill the telling with regret when I felt none as a young man would be unfaithful, would it not?"

"I suppose."

"Do you wish me to tell you a little more?"

Kurt straightened. He couldn't keep the anticipation from his voice. "Right now?"

Herr Brandt poured himself more tea. "Will we get in trouble with Marta?"

"I can tell her whatever you tell me later, if that's okay."

"That would be fine. But you might want to shorten the story, if there are any parts you think might embarrass her." Herr Brandt winked.

Remembering Marta's deep blush the night before, Kurt bit back a chuckle. He picked up another *Apfelstrudel* and settled back, eager to be swept into his grandfather's past. Herr Brandt's gaze drew distant; it was many moments before he spoke.

Chapter Seventeen

In February of 1940, Jäger and I got our wish. We folded our *Hitlerjugend* uniforms for the last time and tucked away our ceremonial daggers. Because we had joined the Hitlerjugend early, we were leaving it the same way, at seventeen. Our ScharFührer handed us our marching orders; we would serve our six-month term in the *Reichsarbeitsdienst* – the Reich Labour Service – near the mouth of the Peene River. We puzzled over the map, wondering why a work camp was even on the spit of land, inhabited by only two small towns, Zinnowitz and Peenemünde. We decided the army must be building fortifications to protect the Oder River, which flowed so close to Berlin and joined the Baltic in the same region. It was exciting to think we would be part of something so important.

It was bitterly cold that last morning on the platform of the Zethen train station. Jäger's father patted his mother's back while she sobbed into her second handkerchief of the morning. My mother dabbed at her eyes. My father was not there.

When the train's white plume could be seen, announcing its near arrival, Hedda rushed onto the platform and threw herself at Jäger. She clung to him and wept. Jäger turned a bright red that matched nicely with his dull grey work uniform. When

I pointed that out, he gave me a look that said the remark would not go unpunished. I grinned.

What a relief I didn't have a girl embarrassing me like that. Jäger had to promise to write every day before Herr Schreiber could coax Hedda to release him so he could get on the train. On board, we stuffed our rucksacks under the seat. I tried to get comfortable on the hard bench while Jäger hung out the window and waved to Hedda. Steam hid the platform as the train pulled out of the station. Jäger dropped onto the seat and his breath huffed out.

I pressed my shoulder against Jäger's and, in a high voice, whispered, "Oh, Jäger. How will I ever live without you? I will cry into my pillow every night."

"No, you won't," Jäger muttered, "because I'll use that pillow to smother you."

I laughed, which earned me an elbow in the ribs.

"Shut up, Wolf," he said. "What do you know about it? Your idea of love is trying to get your hand up Gertrude Reimer's skirt."

The thought made me smile. I said, "I came very close. You leave only one broken heart behind. Not even broken, because you promised undying love. While I leave a string of broken hearts. This morning, pillows are being soaked all over Zethen because of my leaving."

Jäger replied, "And fathers all over Zethen are rejoicing."

I pretended indignance and demanded, "Why? I soiled no one's reputation."

"Not for lack of trying," was Jäger's response.

Arms crossed, I slid down in my seat and grinned. I was the Aryan ideal – blond hair, blue eyes, tall and fit. Girls flew to me like bees to wildflowers. The train was carrying me into a new meadow with a new hive of bees. Nineteen forty looked to be a good year.

I don't think we were ever warm that first month. February on the Baltic Sea is not holiday weather. Storms attacked the shores. Waves crashed over the wide beaches and sometimes threatened to swamp our nearby camp. A chill settled in our bones. The damp clung to everything. Each evening we would hold our sleeping bags open in front of a fire, if we could get one going, trying to dry them out, until a supervisor told us to douse the flames. Blackout rules were strictly enforced.

Every morning we were up before daybreak to gulp down a bowl of *Haferschleim* – oatmeal – and a scalding cup of bitter coffee. We would march to our work site and spend the morning digging ditches or building up berms and roads. They allowed us only a few minutes for a lunch of bread and cheese and more coffee. Each afternoon passed as the morning had. We would arrive back at camp too tired even to eat, though we quickly learned to do so anyway.

Our supervisors were military. A *Luftwaffe* base, called Peenemünde West, took up the north end of the Usedom penninsula. Peenemünde East and South were a mystery – a series of buildings and barracks that we could get in trouble for looking at. The work camp was several kilometres southeast of the outermost barracks. Because we were sometimes required to restore shore defences ravaged by winter storms, we knew the settlement was a military installation. We knew not to ask questions. In truth, we were simply too tired to be curious. Jäger was even too tired to write to Hedda.

Blisters became calluses. Muscles hardened and the weariness grew less consuming. Winter loosed its grip; the seaside became pleasant. Jäger found the energy to pick up his pen.

Except on the weekends, we were confined to camp, not that anyone had the desire to go anywhere after a hard shift. As the days lengthened, so did the hours we spent over a shovel. I needed an outlet for my frustration at being unable to discover the delights of nearby Zinnowitz. Since we were camped by the beach, I convinced the supervisor that swimming didn't qualify as leaving camp.

I towed Jäger over the grass-covered dune that stood between our tents and the beach. Jäger pointed out that it was mid-March and the water would be icy. I told him to quit whining like a boy.

He said, "I'm not whining. But it's foolish. We'll get pneumonia. If you need something to keep your mind off girls, why don't you...write a letter to your parents or read a book?"

Our schooling had focused on science, mathematics and physical fitness. I scoffed at the idea of writing a letter. A painful exercise I would do for no one – not even my mother. Reading a book held even less appeal. I told him to write a letter for me as I halted on the beach and released him. I said, "But now, you'll swim with me."

He said, "If you weren't my best friend I'd tell you to go wrestle a wild boar."

My grin was hidden from Jäger's sight by the cloudy night. He was little more than a silhouette and the water a slick of unruffled blackness. I stripped off my shirt. Cool air painted goosebumps over my skin. I said, "But I am your best friend, so unless you want me to toss you into the sea fully clothed, I suggest you undress."

He tried to bribe me with an offer of a week's stipend, but what was I going to do with another puny fifty *Reichspfennig?* I had not been able to spend what I had earned as it was. I told him to shut up, quit stalling and start stripping.

I tucked my socks in my boots, peeled off my trousers and smiled when I heard Jäger muttering as he undressed. I waited in my shorts, rubbing my upper arms and shifting from side to side, until Jäger was in the same state. He asked, "The shorts, too?"

I replied that I was not going to sleep in wet underwear. Jäger chuckled. In unison, we sloughed off our shorts and dashed into the sea. I lunged over the first waves, and leaped again when I touched down. I landed in waist-deep water and plunged under, arms pumping before I surfaced, in a bid to keep from turning into an ice cube.

Off to my right, Jäger called my name. I swam toward the sound.

Jäger sputtered, "Y-you're crazy."

"You're the one who c-came with me," I said as I treaded water. My voiced trembled as I added, "F-five...no, two minutes."

We were strong swimmers, but by the time we left the water, my legs were as heavy as railroad ties. I said nothing because I didn't want Jäger saying, "I told you so." I dragged him to the water three times per week. When May arrived, either the water had warmed up or we had gotten used to it; we were swimming every night unless it was too rough.

In May, the brilliance of the Führer shone for all to see when our armies rolled through western Europe in weeks, virtually unchallenged. Only the British remained unconquered because they cowered on their little island fortress. All

Germany celebrated a quick end to the war. Parades and celebrations. The camp chafed at being stuck far from the festivities, working on a spit of land that seemed worthless.

The sun warmed the beaches and lowlands of Usedom, and seemed to envelope all Germany in a warm glow. Summer unrolled in a series of hard days and short nights. When we worked out of sight of a town, we stripped to our waists. Soon our skin was as golden as the sand. My hair bleached pale yellow while Jäger's was streaked bronze. Like the other labourers, we became sleek and muscular.

My only regret was that this failed to impress the girls of Zinnowitz, who behaved with strict German Maiden propriety. I often caught them looking when we tripped into town, but they kept their distance. Only the barmaids were welcoming, but they were claimed by labourers who had been there longer than Jäger and me. One barmaid kept her eye on me anyway. Cornelia – Corny, we called her. She was a wide-faced girl, with thick brown braids and an hourglass figure that her boss insisted she show off with laced bodices and low-cut blouses. I enjoyed the view.

One Saturday night, a mug of beer slammed onto my table and a body blocked my sightseeing. Corny's man scowled down at me. Jäger tried to keep me in my seat, but I shook him off and stood. The fellow was my height but wider, with heavy brows and black piglet eyes.

He growled at me to keep my eyes off his girl. I smiled and said, "A guy can look, Mertel. I hear you're off to the army next week."

Before I saw it coming, his fist tumbled me over my chair. I sprawled on the floor, waiting for the room to stop spinning. Mertel leaned over me and said, "Get up and fight, boy."

Before I could reply, a screaming Corny flew at the lummox and began beating on him with a wooden tray. She yelled, "Brute! Pig! I never want to see you again!"

It took two men to haul Corny off Mertel; three to man-handle him out of the beer hall. By that time I was sitting, poking at my already-swelling eye. Corny helped me to my feet, crooning over how she would get me fixed up. I gave Jäger a pleased shrug and he rolled his eyes. She led me through the kitchen to a tiny bedroom that had probably been a storage room. She left me with a cool cloth laid over the bruise and orders to stay put. I dozed. When I woke, Corny was half undressed, smiling at me as she continued to peel off layers. Hers and then mine.

When I snuck back into camp, it was almost dawn. Thankfully, Sunday was a free day. I stripped down to my shorts and had just crawled into my sleeping bag when Jäger said, "Don't do anything stupid, Wolf. One of the locals told me she goes through the same performance every time she wants to change lovers."

I propped myself up on my elbow, irritated that Jäger wasn't congratulating me for finally getting what I'd wanted for so long. "Don't talk about my girl like that," I warned. "If you want to pine away after Hedda, go ahead. I know what I'm doing."

He mentioned that, this close to Peenemünde, the patrols were serious. When I told him I had had to avoid one that night, he sighed.

His worry proved unfounded. Mostly. The odd time I had to hide from a patrol when I returned from visiting Corny. Sometimes we would meet midweek, in the sand dunes between the camp and town. Jäger always covered for me, though I knew he wasn't happy about it.

August trickled into September with no word of our release from the Labour Service into the *Wehrmacht*. It was midmonth before we finally heard that our term of service had been extended to nine months. Something about a backlog of trainees they had to move through before bringing in more. I was secretly pleased. That meant I could keep seeing Corny.

The last Saturday of our labour stint, we walked into Zinnowitz, as always. The beer hall was humming. I was looking forward to one last night with Corny. When I saw her eyeing one of the recently arrived labourers, I guess I shouldn't have been surprised, but I was. Jäger laughed at me. I considered decking him, but remembered what he had told me after my first night with the lusty barmaid. I joined in his laughter.

Still grinning, I headed over to congratulate the newest object of Corny's affections. I saw the locals watching me, wanting a fight. When I held out my hand to the surprised fellow, a wooden tray slammed into my arm. I turned from Corny's attack. She hammered my back with the tray, yelling, "Heartless pig! Brute! Get out of my sight!"

I yanked the tray from the crazy woman, threw it under a table and asked, "Is that any way to say goodbye, Corny?"

She lifted a hand to slap me. Two men grabbed her arms and she strained at them, giving me one last view of her heaving chest. I leaned over to give her a kiss, encouraged by hoots all around. Shadows flickered through her eyes and I realized I was seeing pain. She didn't want me to leave, probably hadn't wanted any of her lovers to leave. She wanted one of us to rescue her. I shook my head and turned away. She was only two years older and I liked her, but not that much.

Hands in my pockets, I headed to the door where Jäger waited. With Corny crying behind us and the beer hall sounds swelling to drown the sound, we stepped into the cool October night. The wind was rising. There was going to be a storm. But come Monday morning, we wouldn't be the ones repairing the damage. We'd be on our way home.

"Did you have to humiliate her?" Jäger asked.

I peered at the starless sky, feeling like scum, and said, "She attacked me."

He whispered, "I think I would have punched you if you had actually kissed her."

I would have deserved it. I slapped Jäger's back and said, "It's good our ScharFührer's recommendation got us posted to the same unit. You keep me honest. I couldn't imagine army life without you, Jäger."

"As you said when we left Zethen," he said, "you'd cry into your pillow every night."

I could hear the grin in his words and had to laugh. I had been right nineteen forty had been a good year, and there were still two months left. November was ours. We didn't officially join the Ninth Army until December 1.

We spent November in Zethen. I felt like a third wheel on a bicycle whenever Jäger spent time with Hedda, which was as often as possible. At home I realized how much nine months away had changed me. I was a man, and didn't appreciate the way my parents still tended to treat me like a boy. My father and I often clashed.

I had only been home a week when I stormed out of the house after arguing with my father over my choice of beer as a supper beverage. Father insisted wine accompany the evening meal. I despised wine. Before I had cooled off, I was two kilometres west of town.

The small town, my family, Jäger's occupation with Hedda, everything was conspiring to drive me crazy. I leaned on a fence and stared at a crack of light spilling into the night from a dairy barn across the pasture. Not good observation of blackout rules. Maybe some cowherding *Dummkopf* needed to learn a lesson. I hoped he was big. A fight might release a little tension.

I slipped into the barn, banged the door shut and yelled, "Hey, *Dummkopf!* You want to let the British know where your barn is so they can blow it to pieces?" That should have been an idle accusation; Goring had promised that no British airplane would darken German skies, but they had managed to bomb Berlin in September. The blackout was deadly serious.

A Fräulein popped up from behind a cow, knocking over her milking stool. The horror on her face was almost comical. I glanced around. No big cowherder to be seen. I smiled.

Her eyes rounded. She said, "You're Wolf Brandt."

I asked how she knew me; I didn't know her. She replied that I had dated her cousin, Katrina Mueller. Hedda's friend, Katrina. I had the feeling my reputation had preceded me. I kept my face expressionless and asked if Katrina had spread rumours about me.

"Oh, she isn't the only one who has done that," the milkmaid said with a smile, and added, "Katrina didn't exaggerate about how handsome you are."

That brought a smile. "What else did she tell you?" I asked.

The milkmaid bit her lip, then said I was supposedly a good kisser. I offered to let her find out, but she blushed and said she had work to do. So I offered to help, if it would give her some free time. She considered me for a moment, then nodded.

Bertha Mueller was her name. It took a week of helping her each night before I talked her into putting the hayloft to good use. She was sweet and loving. I should have known she would be trouble. That last night we took a last roll in the hay. Afterwards, I said goodbye and told her not to show up at the train station. Her tears soaked my shirt. I finally had to push her away.

The next day on the train, Jäger asked me what was wrong. Instead of keeping quiet, I blurted, "I didn't know she was a virgin." When he asked if I meant Bertha, I said, "She didn't act like a virgin, flirting and such." I stared out the window at pine trees darkened by the rain that matched my mood and explained how she had promised to wait for me. And wanted me to write.

Jäger asked, "And you said...?"

"I don't write letters," was my reply. It angered Jäger, who demanded to know if that was all I had said, so I added that I had told her not to wait.

He voiced my fear when he said, "What if she's pregnant?"

"Don't even think it," I replied. "I'm not going to end up married to a milkmaid."

"Don't be such a louse, Wolf," Jäger said. He got up and moved to the other end of the car. I returned to staring out the window. I had learned my lesson. I'd be more careful next time.

That night, in crowded barracks, I tried to get comfortable on my bunk. The first thing our commander had done was order us to stretch out on the ground, then he had strolled over every part of his human carpet while he had lectured us on expectations.

Our commander was a big man. I settled on my stomach and whispered to Jäger in the bunk under mine, "I'm sorry."

"I'm not the one you need to apologize to," he said.

I told him, "She was a mistake. You're my friend."

He said he'd forgive me if I wrote to her and apologized. It was tempting to wring his neck, but I knew he was right. I said, "Only for you, Schreiber."

"No," came the whispered reply. "You have to live with yourself, Wolf. This is for you."

He was annoying when he was right. He sometimes said the same thing about me.

We were both wrong in thinking we were tough. The nine months in the Labour Service had beaten us into steel, but now the army sharpened us to a fine edge. We marched on little or no sleep, we learned to fight above and beyond everything that had been taught us in the *Hitlerjugend*. That had been four years of fun and games compared to the grueling training the army put us through.

Responses became automatic. Shout and we snapped to attention or hit the dirt. Come at us with even a fake punch and we blocked and struck. Obedience was absolute. Punishment for disobedience was immediate, and impressed upon all by having us watch the offender suffer. Seeing one soldier dragged to the infirmary for treatment was enough for me. There would be no sneaking out of this camp to visit local barmaids.

But pride and confidence replaced youthful uncertainty. We were part of the greatest army the world had ever seen. And by April of 1941 we knew something was being planned.

I remember one evening when Jäger and I sat on the barrack steps, backs to the wall, collars undone to catch the breeze. Soldiers lounged around, enjoying the rare chance to relax after a light day of battle exercises. The smell of cigarette smoke wafted on the air.

Liedke, also a private, joined us and wondered aloud if they were planning to send us to Holland, or maybe France. I scoffed, "To patrol occupied areas?"

Jäger said, "They're working us too hard for that. We're going to see action."

Liedke suggested Africa.

I replied, "Rommel is in Africa and has already had his first victory. He doesn't want or need the Ninth's help."

Jäger leaned forward and said, "Do you want to know where I think they're going to send us?" Liedke nodded. Jäger relaxed against the wall and crossed his arms. "England."

Liedke protested, "But they were going to invade last fall and postponed it."

"True, but it's the only thing that makes sense," Jäger said. "We weakened England with aerial attacks all last year and are continuing to do so. Last fall must not have been the right time. This year we will show those British bulldogs what German land troops are capable of."

I agreed, saying that England would fall in weeks, months at the most.

Jäger said, "They're tougher than the French, but not so tough as us. We're Krupp's steel." He pulled his knife from its sheath, letting the sun glint off its edge to stress his point.

Liedke laughed that we would slaughter them like the dogs they were. Someone called his name and he waved to us as he marched away. I watched him go and asked Jäger if it would really be that easy. He said no, but that it would happen. A few moments of silence and Jäger decided to go write a letter to

Hedda. I had little use for letters, especially after the last one I had received. As Jäger started to get up he glanced at me, sat back down and demanded to know what was wrong. I told him to go write his letter.

Instead of leaving, he guessed that I was troubled by the letter I'd received from my father. We had known each other too long. I couldn't keep any secrets from him.

He said, "Don't make me drag it from you, Wolf."

So I explained how Father was furious because Bertha had come to him early in January. She thought she was pregnant and I hadn't answered her letters. I hadn't read them, just thrown them out. I didn't even know.

When Jäger sighed and asked what my father had done, I told how he had offered to pay to get rid of the baby. I didn't love Bertha, but it galled me that my father would offer to destroy my child. Motherhood was a sacred calling. If Bertha had given me a son, I would have honoured that by supporting her, no matter how I felt.

Jäger wanted to know why he had waited so long to tell me. Bertha had refused his offer. Time had proven her wrong. She wasn't pregnant. Father was only happy about one thing – he'd saved himself that money. I explained how the rest of the letter was a lecture on making sure I didn't get caught in some other milkmaid's trap. It wouldn't do for Dietrich Brandt's son to be saddled with...an inappropriate wife.

Jäger said, "Just what you told me when we were headed here."

I told him to shut up, that I wasn't like my father. All he wanted was to thicken his wallet, but we stood for something bigger. Blood and honour. Not just filthy money. Honour.

Jäger wondered aloud whether Father supported rebuilding the Fatherland. His tone was mildly curious, not accusing. I said, "He supports it fine, so long as it lines his pockets. He's using labour from the prison camp near Berlin, Sachsenhausen, in one of his factories now. He spends more time at his apartment in Berlin than he does at home with his wife and daughter. I think he has a mistress."

Jäger lifted his shoulders, as if to say, "Would you do any differently?" My anger was cut off when Jäger stood and stretched and warned me to not stay up too long, that he had the feeling our faithful captains were going to make up for this easy day.

I agreed. I had learned long before to trust Jäger's instincts. Being unable to resist a pretty girl didn't make me like my father, not in a way that mattered. And honour made me different. I vowed I would hold onto my honour, like Jäger did. I retired knowing I had something to help me that my father didn't; I had Jäger as a friend, forcing me to be honest.

And I was honestly sorry I had hurt Bertha. Though that didn't stop me from wondering if I would ever get to find out how much girls liked a man in uniform. Eight weeks later, girls were the last thing on my mind. The troop trains were on the move, but they were carrying us the wrong way. East, not west. Everyone in our company was tense, edgy. Rumours ran rampant.

Operation Barbarossa. Our superiors said the Bolsheviks were preparing to attack, so the Führer was beating them to it, breaking the non-aggression pact Germany had with Russia. We understood the evils of Communism, but it made no sense. The threat on our western flank had to be eliminated before we faced another enemy. Anyone could see that. What was the Führer thinking? We sat, eyes downcast so no one would see our doubt, because doubt was a traitorous state of mind, one none of us dared own up to.

Doubt vanished in the smoke of victory. Another *Blitzkrieg*. In days the Red Air Force was wiped out by our *Luftwaffe*. Tanks advanced so quickly that we foot soldiers struggled in vain to keep up through gruelling hikes across endless distances. Tired legs. Sore feet. Sweat. Heat. And frustration – for the fighting seemed always to be to the right or left of us.

Our unit came to a larger town on the fourth day. The tanks had rumbled around it in their eastward race, and we were under orders to secure it. We approached the main street, a dirt road. Crude houses with thatched roofs faced the roadway. A few pigs rooted in flower beds and gardens. The townsfolk had apparently fled. Captain Rothe ordered us to advance in pairs.

Liedke and another private took point. Jäger and I were close behind, scanning every window and nook. The silence buzzed. I rolled out my steps to keep quiet. A breeze carried the smell of pig manure. As we neared the town's centre, where a communal barn stood, tension began to coil in my gut. They were only Russians, I told myself. They had likely retreated.

Halfway down the street, Jäger touched my left arm. I froze. My heart pounded as I studied the street, trying to see what he saw or sensed. Sweat trickled into my eyes.

Suddenly, Jäger shoved me right. He dived left and yelled, "Snipers!" Something nicked my sleeve and I heard a zing. As I hit the ground, I saw Liedke flung backward by an invisible force. I rolled and scrambled to a doorway. Across the road,

Jäger also pressed himself against a door. Liedke didn't move; his blood moistened the dry Russian dirt. His partner was also hit. He moaned and tried to crawl away. Two bullets ripped into him. I fired a shot down the street, just to let the Russians know they hadn't gotten me, then stared at Liedke. I had seen a few corpses already, but never someone I knew. Vomit clawed at my throat.

"The barn," Jäger shouted, drawing my attention.

From down the street, the captain yelled, "Keep them busy! Lay down covering fire!"

I gave Jäger a puzzled shrug. He made a circling motion. The bulk of the unit would circle around and trap the Russians. I aimed at a window of the barn. My shot was answered by half a dozen. Plaster chips sprayed me in the face when a bullet shaved the door frame. More than just one or two snipers hid in that barn. I glanced at my left sleeve and noticed the tear. Jäger had saved my life. Behind us, more German guns joined the battle. The pop and whine of bullets became constant.

It was over almost as suddenly as it had begun. A pair of explosions, followed by a hail of gunfire, and the doors of the barn burst open. Three Russians fell to our guns. The rest threw down their weapons, shouting and holding their hands high as they poured onto the common.

Jäger and I stepped into the clear, advancing cautiously until we saw German uniforms emerging from the barn, led by Captain Rothe. Only then did I relax. While a few of us guarded our thirty prisoners, the rest did a quick house-to-house search. My finger twitched on the trigger as I eyed the enemy. I fought to keep my limbs from trembling – a delayed reaction. I hated that I felt any sign of weakness at all.

The captain pulled the radio man aside to contact Command and find out what he was supposed to do with the prisoners. When he returned to the center of the square where we had the Russians sitting cross-legged with their hands on their heads, his expression was stony. He ordered that we separate the officers from the enlisted men.

We had studied Russian insignia, along with British and French, so the order was carried out quickly. The captain singled out a dozen men and sent them to the edge of town with the Russian enlisted men. A transport was on its way to pick them up. When those prisoners had been marched away, the rest of us awaited the captain's next order, while the Russian officers exchanged worried looks. Jäger looked as curious as I felt.

Rothe ordered us to line the officers up against the barn. My stomach clenched. Someone whispered what I was thinking: "But they surrendered."

Fury swept over Captain Rothe's features as he drew his pistol and yelled, "I know they surrendered! Line them up!" More quietly, he added, "If anyone wants to question Command's orders, I'll gladly send you there to do it."

That whisper had been grounds for execution; one did not question a superior's orders, but Rothe obviously disliked the order as much as we did. Four men herded the six Russians up against the barn wall. The full realization of what was happening was reflected in their faces. One babbled, not realizing none of us spoke a word of his language.

The captain motioned for the ten of us standing to the side to take our positions.

We lined up facing the unarmed Russians, who watched us with varying degrees of fear. One had pissed his pants. A part of me seemed to be watching from outside my body, amazed that this was happening at all. This wasn't what happened when one surrendered. I had never heard of our troops doing this to the French or the British.

Rothe yelled, "Ready!"

We snapped our rifles up. Beside me Jäger's breath hissed between his teeth.

Then came the order to aim. I sighted down the barrel of my *Mauser*, stretched my finger and rested it against the trigger, noting how natural it felt. I aimed twelve centimetres below a bobbing Adam's apple, then closed my eyes. Jäger drew another loud breath. I held mine and awaited the inevitable.

Rothe yelled, "Fire!"

Chapter Eighteen

The phone rang. Kurt startled. He was breathing hard when Herr Brandt got up to silence the insistent ringing. Elbows on the table, Kurt hid his face in his hands. In the background, Herr Brandt's voice droned, paused, droned again. A click. Silence.

Kurt flinched when a hand rested on his shoulder.

"I am sorry, Kurt. I thought you wanted me to tell you the truth. I wish I could say everything Jäger and I did on the eastern front was honourable. But there were times when all we did..." The old man sighed.

Not lifting his face, Kurt said, "You followed orders. It's not that. It's..."

A chair scraped on tile. Herr Brandt sighed again as he sat down. "What is it?"

"My dream. The execution was...so much like part of the dream that..." Kurt took a deep breath and sat back. "I'll be okay. Who phoned?"

"Marta. Her mother is wondering why I have not arrived. I am expected for supper." Herr Brandt glanced at the clock. "We lost track of the time, it seems. Now my son-in-law has been dispatched to pick me up."

Kurt stood up. "I'm sorry. I'll leave." He retrieved the bag from the counter and stuffed the two remaining *Apfelstrudel* into it. Herr Brandt's touch on his wrist stopped him. Kurt stared at the long fingers – fingers that had felt natural touching a trigger. As in his dream, when holding the *Mauser* felt so comfortable. Kurt's stomach turned over.

"Tell me about the dream." Herr Brandt's voice was quiet, insistent.

"It's stupid. Just a dream."

Tell me."

Kurt lifted a bleak gaze, knowing the dream would haunt him tonight. "Have you ever seen the movie, *Schindler's List*?"

"No, though I have heard of it. And I have read of the man." He smiled sadly. "The kind of man you wanted your grandfather and me to be, yes?"

The door knocker clanked. Kurt shrugged. "I have to go. Thank you. For telling me so much. I do want to know. It's just..."

"It is hard to hear."

With a nod, Kurt hurried to the door and let Marta's father inside. He muttered a greeting to Herr Fischer and headed to the Klassens', wishing he had time to go for a jog. Running made almost anything seem bearable. He doubted he could outrun this, though. He glanced at a parked car and, for a second, the shadowed reflection of himself turned into the soldier in the mirror. Kurt shuddered.

I am not Jäger. But when the young Wolf's voice lured him into the past, he almost felt as if he were there. Beside Jäger and Wolf, if not in Jäger's boots.

Frau Klassen was pleased to have *Apfelstrudel* for dessert. Kurt wasn't hungry and only nibbled at the simple *Abentbrot* of cheeses, sausages and bread. Frau Klassen had a meeting to attend so Kurt offered to clean up. He had just turned on the tiny dishwasher when the phone rang. Kurt answered it. Marta greeted him and asked if he could come over.

"I'm releasing Rick and thought you might want to help," she said.

"Rick?"

"*Casablanca* Rick. The little hedgehog I've been nursing."

"Oh, right. Yeah, I'll come over."

The sun was dipping below the horizon when Kurt got to Marta's house. Clutching a small cage, she met him by her front gate and indicated the stand of forest a half block away. Kurt fell in beside her without talking. They took a trail that cut through the trees, entering a world of semi-darkness. Pine scent wrapped around them. Ten metres down the trail, Marta stopped. They knelt together and Marta opened the cage door. The hedgehog didn't move.

Marta pulled a garden glove from her jacket pocket and put it on. She cradled the curled up creature in the palm of her hand. It wasn't until she set it under a fern that it poked its pointy nose out and sniffed. It seemed to regard her for a minute, then scuttled away.

"Well. That was exciting." Kurt sat back on his heels.

"Maybe not exciting," Marta said, "but satisfying."

"It's good you like releasing your strays back into the wild. Your room isn't big enough to run a zoo."

"Am I going to have to release you?"

Kurt searched Marta's face. Her eyes were black in the growing shadows. He often teased her about adopting the stray from Canada, but he knew that wasn't what she meant. "I don't know, Marta. I do have to go home so I can finish high school. I need Math and Chemistry for university. We can write and email when I'm gone."

Marta sighed and looked down. "It's not the same."

"No." Kurt lifted her chin and kissed her. Is this how the young Jäger had felt about Hedda? Had the thought of leaving her felt like being kicked in the gut? Kurt stood and pulled Marta to her feet. "Do you ever find it weird?" Kurt asked as they strolled down the trail.

"What?"

"That we ended up as friends when our grandfathers were, too?"

"And we had no idea they had even known each other. I guess it's a little weird. Or maybe it was meant to be – like a circle being completed."

"Maybe." Their grandfathers' first day of battle came to mind. If not for Jäger, Wolf could have died that day. And that would have meant Marta wouldn't have been born. Kurt squeezed her hand as he silently thanked his grandfather.

"What were you doing at Opa's house today?"

"I met him downtown and we ended up sharing tea and *Apfelstrudel.*"

"Opa is rarely late. What were you talking about that he forgot the time? The war?"

"Yeah." Kurt smiled. "He was afraid he'd get in trouble with you for it."

"You're both in trouble. I said I wanted to be there to hear."

She didn't sound angry. Kurt glanced at her and she gave him an expectant look. He shrugged. "You didn't miss much. He told me about 1940 and his time in the Labour Service. They were stationed near Peenemünde. Isn't that amazing?"

"What was at Peenemünde?"

Kurt tsked in mock disappointment. "The German military's rocket program. I thought you liked history."

"Do I care about rockets?"

"But those rockets led to the space program."

"And was Opa building rockets?"

"Well, no, he was digging ditches, and everything there was very secret so he didn't actually know what was going on, but it's still pretty interesting."

"What else did he tell you?"

"About his...girlfriends. He –"

"I do *not* want to know."

Kurt chuckled and paused by Marta's gate to open it for her. "I thought you would say that. Too bad. It makes for some interesting stories. And I like seeing you blush."

Marta ignored the comment and arched her brows. "That was it?"

Kurt leaned against the gate. "He told about joining the *Wehrmacht* and their first combat."

"So tell me."

Looking over Mara's shoulder, Kurt said, "Maybe tomorrow. I should go."

"Was it that bad?"

"It could have been worse, I guess."

"But you don't want to talk about it." Marta crossed her arms. "Talking helps, you know."

Kurt rolled his eyes. "So now you're a psychologist, not just a rescuer of strays?"

She pursed her lips. "I thought we were friends."

"I just need to work through this on my own."

"Typical male."

"Guilty as charged. And I'll be more typical yet." Kurt took her hand and pulled her away from the street light into the shadows. "I'd rather kiss you good night than talk."

"Oh?" Marta placed both her hands on Kurt's shoulders and gave him a quick kiss on the cheek. She stepped back. "There you go. Good night, Kurt." She headed for the house.

"That's not what I had in mind," Kurt called after her.

"Life is full of disappointments." Marta waved and disappeared inside.

"No kidding," Kurt whispered. He stared at the door and realized that leaving Germany would be one of those disappointments. Not just because of Marta, though she was a large part of that. In some odd way, he felt like he belonged here. Maybe because of the growing connection he felt with the young man his grandfather had been. He only had eight weeks left.

Kurt wandered the streets, soaking in the evening quiet, the warmth of the lights shining out from windows, wishing it could calm his thoughts. Erase his dreams. He wound up in the park at the end of Freidenstrasse and sat on the bench where he had first confronted Herr Brandt. Wolf – he still found it hard to think of the old man as anything other than Herr Brandt, even though he had been invited to do so. Wolf was his younger self. Wolf and Jäger.

The more Kurt heard about his grandfather as a young man, the harder it was to believe Peter's accusation. What had Grandfather run from all those years ago? Not his duty. He had been trained to follow orders, and he had, just like so many others.

Would Kurt have done the same, if he had lived then? He feared he dreamed the answer to that question. Over and over again.

The dream starts the same. Rounding up the Jews. Seeing the girl in the red coat run away. Beginning the house-to-house search.

Kurt approaches the second apartment building. It begins to shrink, fades to dirty white and the top floor melts into a thatched roof. He spins around. All the apartments on the block are doing the same. Transforming into peasant houses. Dirt blows in and covers the cobblestones. At the end of the street a barn starts rising from the ground.

His chest heaves as he watches the barn until it stops. He shouts, *"Juden! Raus!"*

In front of the barn, a cluster of German soldiers turns at the sound of his voice. Where did they come from? As Kurt advances, they step aside. Seven people stand with their backs to the wall and their hands on their heads. Seven? No, that's wrong. Wolf said six.

His breathing is louder now. The *Mauser* is heavy in his grasp. His legs feel like dead weights. Still, he walks forward. He can't stop. He tries, but he can't.

A soldier draws his pistol. "Take your position!"

Kurt steps forward alone. One facing seven. He gapes at the person in the middle of the lineup. The little girl in the red coat, hands on her head, brown eyes fixed on him. *No! Run!*

"Ready!"

He raises his rifle.

"Aim!"

He sights along the barrel to the second button on the red coat.

"Fire!"

His finger trembles against the trigger. He feels a pistol pressed against his temple. The captain shouts, "I said, Fire!"

Kurt closes his eyes. His finger stops trembling.

The gunshot flung Kurt from his dream into wakefulness. He gasped in air. Who had fired? He or the captain? He raked his fingers through his hair. He didn't know.

The clock said 6:00 a.m. He flung back the covers, threw on a T-shirt and shorts. Downstairs he scribbled a quick note so Frau Klassen wouldn't worry, then headed out to run around the lake. As he passed the large houses fronting the lake in the older part of town, he wondered if one of them had been Herr Dietrich Brandt's house. A rich man would not have lived in the small house his son, Wolf, had lived in – since 1946, Herr Brandt had said.

A dog barked; Kurt sped up. He glanced over his shoulder, half expecting to see German soldiers chasing him. He tried to laugh, but it wasn't funny. None of it was funny. Especially the dream. Maybe he needed professional help. Not just a coward, but a crazy coward.

Would hearing more of Herr Brandt's story make the dream go away, or add to its growing weirdness? It didn't matter. Kurt knew he had to hear the rest, however awful.

Kurt tried to set his thoughts aside and focus on the run. He counted steps. Breathe in – one, two, three. Breathe out – one, two, three. Breathe in. Count. Find the rhythm. He knew he was running too quickly, but he couldn't seem to pace himself. He pushed, and pushed more.

Three-quarters of the way around the lake, a cramp almost doubled Kurt over. He staggered to a stop and pressed his hand to his stomach, fighting nausea. He forced himself to keep walking, head down, sweat cooling against his skin and clogging his nostrils. His vision blurred and the little girl from his dreams swam into view. He dropped to his knees and retched.

When his stomach quieted, Kurt slumped against a tree. It was just a dream. A stupid dream. But he didn't know who had pulled the trigger. Kurt scowled at the pale orange sky.

Had his grandfather been a coward because he had pulled the trigger? Hadn't stood up for what was right? But most people would follow orders. Kurt remembered his father talking about experiments psychologists had done back in the 1960s, or maybe the 1970s. Even when they thought it was deadly, people pressed a button to shock a subject when some guy in a white coat told them to. At the time, Kurt had declared he'd never be such a stooge.

But his dreams said otherwise.

A green and white car rolled to a stop in front of Kurt. The policeman he had met the day before stepped out of the vehicle. He said, "Are you okay?"

Kurt stood. "Yes. I was running too fast. Got a cramp."

"I'll give you a ride. I have a few minutes before I have to be at the station."

"Thanks." Kurt slid into the front seat and reached for the seat belt.

"Where to?"

Without thinking, Kurt replied, "Herr Brandt's house."

"It's not even seven o'clock."

"Oh." Kurt glanced at his wrist. His watch was on his bed-side table. "I won't knock if there aren't any lights on. I just need to ask him a question."

"You'll have to give me directions. I only see him when he's out walking."

"Mozartstrasse. Number twelve."

They drove in silence. The early morning sun painted the houses with rainbow shadows. Most of them were similar – some variation of white masonry with red tile roofs – but each yard had a distinctive fence. Stone. Hedge. Wrought iron. Some combination of the three.

The car halted in front of Herr Brandt's familiar iron gate. The dining room light was on. Kurt thanked the officer for the ride.

"Take it easy next time."

With a nod, Kurt trotted up Herr Brandt's sidewalk. The door opened before he could knock. "Good morning, Kurt. I wondered why a police car would be stopping at my house, and so early. In trouble with the law, are you?"

Kurt smiled. "No. I got a cramp. He offered me a ride."

"And you came here. Why?"

"To see if you still eat porridge for breakfast."

The old man huffed and turned away, leaving the door open. "Too many smart answers too early in the morning. It is no wonder people want to beat you up." He motioned for Kurt to follow him to the kitchen. "I have *Brötchen* and cheese. Join me. I will not, however, ask you to share in my second break-fast of pills. When you get old, you have pills to start you, pills to stop you, pills to thin your blood and thicken your bones, and who knows what. I barely have room for normal food in the morning, and certainly not something so filling as oatmeal."

Kurt chuckled as he stepped into the cheerful kitchen.

Herr Brandt eased onto his chair. "Get yourself a plate. To the right of the sink. Then sit and tell me the truth of why you came. Do you always run so early in the morning?"

Kurt pulled a plate from the cupboard. "No. I woke up early and didn't want to go back to sleep. I usually run after school if I'm going to." He sat at the table. Curious eyes watched him tear a bun in half and lay cheese on it. He met the grey blue gaze when he took a bite. After swallowing, he said, "What happened to Bertha?"

"That's what you came to ask me? You think I kept track of all my conquests?"

"I think you kept track of Bertha." Kurt took another bite and waited.

"Yes, yes. You are right, of course. My guilt would not let me forget how I had almost ruined her life. I hope she found happiness, but I do not know."

"You just said you knew what happened."

"What she did, yes, but not if she was happy. And you are asking me to jump ahead in the story. I do not like doing that."

Kurt rolled his eyes and piled cheese on the other half of the bun.

Herr Brandt took a sip of tea and sighed. "After the war, Bertha came to me and told me she had waited. But I told her I did not love her, that I wanted a love like Jäger had. She left in tears. And then she married a Russian. Not right then, of course. Maybe two or three years later. She went to Russia with her husband, to a farm south of Moscow, if I recall correctly. I was told she died in a farm accident. 1970, I think." He took a *Brötchen* and tore it open. "I hope she was happy." He buttered the bun with great care.

"Did you find your love?"

The old man paused. "I found a love. I do not know if she was the love of my life, as Hedda was Jäger's, but we were happy. And before you ask, I did not have a mistress after I married."

Heat crept across Kurt's cheeks. "I wasn't going to ask."

Lines crinkled out from Herr Brandt's eyes, now blue with silent laughter. "Why not? You do not hesitate to ask anything else." Kurt gave him a sheepish look and took a big bite of his bun. Herr Brandt chuckled. "And for the next question, you use my name as I have requested or I will not answer." He sipped his tea. "Continue the interrogation."

"When did she die, Wolf?"

"My wife? She is not dead. Luise is in a hospital for the aged. I try to visit once a week, but it is hard. She lives in her childhood now. Alzheimer's, they say." He wrapped his hands around his teacup and stared into it. "She once told me that when she was small – I am eight years older – I came across a boy stealing candy from her. She said I chased him, booted his rear and returned the candy to her. I do not remember it." He sighed. "When I went to Greece over the winter it was the longest we had ever been apart, and she did not even notice."

Kurt vaguely recalled Marta, last fall, saying her grandmother was in a home. "I'm sorry."

"You did not know. There is no need for apologies."

Several moments passed, filled with the sounds of chewing and sipping. Though he thought he knew the answer, Kurt felt compelled to ask, "Why did you pull the trigger?"

Dark eyebrows raised, almost joining the silver hair above them. "You said yesterday you understood I was following orders. It was what I was trained to do. It was what I did. To do otherwise was to die a traitor's death." Herr Brandt leaned forward. "Do you think you would have refused, if you had been trained as Jäger and I had been since we were ten years old? Would you have gone against eight years of training?"

Kurt dropped his gaze. He whispered, "No."

"And that bothers you. Your grandfather was not a monster, only a man. He was no different than you. But you want to be different. You do not want to realize how easy it is."

"I know how easy it is. I dream how easy it is." Kurt paced to the doorway between the dining room and kitchen. He leaned against the door jamb, his back to the table. *It helps to talk*, Marta had said. It couldn't hurt. Kurt swallowed. "I dream I'm rounding up Jews. It's a scene from the movie, *Schindler's List*. I search house-to-house and find a little girl. Our orders aren't to round up those hiding. Our orders are to kill them. And I do. I find the little girl and I kill her. I never see her die, though. I always wake up to the sound of the gunshot." He closed his eyes. "There have been small differences in the dream, but last night it was a lot different. The street changed into a Russian village, and I was ordered to kill those captured Russians. But the little girl was there and I aimed at her first. I couldn't pull the trigger. The captain held his pistol to my head and ordered me to fire."

From right behind Kurt, Herr Brandt whispered, "Did you?"

Kurt opened his eyes and stared at the dark table bright with a fresh bouquet of tulips. "I don't know. I woke to a gunshot, but I don't know if it was mine or his. I'm afraid it was mine."

"It is a rare man who finds the strength to stand against a swift-flowing river. Most are swept away by the current. I had to make peace with myself about that a long time ago. Do not hate yourself because of a dream." Herr Brandt paused. "I think I should not tell you more."

"No!" Kurt spun around. "I can't know this much and not know the rest. I need to know." His throat constricted. "I think, I *hope*, if I know the whole story, the dream will go away."

"Perhaps you are right. Perhaps you are wrong."

"The dream started before you told me anything. It's been getting better. Sort of." Until last night. Kurt whispered, "Please, Wolf."

"Ach. Now you are not playing fair, sounding like Jäger and pleading with his eyes."

Kurt smiled. He knew he had gotten his way. "Can I ask you one more question?"

"Can I stop you?"

Kurt shrugged. "This couldn't have been your house when you were a boy. It sounds like your family was quite wealthy. Where did you live?"

"So now you are a detective."

"Sam Spade, at your service."

"I saw that movie on television. I preferred Humphrey Bogart in *African Queen.*"

"Yeah, that was a good one. He was a Canadian in that movie, you know."

"Oh? I don't recall that. Marta warned me you are an old-movie buff."

"My mom thinks it's part of my education to watch them. The house?"

"Yes, yes. It was number twenty-three, Zethensee Strasse. It was abandoned for many years. Now they are renovating it, turning it into apartments."

Kurt squinted one eye, recalling the street that was part of his running route. "I think I remember which one it is. Why didn't you live there after the war?"

"You are asking me to jump ahead in my story again." When Kurt's expression turned to exasperation, Herr Brandt smiled. "Just like your grandfather. You pull words from me whether I want to say them or not. I did live there near the end of the war, for a week. Then the Russians came and one took a liking to the lakeside view. Father was dead and I was not about to die for a mere building. I had always felt more at home in Jäger's house than in my own. There was real love in his house. Maybe that is why he found love so early in his life."

"And where did Grandfather live?"

"Number twelve, Mozartstrasse." Herr Brandt pointed at the kitchen ceiling. "His bedroom was right above us, overlooking the garden."

Chapter Nineteen

Kurt drifted across the dining room and gaped at the staircase facing the front entrance. He grasped the wooden post and rested his foot on the first step as he studied the stairs his grandfather had climbed every day of his youth.

"Go look if you want," Herr Brandt said. "The front bedroom has been renovated into a guest room with a bathroom. Jäger's room is little changed. A coat of paint. A new window."

"Why didn't you tell me?"

"You did not ask. And it did not seem important before now."

Kurt gave the old man a wry look and trotted up the stairs. The staircase was almost a spiral, with the incline changing direction every four steps. Kurt paused on the last step and eyed the print hung across from the stairs. A ruined church in a misty graveyard surrounded by skeletal trees. A haunting image in shades of brown that Kurt found unsettling.

The guest room door was on his left. He swung right into the narrow hallway to face a brown door. Two panels and a brass knob – likely the same door Wolf had knocked on, a secret knock shared by best friends. Kurt slid his feet across the wood floor and pushed the door open, half expecting to see sixteen-year-old Jäger hunched over the radio he had repaired.

The room was empty except for a low trundle bed under the window and a dresser beside the door. To either side, the walls rose straight for a metre, then leaned inward. In the middle of each short wall was a miniature door. Kurt rubbed the wood grain of the dresser as he looked around. He leaned over and checked each drawer. They were all empty. He crossed to the small door on the left and leaned to look inside. The cramped storage area was stuffed with boxes, most labelled "Christmas." He approached the other small door and knelt beside it.

An indent in the wall caught his eye. Kurt brushed his fingertips over the blemish, imagining this was the very spot damaged by the radio Wolf had kicked. He opened the door to the metre-deep storage area. It was also filled with boxes to either side of the door, mostly unmarked. Kurt noticed a familiar square box. He knew it contained a German helmet, World War Two vintage.

Kurt crawled into the cubbyhole and leaned against the outer wall. He laid the helmet's box on his thighs. Downstairs, the phone rang. Kurt removed the dull green helmet from its nest and rubbed the surface, feeling the scratches and dents. The metal smell teased Kurt's nostrils.

Setting aside the helmet, Kurt pulled out a flat box he suspected held his grandfather's uniform, and opened it. Something wrapped in tissue lay on top of the grey tunic. Kurt peeled the white layers back. His throat constricted. A dagger. He didn't need to see the insignia on the handle or the inscription on the blade to know what it was. *Blood and honour.* An HJ dagger.

The door creaked. Kurt looked up. "Why did you keep all this?"

Herr Brandt gripped the dresser and bent over to peer into the closet. He crossed to the bed, out of Kurt's sight. Bedsprings creaked. "It was all I had left of my friendship with Jäger."

"The dagger was his?"

"Yes. Mine was left behind at my house."

"Couldn't you have gotten into trouble with the Russians over this stuff?"

"Yes, yes. Especially our campaign medals from the eastern front. I lied to them and said I had fought on the western front. They would never have given me the position they did if they had known I had killed their countrymen. Everything was well hidden for many years. And forgotten for many more."

Kurt touched the dagger's swastika emblem. He had gotten an email from Tyler the day before. To *Sour Kraut*. He had signed it: *Tyler – call me Jew-boy and I'll break your head – Green*. He recalled Tyler in the catacombs, looking haunted by the bones...of six million bodies. The number Jim had quoted was also the number of Jews estimated to have died in World War Two. Is that what had bothered Tyler? Being surrounded by six million –

Throat dry, Kurt swallowed. "You've never mentioned..."

Herr Brandt's voice was sharp, making Kurt wince. "Mentioned what?"

"Anything about...the Holocaust. The camps, or Jews being arrested, or..."

The old man sighed, a drawn-out sound filled with sadness. "I knew someday you would ask this. Even knowing, I have no good answer for you."

Kurt rewrapped the dagger, tucked it under the tunic, then traced the eagle over the right breast pocket, a swastika clutched in its embroidered talons. Symbol of death for so many.

Finally, Herr Brandt said, "That I recall, there were only two Jewish families in Zethen. They moved away around 1935. I never much noticed their leaving, and have no idea where they went. I do not know their ultimate fate. I was young, Kurt, and cared for nothing beyond my HJ unit. And the government made it so easy. Their concentration camps were in the country, out of sight, easy to ignore. From what I've heard, if you lived close to one, you were *expected* to ignore what was going on in the camps. Is that an excuse? Perhaps."

Another sigh stretched through an awkward silence. The wool in the tunic itched Kurt's palms; he kept his hands splayed over the rough material and tried not to let Tyler's haunted expression fill his mind's eye.

Herr Brandt said, "You always make me race ahead in the story, but this needs to be said. You like history, so you might know that part of Operation Barbarossa was to carry out the Final Solution, as it was called. Behind the eastern front, the SS destroyed Jews and other 'undesirables.' Terrible times." Another sigh. "On the front lines, Jäger and I never saw any of the mass murders, though we heard about some. We witnessed some hangings, executions. Partisans, mostly soldiers behind our lines, who organized their countrymen to fight against us. But I remember one girl...Marta's age. Her captors had obviously...used her before the hanging." A pause. "It pains me to speak of such things, Kurt. It is easier to let myself remember the battles."

Kurt stroked the uniform. "Did you agree with what was happening?"

A huff sounded from beyond the closet. "So you refuse to let me off easily. I was taught to see Aryans as superior to everyone else. Four years on the eastern front taught me the Russians were inferior to *no one*. As for the killing...I did not think about it. Those decisions were made by our superiors and meant nothing to me, or so I thought. The death camps were not fully operational when Jäger and I headed to the front. After, when I heard the numbers of people that had been murdered, I wanted to deny it. And I did, for many years, but the evidence could not be denied."

Another silence. Herr Brandt shifted and continued speaking.

"I went, once, to the biggest death camp. Auschwitz-Birkenau. As an official in the Soviet regime, though a minor one, it was easier for me to get a travel permit than for many. I travelled to Poland by myself, shortly after Marta's mother was born. I wanted to see this supposed death camp, to scoff because it was no different than any of the concentration camps, no different than the Soviet prison camps." His voice dropped and Kurt had to strain to hear it. "How wrong I was."

After a moment's pause, Herr Brandt said, "I saw Auschwitz first, the original camp with its execution wall, hanging posts, crematorium ovens. It was all quite sad but did not convince me of the horrific numbers they claimed had died – one and a half million at Auschwitz alone. But Camp Two was also part of Auschwitz, so I went to see it. Birkenau it was called. Its size was staggering. I explored what buildings still stood, for the retreating ss had destroyed much of the camp – to hide their crimes, it is said. The mass graves, the pits of human ashes, the four collapsed crematoriums, all pointed to the truth of how many had died. The last building I toured was the 'sauna' where prisoners kept for slave labour were deloused. When I walked out, it was to face a field of neatly laid out brick foundations of buildings that had been burned. There was a plaque on a post beside the field. By then, I knew Russian and had taught myself as much English as I could, so I went over to read it."

Silence vibrated in Kurt's ears.

When Herr Brandt spoke again it was in a quiet voice. "What happened then, I have never told anyone, not even my wife, and certainly not Jäger, for we only corresponded by letters and I knew they were sometimes read by my socialist masters." Herr Brandt's breathing grew loud. The stink of mothballs made Kurt's eyes water and he squeezed them shut.

Herr Brandt continued in that same hushed tone. "The name hit me – a name given to buildings that no longer existed. They had been warehouses, used to store goods taken from the prisoners. Suitcases, shoes, silverware, photographs, hair even. They had been named after a country the Poles saw as a land of plenty: Kanada. I stared at that name for a long time. I was shaking when I dropped to my knees beside the brick outline of one destroyed warehouse, with pieces of lives still scattered inside the foundation. That name ricocheted through my mind like a bullet glancing off metal. Kanada."

Silence again. Kurt scowled at the uniform. Buildings called *Canada*, a part of Auschwitz? A part of the biggest death camp of them all? Ice trickled down his spine.

"Kanada," Herr Brandt repeated. "The place that had taken Jäger from me. Almost twenty years had passed by then and I had never mourned…any of it. My lost youth, the war, the loss of my best friend. I had been too busy surviving under the Russians. If Jäger and I had grown up in peaceful times, we might have drifted apart and never noticed. But our youth had made us like brothers and our time on the eastern front had woven our souls together. It sounds like foolishness to someone who has never experienced such a thing, but it was what had kept me sane, had kept me alive. I had forever lost part of me and suddenly the pain of it threatened to crush me. I could feel the dam within beginning to crumble. The shaking grew worse. I could not breathe."

Kurt's throat constricted as Herr Brandt's pain washed over him.

A breath shuddered through the room. And another. "That is when the cloud of witnesses descended. I do not know how else to describe it. I could feel the eyes of thousands, tens of thousands – and yet I was alone. But…I was not alone. I was not. I felt them all around, sharing in my pain, sympathizing with me. How could they sympathize with me, one of their tormentors? But they did. The dam burst. Forty years old and I sat in a field, crying like a child, helpless to stop."

The sound of the old man's laboured breathing drifted into the closet; Kurt's insides twisted.

And still Herr Brandt continued, "I heard a Russian voice behind me say, 'Poor fellow. He must have had family killed here.' I wanted to laugh at how wrong he was, but could not stop the sorrow pouring from me. My tears streamed onto ground that had soaked up countless tears. When at last I regained control of myself, I felt the cloud lift. And I was truly alone again. Alone in a field called Kanada. I walked away, knowing I could never tell anyone what had happened, that they would say I had gone crazy and needed to be locked away." He quietly added, "But I am old now and it does not matter so much any more what people think of me."

Kurt swiped at his eyes with the back of his hand, surprised by the wetness there. Was it crazy to sense ghosts? He tried to find his voice, but his throat was closed tightly.

Herr Brandt blew out his breath. "When I returned from Auschwitz, I got out my uniform and Jäger's, our medals, everything. Looking at them, I could not bring myself to throw away what remained of my youth, of Jäger's youth. So I kept them. But what remained of my beliefs had been washed away in that flood." He sighed. "What did you ask? Did I agree with what was happening? I did not disagree because I did not think about it, so perhaps that is agreeing. It is sad to say, but I was so absorbed by my own fight to survive that I did not care about anyone else's. One thing I know. After seeing Auschwitz and Birkenau, my *Wehrmacht* uniform took on a new meaning. It reminded me how fortunate I was not to have joined the ss. If I had, I might have been one of the guards at that camp. So many lost their lives, but those guards must have lost their souls."

Kurt fingered the dark green collar with its light grey bars, silently thankful with Herr Brandt that neither Wolf nor Jäger had joined the ss. "This stuff should be in a museum."

"When I die perhaps. But that uniform is Jäger's. The choice should be his. Or yours."

Kurt cringed. He didn't want to think of the uniform as having anything to do with him, no matter what the soldier in the mirror thought. He closed the lid.

Herr Brandt said, "Ach, I forgot. Frau Klassen phoned

looking for you. It seems you are late for school. I took the liberty of informing her that you weren't feeling well. A cramp. She is going to phone the school to let them know you might not make it to classes today."

Smiling, Kurt picked up the helmet and set it in its box. "Are you encouraging me to skip classes, Herr Brandt?"

"The name is Wolf, and you can do as you please."

Kurt slid the boxes into their places. Nothing major was happening in his classes today; he could get copies of notes from other students. Right now, spending time with... Wolf...felt more important. He scuttled out of the low closet. "What I would like is to have a history lesson. I know very little about the eastern front."

"Not every hole in one's education needs to be filled."

"This one does. Please, Wolf."

Herr Brandt braced his hands on his knees and pushed to his feet with a groan. "That bed is not made for old men. If I tell you anything, it will be from the comfort of my easy chair."

Kurt grinned.

Herr Brandt pointed his finger at Kurt. "And stop looking like Jäger, young man, before I forget your name." He patted Kurt's shoulder blade. "Go put on the kettle. I cannot talk for hours without some tea to soothe my throat."

December 1941. That winter is frozen into my memory, one night above all.

I remember shoving my gloved hands under my armpits, a shudder raking across my shoulders. Even on a moonless night, objects were silhouetted against the snow. I peered down what looked to be a quiet street. My whisper was hoarse when I asked Jäger where we were. We were supposed to be on patrol, but I knew we had ranged farther than usual. We had taken so many twists and turns and backtracks, even a few cuts through trenches guarded by barbed wire, that I didn't have a clue which way camp lay.

Jäger stifled a cough and said, "Not far outside Moscow, I think."

"Moscow!" I almost shouted. I peered down the street again, searching for the Kremlin's spires and said, "What were you thinking? We're behind enemy lines."

"I don't care," was Jäger's reply. He sank to his knees and hunched over to muffle another cough. I crouched beside him. He whispered, "I'm so cold, Wolf. I can't warm up. Our side of the line is picked clean. I dream of finding a blanket. Or a dead Russian's snow gear."

"If you want to be mistaken for a Russian and shot," I replied, and shivered in sympathy.

Berlin had sent us nothing to fight the cold and we had little shelter – the retreating Russians had made sure of that. Our greatcoats and gloves were too thin to fend off the frigid Russian winter. In November the sea of mud had frozen almost overnight, and temperatures had dropped. The Russians didn't have to shoot us – winter was killing us one by one. But they helped anyway. Their fierceness was alarming. They had stalled the *Wehrmacht* less than thirty kilometres from Moscow. We were trapped between Russians eager to die for their capital and High Command's refusal to let us withdraw until the cold released its grip.

Jäger started coughing. I pounded his back until he

stopped, then studied the street in case the noise had been noticed. He needed to warm up before pneumonia set in. I said, "What's your plan?"

"No plan," he said. "Just search empty houses. Pray the owners left something behind."

I asked how far we were from camp. He said, "Barely eight kilometres."

Not as close to Moscow as I had feared, but still in Russian territory. I pointed out that we needed to get busy so we could get back under cover of darkness.

Jäger led the way down a street of small white houses. We slipped past one that was boarded up. In the second yard, Jäger jiggled the handle of a low door. It protested but opened. Inside it was coal black. He circled left; I went right. We felt our way along. I bumped into a table, knocked my head on a pan hanging from the ceiling. Wood groaned. Something creaked. Jäger whispered, "A bed."

I stumbled through the dark toward his voice, cracked my shin on a post and bit my tongue to keep quiet. I ran my hand over Jäger's find – a straw-filled mattress – and almost shouted my joy.

We both yanked off our boots. I cut a hole in the mattress and we stuffed as much straw inside them as we could. My fingers were so numb I could barely pull the boots back on. We sliced the mattress wide open and salvaged the rough cotton covering, then crept outside, each with a swath of homespun tucked under our belts. The cloth would make good lining under our greatcoats.

At the next house we walked in without hesitating. Jäger halted. I almost bumped into him. Weak light from a low fire washed over the room. On the other side of a crude fireplace, an old man sat up in his bed. He opened his mouth as if to sound the alarm. Jäger aimed his rifle. The old man closed his mouth, but his eyes became circles. I was glad he couldn't see how Jäger trembled. My friend couldn't pull the trigger on an old man. I whispered, "What now?"

He told me to close the door. I did, then propped a chair against it. Now that he realized he wasn't in immediate danger, the old man seemed confused. How did we look to him? White cloth swaddled our helmets; likewise, we had fitted sheets over our greatcoats in an effort to blend in with the snow, but the sheets only hung halfway to our knees. The ridiculousness of the situation struck me and I choked back laughter.

Jäger shot me a dark look and paced to the fire. He stripped off his gloves to hold his now shaking hands over the heat. The old man started to get up; I motioned him down with my rifle. Near the fire, I spotted a wooden bucket with a rope tied to the handle. I cut the rope and used it to tie one skinny ankle to the bed frame, then noticed a second lump under the blankets.

With my rifle touching the old man's chest, I eased back the covers. The old man had a wife who was either deaf or a very sound sleeper. She didn't stir, so I dropped the covers back over her head. The man whispered something. Thank you, maybe, but I wasn't sure.

With my rifle laid across a rocking chair, I added wood to the fire. The high stack in the corner looked more enticing than a pallet of gold bars. But dragging a load of firewood for eight kilometres through enemy territory was impossible. I said, "Get your outer gear off, Jäger. Warm up properly, then we'll go."

Jäger didn't need prompting, but he was shaking so badly

he almost needed help. He sat in front of the flames with bare feet exposed, hugging his legs to his chest. I lifted a folded woolen blanket from the seat of the rocker and laid it across his shoulders, then settled on the chair, my rifle across my legs. The old man lay back down but kept his eyes fixed on me.

The one-room hovel was warm, at least compared to the outside. I had never experienced such cold. Icy air that froze your nose hairs, any exposed skin, your lungs, then cut through your clothes to freeze the rest of you. I wondered why we even wanted to capture Moscow. Who would want to face this winter year after year?

Jäger's head lolled. He curled onto his side. I rearranged the blanket over him, added another log to the fire, and sat down to keep vigil. Me and the old man, who remained alert. One hour, I told myself. I would let Jäger sleep for one hour.

Loud crunching woke me up. I jumped to my feet, rifle seeking a target. The sound came from outside; it was accompanied by quiet voices. Heart thudding, I sidled to a shuttered window facing the street and cracked one shutter open. Six Russian soldiers walked down the middle of the road, their thick white uniforms stark against the silhouetted houses. I realized the houses were dark outlines because the sun was rising behind them. I leaned my head against the closed shutter and watched the soldiers until they disappeared around a corner.

Muttering, "Oh, God," I returned to the fire, added wood, fanned the flames and considered our next move. There was no next move; we were trapped here until darkness returned. Jäger still slept. The old man's watery gaze still followed me. His eyes were pale and unnerving. I said, "Stop watching me."

He stared, clearly not understanding. I removed my helmet

and rubbed my neck. My stomach rumbled. It would be a long day. The old man fell asleep; his wife had yet to wake up. Maybe they survived such brutal winters by sleeping most of the time. Hibernating. I fed the fire until Jäger woke up at mid-morning. When I explained, he was angry that I had let him sleep. I wasn't pleased with myself, either.

Suddenly, Jäger's grin flashed. He said, "At least I'm warm."

"Wonderful," I said. "If those soldiers return, we'll die warm."

His response was to suggest we find out if there was any food. On the other side of the room, in an open cupboard, Jäger found a small cast iron pot half full of frozen cooked oatmeal. We hung it on a hook over the fire and waited for the gruel to thaw. The milk we found was also frozen. The fireplace only heated half the room. By the time the oatmeal was warm, the old couple was awake. The woman sobbed while the man held her close and whispered.

Jäger found four bowls, filled them all and offered one to each of our hostages. The man took both with a nod, while the woman continued to blubber.

I said, "We'll have to gag her if she doesn't shut up."

Jäger insisted we let her eat first. The sound of our German voices set the woman to wailing. I picked up my *Mauser*, pointed at her, then touched my finger to my lips. The man understood that. He clamped his hand over her mouth and whispered. Whatever he said, the woman quieted. I returned to eating oatmeal.

After we had eaten, Jäger put his outerwear back on and sat back from the fire. We would have to move quickly if we were discovered. Daylight couldn't breach the stout shutters, so we lit candles.

Then we spotted the outerwear hanging in the far corner. I gaped at the sight of the shaggy fur coat, moth-eaten but use-able, and a pile-lined cap with earflaps. Jäger and I exchanged wonder-filled looks, then Jäger's expression changed to guilt. He said, "We can't take his coat. How will he keep warm?"

I reminded Jäger the old man would bring soldiers down on our heads if his own life wasn't threatened. He didn't care if we died. But Jäger disagreed. We argued quietly for several moments, but there was no changing his mind. We retreated into silence, the old man's eyes following our every move. Shortly after noon, a truck rumbled past. It spurred us into motion. We rummaged around, found some turnips and onions.

"How do you cook turnips?" Jäger asked.

"I don't know," I said. "I hate turnips. Ask the old man."

Jäger glared and set a pot of water to boil. When it was bubbling, he added vegetable chunks and sat beside the fire, stirring his mixture. The old man used the chamber pot for a second time, then went to the sack of turnips. From the bottom, he produced a few potatoes and a chunk of cabbage, and handed them to Jäger, who eyed the fellow with surprise.

By midafternoon, the hovel reeked of sour vegetable stew and urine. The chamber pot was almost full, but I refused to let anyone go outside to empty it. The old man dribbled in it yet again. On his way back to the bed, he picked up the wool blanket, handed it to me, then pointed between me and Jäger, who said, "I think he wants us to have it."

I scowled at the old man, not understanding his kindness. He patted my hand and nodded, then crawled back into bed. I muttered my thanks, cut the blanket in half and sliced a hole in the middle of each piece. Jäger and I stripped off our greatcoats and pulled the woolen cloth over our heads like capes. We did the same with the cloth pieces from the straw mattress, then donned our outerwear again. The layers made us almost uncomfortably warm, especially with the fire banked high. But Jäger's cough didn't sound nearly as ragged as it had earlier.

Again, soldiers passed by outside. Jäger guarded the window; I trained my rifle on the old man, who kept his wife quiet. When the street was empty, we shared the stew. The thin broth was bland and coated my tongue with the taste of turnips, but I ate every morsel, drank down the broth and had another bowl. Poor as it was, it was better than what we usually ate. For one thing, it was hot instead of lukewarm. The pot was a quarter full when we set aside our bowls and put on our helmets.

The sun set in the late afternoon. The darkening sky made me restless. I prowled the room, pausing by the fur coat each time I circled around. Jäger needed it. When Jäger signalled that we should go, I pointed at the bed with my rifle and asked, "What about them?"

"Leave them," he said.

"They'll sound the alarm."

Jäger's green eyes narrowed as he said, "Are you going to shoot them?"

I lifted my rifle and aimed. The old lady, quiet most of the day, began to sob. I lowered the *Mauser*, raised it again...and looked away in disgust. The old man got up – I had forgotten to bind his ankle after his last trip to the chamber pot – and padded to his coat. He lifted it and grabbed another from underneath it. This one was dirty white and quilted. He took the knee-length coat and his pile-lined cap, and pressed the clothing into Jäger's arms. The man touched his finger to his lips. I figured he was trying to bargain for their lives. Jäger agreed.

The bony old finger indicated a rough cross hanging above the bed, then pointed to us. Gnarled hands clasped together. I said, "He's even offering to pray for us."

Jäger smiled at the old man. "Maybe all Russians aren't godless Bolsheviks. We could use some prayer." He slipped into the coat. It was broad enough to fit over his gear, but short in the sleeves. He touched the man's shoulder and thanked him. Incomprehension entered the pale eyes.

I told Jäger to put the hat on. He did so, lowered the earflaps and jammed the helmet overtop. It looked ridiculous, but neither of us cared. Just the thought of re-entering that bitter Russian winter made me shiver.

Jäger opened the door a crack to make sure the way was clear. Cold air surged into the hovel. Jäger stifled a cough and motioned for me to come. He nodded to the old man and slipped outside. I gave the man a long look, half warning, half puzzlement, then left our refuge.

The cold grabbed me by the throat and I gasped. I took a loose end from the cloth covering my helmet and wrapped it across my mouth. Jäger's breathing sounded harsh.

As usual, Jäger led and I continually checked over my shoulder. We darted through alleys, quickly escaping the town. No alarm sounded. A relief, but I still couldn't relax, knowing how deep in enemy territory we were. Two hours later, we skirted another town and hunkered in a graveyard to rest. Avoiding main roads often meant having to break trail through the snow.

I asked how far back to camp. Jäger figured three kilometres at the most. I leaned against a tombstone and asked "Do you think they will tell anyone?"

Jäger was quiet for a moment. "No." He muffled a cough.

We set out. Twice in ten minutes we had to hide from patrols. "Must be close," I muttered. Jäger shushed me and listened to the night. He started out, paused, changed direction. I dogged his footsteps, peering backward often, wondering what had he heard or sensed. I did not break the silence.

We were circling around another village when Jäger hauled me down. We flattened ourselves against the crusty snow. Faint grumbling became a roar. Three trucks swept darkened headlamps over us as they lumbered into the village. The engines cut off; the silence hummed. Voices drifted down the short street. They could only be Russian soldiers.

Jäger nudged me and began to crawl forward. Both hands on my rifle, I wriggled after him. Progress was slow. The snow crackled under us. Beads of sweat chilled against my neck.

A dog barked. I froze, as did Jäger. His breathing rasped. We waited a moment, then Jäger tapped me again and started out. He stopped to smother a cough. One escaped – a hoarse bark that set the nearby dog yapping. Human voices joined the clamour.

Snow seems to carry sounds for great distances, particularly at night. I tried to judge how far away the voices were. Boots scraped the snow. Ten metres or one hundred? The dog worked itself into a frenzy, trying to alert someone to our presence. It yelped and fell silent. Crunching footsteps grew louder, then stopped. My heart hammered *run! run!* Instead, I turned my head very slowly, hoping to spot whoever was near. From the corner of my eye, I saw a match flare barely three metres away, saw a cigarette being lit, saw its glowing tip illuminate dark eyes and ruddy cheeks. The match flipped through the air in my direction. The eyes watched it, then narrowed.

I rolled onto my back as the soldier shouted what sounded like "Nee-yah-mitz!" – a word I recognized as meaning "Germans!" My rifle coughed. The soldier fell backwards.

Jäger was already up and running when I scrambled to my feet. He slowed for me and we fled into the darkness, away from the buildings. Behind us, trucks roared to life, shouts bounced down the streets and rolled across the fields. Lights flashed over us. We zigzagged toward a stand of trees, scrambling in the snow. Twenty metres. Ten. The lights found us again.

Something slammed into my leg. I stumbled, rolled, forced myself to my feet. My leg throbbed with each step. Now the air hissed with bullets. The trees hid us from sight, protected us from whizzing death. Still we ran. I fell again, called to Jäger. He appeared back at my side.

"My leg," I whispered. "I think I was hit." Glove off, I touched my leg above my knee; my fingers came away sticky. I added, "A graze. Deep. Hurts." I hissed when he touched it.

He reached under his coat, ripped off a piece of the mattress cloth and begged, "Don't bleed, Wolf. They'll follow the blood trail. Stop bleeding."

"Right," I scoffed. "Maybe the air will freeze it. Bloody cold air has to be good for something." I winced when he tied the rag around my lower thigh.

Voices floated across the field. Jäger pulled me to my feet.

We had to run.

Behind us torches – flashlights – swept beams of light over the trees. To shoot was to reveal our position. We ran. I tried to ignore the fire in my leg, the jolt of pain when my boot struck the ground. I ran because I had no choice. Jäger stuck beside me, urged me on, whispered each change of direction.

We came to a frozen creek and followed it, the level surface allowing for more speed. The trees disappeared. Still we followed the ice. "Left," Jäger whispered. "Should be less than a kilometre."

Across a field, over a fence. I fell into a ditch. Jäger pulled me up, cut an opening in coiled barbed wire, and pushed me through.

"Can't," I choked. I lay on my back and sucked ice into my lungs. My leg was screaming. I whispered, "Go. Run."

Jäger pulled me up and began to drag me forward.

No voices behind us now. The Russians knew how close to the line we were. I stumbled just as a shot rang out. It shocked me into running again. Another gunshot, this time from in front of us.

Jäger sprinted ahead of me yelling, "Two Germans! Don't shoot! Ninth Army! Schreiber and Brandt! Don't shoot! Don't shoot!"

The dark slash of trenches and bulwarks was visible now. I lurched and fell. More shots from behind. Suddenly the air above me filled with the whine of gunfire. I heard Jäger calling, "Crawl, Wolf! They're covering for you." This was good, so long as I didn't lift my head too high.

I crept forward, dragging my rifle. In an abrupt silence, two shadows rose from the ground and grabbed my arms. They dragged me over the mound of dirt and snow. I tumbled into the trench, landed on my injured leg and cried out.

"Quit whining like a boy," Jäger said.

I dragged myself to my feet and reminded him that he had gotten me into this mess.

Jäger persisted. I could hear the grin in his voice: "Headline: Zethen, December 1941. Local soldier snivels over scratch. Thinks he should get medal."

"For putting up with you," I muttered. He offered to help and I knocked his hand away.

Halfway to our quarters, which was little more than a hole in the ground, Captain Rothe appeared before us, torch in hand. He barked, "Why are you two still alive?"

"Schreiber's fault, sir," I replied.

"You were the one who let me fall asleep," Jäger said.

I replied, "I meant it's your fault that we're still alive."

The captain eyed Jäger's newly acquired coat and said, "You were missing for a day and a night because you decided to go foraging?"

We both stiffened into attention. My injury pulsed and I shifted my weight to my good leg. Together we intoned, "Yes, Herr Kapitän!"

The moment stretched. I stared over the captain's shoulder, waiting for his response. A puff of frosty breeze nipped at my cheeks. Jäger suppressed another cough.

Finally Captain Rothe said, "I want the coat."

My gaze snapped to his. Without thinking, I blurted, "You didn't risk your life for it." As an afterthought, I added, "Sir."

The captain held out his hand. Jäger handed me his rifle. I pushed it back at him and said, "Jäger will get pneumonia if he doesn't keep warm. The unit depends on him." Rothe's hand beckoned. I gritted my teeth, knowing I walked a dangerous line, then said, "A trade."

Captain Rothe eyed me skeptically.

I said, "That woolly vest under your greatcoat for Jäger's quilted coat."

Rothe said he could charge us both with disobeying orders. I held his gaze and hoped. I couldn't offer another protest. Soldiers were shot for less. It galled me. Jäger would just give him the coat; I had to try to get something from the deal. Between the wool blanket already warming him and the captain's vest, Jäger would be okay. He had to be okay.

The captain nodded and said, "We'll switch in my tent."

My shoulders slumped in relief. I gave Jäger a half smile. His eyes jigged toward his eyebrows, indicating the pile-lined cap. I gave him a warning look to keep quiet. As I gritted my teeth and limped after the captain, Jäger fell behind me and hid the cap under his greatcoat.

The captain glanced over his shoulder and asked, "What's wrong with you, Brandt?"

"Shot in the leg, sir. A graze."

He said, "Clean it up when we're done our business. Glad you aren't a whiner."

I gave Jäger a superior look and he grinned.

Chapter Twenty

The train was going to be late arriving in Berlin. Only a few minutes, but enough that Kurt silently urged it to greater speed. The weekend in Amsterdam had been...empty. Weird how you could be with a group of people, yet still feel lonely. Weirder still that his favourite times during the past few days had been when he was alone, jogging beside the canals in the early morning, mist curling off the water, lifting fog hanging over ornate rooftops, narrow houses crammed together like books on a full shelf.

Marta would have loved Amsterdam and how easily the old city could be walked. It wasn't that Amsterdam was boring, Kurt realized. He pressed his forehead against the window and frowned at the slightly blurred countryside. Amsterdam wasn't boring at all – it had just been missing something. Someone.

When the train pulled into Hauptbahnhof, Kurt was the first out of his car. He slung his bulging backpack over his shoulder and joined the flow of people, off that platform and down to the level he needed to catch a train to Ostbahnhof. Once there, he left the train platforms and entered the shop-filled rail station, where he found a pay phone and dialed Marta's cellphone. Her voice was hushed. "Hello?"

"Hi, Marta."

"Kurt. You're back."

"Right. Where are you? You sound strange."

"I'm in the school library, researching that History paper. You know how the librarian hates cellphones in her library. I had mine set to vibrate."

"How long will you be? I'll swing by as soon as I get to Zethen."

"If I'm done in the library, I'll wait on the school steps." A pause and Marta whispered, "She's coming. Bye." The line went dead.

Chuckling, Kurt returned to the access tunnel and checked the schedule. His connecting train, the S5, was leaving in two minutes. He tore toward Track Eight. Taking the steps two at a time, he burst onto the platform and lunged through an open train door just as the whistle blew.

Kurt plopped into a seat by the door and stared out the graffiti-scratched window at the airbrushed graffiti decorating old buildings along the tracks. Yes, the worst thing about Amsterdam was definitely that Marta hadn't been there. Victor would laugh at that. Kurt realized he didn't care. Daydreams of pulling Marta behind a bookshelf to sneak a kiss occupied Kurt to Ostkreuz station, onto the next train, and all the way home to Zethen.

Marta wasn't in the library. Long strides carried Kurt to the front steps. Marta wasn't there, but Stephan Neumeyer was, grinning like that cat in *Alice in Wonderland*. Marta's backpack leaned against Stephan's leg, as if he were watching it for her.

Working his jaw, Kurt edged toward Stephan. "Where's Marta?"

The grin widened. "Peter wanted a word with her."

Kurt's stomach flipped. He hauled Stephan to his feet. "Where?"

"Hey. Let go, will you? It's...a private conversation."

Kurt fought the urge to plow his fist into Stephan's face. He whispered, "Where?"

Stephan smirked. "By the shed."

Kurt shoved Stephan back as he leaped to the sidewalk. He raced to the left, Stephan's laughter goading him on. His backpack fell from his shoulder as he rounded the corner of the school, heading for the back, where an equipment shed sat near a windowless corner of the brick building. The gap between the shed and school was jokingly called "Makeout Alley."

Kurt's stomach flopped again. He gasped for air as he tore around the next corner and sprinted toward the shed, its broad side shielding the alley from view. He skidded to a halt at the head of the two-metre-wide recess.

Peter had Marta pressed against the wall. He was kissing her; his hand had pushed her skirt up and was gripping her thigh. Kurt yelled, "Neumeyer!" and started forward.

Peter lifted his head and said, "Don't forget where we left off, *Liebchen*."

Sweetheart? Rage bubbled up. Kurt charged as Marta pushed the bully away. Laughing, Peter spun. His roundhouse punch hit Kurt's shoulder, steering him into the brick wall.

Kurt smacked against the school's wall, his face grazing the brick, and rolled so his back pressed against it. He glared at Peter Neumeyer. He could never win a physical contest. Kurt licked his lips and met a familiar metal taste. He wiped the back of his hand across his mouth and nose. It came away bloody. He glanced at Marta, saw the uncertainty in her eyes.

That pig had been mauling her. What lie had he used to lure her behind the school?

Peter raised clenched fists to waist level, his stance casual, his smile mocking. Kurt pushed away from the wall and stepped toward the open field behind him, hoping to draw Peter away from Marta. "Let Marta go, Neumeyer. She isn't part of this."

"She is now." Peter sneered. "You've been keeping a secret, Schreiber, not letting anyone know how well she kisses. Well, kiss her goodbye. She's my girlfriend now."

"Marta isn't a book to be passed from one owner to the next. She picks her boyfriend."

"Wrong. She'll be my mine or she'll watch me pound you into mush." Peter's eyebrows arched. "Run away like you always do, Schreiber. You interrupted our first date."

Nostrils flaring, Kurt took another step forward. "I'm not going anywhere, Neumeyer."

"I finally found something to make the coward stand and fight. I know what Marta is to you. Why did you bother about that old man?"

"He's Marta's grandfather." Kurt spat some blood and wiped at his nose again. It had almost stopped bleeding. Without taking his eyes off Peter, he said, "Go, Marta. Run."

"No," Peter said, his bulk blocking her way. "She has to see this. Winner takes all, Schreiber." He grinned. "And believe me, I'll enjoy taking it."

The remark was designed to make Kurt angry. The problem was, it worked. He tried to clear his mind, to remember the self-defence lessons that Tyler had given him and the moves he and Victor had practised. None of them applied to his taking the first swing. He had to get Peter to attack. Kurt moved two metres away. "You're the coward, Neumeyer, using Marta to hurt me. That can work both ways. You hurt her, I'll hurt Stephan. He isn't the lummox you are. He'll go down fast."

Peter's lip curled, but anger flicked through his eyes. "Leave Stephan out of this."

"No." Kurt started to turn away, as if going to find Peter's younger brother.

With a roar, Peter charged. Kurt stepped into the attack, hoping he knew what he was doing. He blocked the punch to his stomach with his forearm, grabbed Peter's wrist, swept his foot at Peter's ankle. Overbalanced, Peter started to topple. Kurt helped him with a shove.

An "Oof!" exploded from Peter when his landed on his side. He was on his feet again in an eyeblink. Rage reddened his face. Kurt backpedalled, knowing he was dead if one of those wrecking-ball fists connected. Peter plowed one at Kurt's head. Kurt ducked, danced behind Peter, landed a tap on his shoulder blade. The bully pivoted, fist extended.

Kurt sidestepped and backed out of Peter's reach. "Is that the best you can do when you don't resort to ambush? If you taught Stephan to fight, he'll be an easy target."

Face twisted, Peter rushed forward again. Holding his breath, Kurt blocked the blow to his head. He grabbed Peter's wrist, twisted, bent over. Peter's momentum carried him over Kurt's shoulder. He landed flat on his back and gaped like a fish on land, fighting for air. Hauling back his foot, Kurt aimed for the bully's ribs. He let his foot drop. He wasn't going to let himself become like Neumeyer, kicking someone when he was down.

Marta grabbed Kurt's hand. He shrugged one shoulder. "Let's go."

They walked away from Peter, still struggling to catch his breath. As they turned the corner, shaking threatened to buckle Kurt's knees. He had done it. He would have to email Tyler and thank him.

Stephan was still on the school steps. Kurt shifted his own recovered bag to his right shoulder and slung Marta's bag over his left. Stephan eyed him with a mixture of confusion and dread. Kurt realized he had to look awful. Bruised cheek, blood on his mouth, chin and shirt. He ignored the younger Neumeyer, took Marta's hand and led her toward the crosswalk.

As they headed toward Marta's house in silence, Kurt felt Marta's tension in her tight grip. Her lips drew into a thin line and her eyes glimmered. *Please don't cry*, he thought.

Kurt had gotten lucky, prodding Peter into losing his cool. But Peter wasn't stupid. He knew now that Kurt only had a few self-defence moves. He wasn't a fighter. Those moves would likely never work again.

Kurt squeezed his eyes shut and almost tripped over a cobblestone. His breathing sped up again. Peter *was* a fighter. He would hurt Marta again because hurting her hurt Kurt. They halted at Marta's gate. He tried to pull his thoughts away from that one awful realization.

Marta unlocked her gate and whispered, "Kurt?"

He realized he wasn't moving. He followed Marta up the sidewalk, each footstep heavier than the last. They stood under the porch roof and searched each other's faces.

Kurt finally asked, "Did he hurt you?"

She shook her head. "He kept his hand over my mouth until he heard you coming. He didn't kiss me until..."

Until I was there to see it. Kurt clenched his jaw.

"I thought you were hurt. He told me you needed help, as if he had already beat you..." Tears pooled in Marta's eyes. "It makes me angry that I was so helpless against him."

Kurt dropped both backpacks and hugged her. She sobbed once against his shoulder, then wrapped her arms around his waist and held tight. He laid his cheek against her hair and inhaled the fresh apple scent even as his gut twisted. This wasn't like Marta. Kurt held her at arm's length and studied her now puzzled features.

"What is it?" Marta said.

"I can't...do this to you."

"Do what?"

"Let you be hurt because of me." Kurt closed his eyes against the ache behind them. "You have been my best friend here in Zethen, Marta." *And you're more than a friend to me now*, he wanted to add, but couldn't get the words out.

"Have been? Does Victor have that spot in your heart now?"

She couldn't be trying to tease him. Not now. Something Marta saw in Kurt's face silenced her. Her brown eyes filled with compassion. She touched his scraped cheek.

"Don't," Kurt whispered.

"You're scaring me, Kurt."

"I don't want to scare you. I want to protect you." He stared at her mouth, her lovely kissable mouth, then looked away. "There's only one way I can do that."

"Yes. I saw. It was beautiful, the way you flipped –"

"No!" Kurt released her and picked up his backpack. "I got lucky today. That's all. Peter will be madder than ever when he catches his breath. But..." Kurt's brow creased with the effort of forcing out his next thought. "If I leave you alone, Peter will leave you alone. It's that simple."

Marta's stare was blank, but only for a moment. "But we're... What are we? Are you my boyfriend? Are you breaking up with me? You can't be walking away from our friendship."

"Not walking. Running. It's what I'm best at."

"You can't do that!" Marta stamped her foot.

Kurt almost smiled at the uncharacteristic show of temper. The tears threatening to spill down her face sobered him. "I'm sorry, Marta. I'm leaving in two months anyway. Just think of me as...already gone." He turned away.

"*Sorry!* If you leave me, then Peter wins."

But you are safe. Staring at the beckoning gate, Kurt said, "Then Peter wins, Marta. He warned me he would."

Kurt told Victor that he and Marta had broken up. He urged him to tell Rebekka. Word had to get to Peter quickly from someone not involved. Kurt avoided everyone and used his self-imposed isolation to keep an eye on Marta, as much as possible, without being noticed.

When Peter ragged Kurt in Sports class, saying Marta had dropped him because she saw him for the coward he was, Kurt just retreated. Peter found this vastly amusing, but his eyes still radiated hatred. Three days and Peter seemed to be ignoring Marta. Kurt started to relax. He had been right. She was safe so long as she wasn't with him.

Walking home from school on Thursday, Kurt felt more alone than he had that first week in September. He tramped into the kitchen to find Frau Klassen leaning against the counter, expression serious. Her voice was firm. "Are you still refusing Marta's phone calls?"

Kurt winced inwardly. "Yes. Did she call again?" Twice on Tuesday evening, once last night. Getting beaten up by Peter had been less painful than saying no to talking to Marta. And seeing emails from her address had been like having scalpels poked into open sores.

"No, she didn't." A sigh of relief escaped. Frau Klassen added, "But her grandfather did. He wants you to join him for supper tonight. He said you have some serious matters to discuss. I accepted on your behalf." Frau Klassen was normally gentle, but the fierce look she gave Kurt was one reserved for her war against the wild boars raiding her garden.

"Will Marta be there? I'm not –"

"I didn't ask and he didn't say. It doesn't matter. You are going, Kurt Schreiber. No arguing. Herr Brandt asked that you arrive at six o'clock. That gives you several hours to run around the lake or whatever you have to do." Frau Klassen set a cutting board on the table and began chopping onions with jerky motions. "I cannot imagine what you two quarrelled about, but I am not putting up with having to refuse Marta's hurt voice on the telephone. I expected more courteous behaviour from you."

She scraped the onion into a frying pan and started on a green pepper. Kurt had only seen this unbending side of Frau Klassen once or twice with Herr Klassen. He took her advice, ran around the lake, then showered and changed into clean jeans and his favourite grey shirt.

The walk to Herr Brandt's seemed extra long. Kurt's feet dragged. He stood at the wrought iron gate, struggling with the desire to run. If Marta was there... His gaze fell from the wooden door. The tulips along the sidewalk had been replaced by bedding plants. Two of them were budding, cheerful gold petals peeking out from green cocoons. Marigolds, maybe.

Kurt strode to the door and grabbed the iron ring hanging from the wolf's mouth. His hand froze as he stared at the knocker. This had to have been something Wolf Brandt had added after he had moved into Jäger's house. Kurt let the ring fall. The quiet *thunk* was barely audible. He didn't want to face Herr Brandt, not tonight, not even to hear another story.

The door opened. The old man's grey blue eyes pinned Kurt before he could turn away. The gaze shifted to Kurt's scraped cheek. "Young Schreiber. Come in." He held the door open wide. When Kurt didn't move, Herr Brandt said, "You are here for supper, are you not?"

"I'm here because Frau Klassen told me to come."

"Ach, the honesty of youth. Step inside before these old bones get a chill."

Kurt shot Herr Brandt a skeptical look. It was a warm evening. He peered inside.

"You are expecting someone else to be here, perhaps? Fear not, young Schreiber, we are alone. I wish to talk with you, man to man."

With a nod, Kurt followed Herr Brandt into the kitchen. The smell of bratwurst and frying onions filled the room. A bowl of cold sauerkraut sat on the table, along with dark rye bread and two narrow-necked brown bottles. Beer. Kurt almost smiled.

"My cooking skills are limited," Herr Brandt said. He crossed to the stove and stirred the onions. "The sauerkraut is my daughter's home-cooked recipe. Quite mild. You do eat sauerkraut, do you not?"

Kurt shrugged. It wasn't his favourite, but he had sort of learned to enjoy it. "It's okay."

"Okay." Herr Brandt snorted. "A neutral word that means neither yes nor no. It tells me that you will put up with it to humour an old man."

"I like Frau Klassen's sauerkraut. It has pineapple in it." Kurt gripped the back of a chair. He wasn't sure he could eat, the way his stomach was churning. Now that he thought about it, *man to man* had an ominous ring. He peered at the beer bottles. They were both a malt brew – almost no alcohol in them, just the taste of beer.

Herr Brandt set the cast iron frying pan on a metal trivet in the middle of the table. He said, "Do we talk first, or eat first?"

The odour of the onion and sausage and grease clogged Kurt's nostrils. His throat convulsed. He whispered, "Talk."

Inclining his silver head, Herr Brandt pointed out the window. "We will sit on the swing."

Kurt led the way down the cellar steps, then outside. He sat on the swing by the outer stairwell and recalled the last time he had sat there, when Herr Brandt had caught him kissing Marta. He braced his feet to steady the swing and hunched forward, waiting to be bawled out.

Herr Brandt sighed as he sat. "My daughter knows I dislike interfering in her affairs. So last night, after my usual Wednesday supper with them, I was surprised when she asked me to talk to Marta. We have a good relationship. I have told my daughter it is because I do not talk, I listen. But like many parents, she likes to lecture and call it a talk." He sighed again. "You promised you would not hurt Marta." Kurt braced his forehead on his fists. The disappointment in Herr Brandt's voice was far worse than a lecture. The old man said, "I would never have expected such behaviour from Jäger's grandson. From mine perhaps, but not his."

"I am not Jäger," Kurt whispered.

"No, but I see the same integrity in you that I knew in him. I would like to hear the explanation for your actions."

In the silence, Kurt relaxed slightly. Herr Brandt didn't plan to berate him; he only wanted to listen. Kurt leaned back. Reluctant to look at the old man, he stared at the tall hedge separating this yard from the next. "You know I've been having trouble with Peter Neumeyer."

"Yes, yes. Though you have never explained why, just that he is a bully."

Kurt nodded. "He likes to pick on a different student each year. This year he chose me. It was only annoying talk until the day he called me a coward. He said I was just like my grandfather. I still don't know why. The bullying has been getting worse. On Monday..." Kurt shifted to face Herr Brandt. "I embarrassed him. Now Peter really wants to hurt me. And on Monday he used Marta to do it."

The old man's face remained bland, but something dark flicked through his eyes. He waited for Kurt to continue. He did, explaining about the fight, the flip, and the realization that the only way to keep Marta safe was to stay away from her.

When Kurt stopped talking, Herr Brandt said, "So you wound her heart to keep her from harm. This matter has gone beyond a schoolyard spat. Perhaps you should involve the police."

"I'll be okay. I'm sure I can stay out of his way for eight weeks, and I know I can outrun him. So long as he leaves Marta alone, I don't care."

"You could leave now. This is not your home."

"I'd lose this term's credits." Kurt peered up at the window of what had been his grandfather's bedroom. He added, "And...it almost feels like home. I don't want to run away." Kurt gave Herr Brandt a small smile. "Besides, if I leave I won't learn the end of your story."

"Ach, is that all that is important to you? An old man's war stories? You do not care that the old man's granddaughter is crying into her pillow?"

Kurt jerked to his feet. He rubbed his neck and turned away, unwilling to let Herr Brandt see the upset caused by the thought of Marta crying. "I care. It's just better this way. I didn't mean to hurt her."

Herr Brandt groaned as he stood. He squeezed Kurt's shoulder. "Come. Our bratwurst will be cold. You are more like your grandfather than you realize, young man, not caring what happens to you so long as your loved ones are safe. You need to explain this to Marta. Be fair to her, Kurt." He dropped his hand. "You did not mention this coward non-sense before. I cannot think why young Neumeyer would say that, but it is one wrong idea I can disprove...if you want to hear another story."

Relief flooded Kurt's thoughts. The man to man talk hadn't been so bad after all. He ignored the niggling feeling that the old man was right; he did need to talk to Marta. Instead he smiled and arched his eyebrows, letting amazement fill his reply. "If...?"

Chapter Twenty-One

1943. We were retreating again, and had stopped to rest. A bad miscalculation. Two companies of Russian infantry were advancing on our position from three sides. I peered out a crack in the back door of the storeroom where the remains of our unit was holed up and said, "Captain, you want to see this."

A T-34 Russian tank stopped at the intersection thirty metres down the alley. Captain Rothe joined me and swore. Where there was a tank, infantry wasn't far behind. Our escape route was being blocked. Jäger asked what was out there. When I told him, he butted a wooden beam with his rifle and muttered something about being trapped.

The irony wasn't lost on the few of us who were original members of the unit. Our backs to the wall...in a barn. Surrender was not an option. We had heard the rumours about how the Russians treated prisoners – revenge for the way their captured men were treated.

Jäger jogged to the newest member of the unit – a boy of eighteen with fear-filled eyes. He yanked both of the boy's potato mashers – his long-handled grenades – clear of his belt. Like me, Jäger had used his to slow down our pursuers.

Captain Rothe announced, "The turret is swivelling. They're going to blow open this side of the building."

Returning to my side, Jäger handed his rifle to the captain and told me, "Shoot the tank commander before he shoots me, Wolf."

My insides twisted. I demanded to know what he was doing. He said he was going for a run. The captain grabbed the door handle and said, "It has to be down the hatch, Schreiber."

Jäger was outside and running before I could protest. He dodged toward the tank. The Russian commander was standing in the open hatch, visible from the chest up. I snapped my *Mauser* into position. Over the rushing in my ears I heard Rothe yelling at the men to get ready to run like Jäger. That's how our unit referred to the need for speed – to run like Jäger.

I saw the tank commander raise his pistol. I fired and only got him in the arm. Jäger was almost to the tank. The commander took aim again. This time I didn't miss.

Without slowing, Jäger swung around the tank's swivelling gun barrel and charged up the sloped front. He dropped one grenade down the hatch as he dashed the length of the track guards and threw the other grenade under the tank as he jumped from the back to sprint away.

The double *whump! whump!* shook the door. I flinched, then yelled my horror when I saw the force of the explosion toss Jäger against a wall. I raced out, the unit right behind me.

Behind us, gunfire battered the front doors of the barn. We raced past the lopsided tank with smoke billowing out of its hatch. I skidded to a halt beside Jäger, ignoring the captain's cry to keep moving. I didn't pause to check for a pulse, just hoisted him over my shoulder and kept going. Two blocks later we rounded a corner into the welcoming arms of another German unit. Someone spotted my burden and waved me toward a captured Russian truck with a crude swastika painted on the side. The captain followed me.

We crawled into the back, where I laid Jäger onto the floor beside a few other injured men. There was so much blood. He had been hit by shrapnel. His arm was broken, or at least dislocated. I tore at his belt. We had to get the bleeding stopped.

The driver poked his head into the back, took one look, and said, "Don't bother. We need the room for the ones who can be saved."

I jammed my rifle under his chin and told him to get us to a field hospital. Captain Rothe pushed the rifle down and said, "This man just saved our unit, *OberSchutze*. We have to try."

The lance corporal gave me an angry look and said, "Yes, sir." As the truck bounced away from the town, Rothe helped me get Jäger's belt and Y-straps off. He regained consciousness when I was peeling off his tunic.

His whisper was ragged, hard to hear over the moans of the other men. I assured him that we had all made it out and chided him for bleeding on my uniform. I reminded him how I hated washing my tunic. His smile was weak. I knew the moisture on my cheeks was not sweat.

I continued to harass him verbally – anything to keep him awake – while we tried to fashion bandages from a few empty meal sacks that had been scattered on the truck bed. The other wounded men watched us with hopeless gazes. I rolled his torn tunic and tucked it under his head. Jäger groaned with each rut we hit. I prayed the hospital wasn't far, pressed cloth against the worst wound and avoided Captain Rothe's eyes. Avoided everyone's eyes.

Medics met us and eased Jäger onto a stretcher. We followed them into a tent where a tired doctor in a bloody apron examined Jäger and told us it was good we had worked to stop the bleeding. He might make it.

The captain leaned over Jäger and said, "You'll get the Iron Cross for this, Schreiber."

I thought he was unconsciousness, but Jäger's eyes opened. His bloody fingers wrapped around Rothe's wrist. "Get me home," he whispered, "I want to marry Hedda."

Rothe looked doubtful and said he'd do what he could. I said, "You'll do it. You owe him. We all do." I met Jäger's gaze and fell dumb. So much to say and I couldn't get a word past my clogged throat. His eyelids drooped; his breathing rasped. I didn't know if I would ever see my best friend again and all I could do was hold his hand until medics chased me out of the tent.

Six miserable weeks followed of trying to hold the line and being forced back, step by bloody step. I had so many close calls that I stopped counting. I knew, without Jäger to guard my back, it was only a matter of time before one of those crazed, fearless Russians got me. They didn't care if it took ten, twenty or even a hundred men to kill one German – and I was sure I had killed many more than that. My turn was coming.

In late May of 1943, the unit had been rotated behind the front lines for a short break, the only kind we ever got. Days, if we were lucky. We never knew whether partisans would attack us behind our own lines, so even breaks were uneasy. The Russians kept growing in strength and ability; the *Wehrmacht* kept weakening. We were our own reserves, while Russian resources and manpower seemed limitless. Only sheer willpower – ours and our commanders' – kept us fighting. Futility and fear loomed like a thundercloud.

I was leaning against a dead tank, eyeing the dark smoke staining the eastern horizon, when I saw Jäger striding through camp, creased and clean, looking as if he had stepped off a recruiting poster. I was stunned. I had heard he had been posted to Denmark.

He hadn't noticed me. Like the bloodhound he was, Jäger had sniffed out Captain Rothe's position behind a rickety table under a tree on the far side of camp. I followed. The captain was unaware, but every line in Jäger's body screamed that he was on the hunt. I broke into a jog and arrived at the table a step behind Jäger, but even that didn't earn me a glance. The captain looked up from reading a letter. He didn't appear surprised.

Without saluting, Jäger said, "*Obergefreiter* Schreiber reporting for duty...sir." Anger oozed from his pores. The Iron Cross, snug under his collar, bobbed as he worked his jaw. Second Class. What complete foolishness did a soldier have to commit to earn First Class?

The captain leaned back and said, "At ease, Schreiber. Speak before you explode."

Jäger did both. He yelled, "I was out of this hellhole! I was posted to Copenhagen until you interfered, you slimy ba –" He cut off, then continued, "I don't know what favours you called in to get my assignment changed, but you can bloody well get it changed back. Now."

Rothe's blunt refusal made fury darken Jäger's face; his eyes flamed bright green. He was headed for a firing squad if he kept at it. I touched his arm. He slapped it away. When I grabbed his wrist and forced his attention to me, the anger subsided to sadness.

Voice suddenly quiet, Jäger told me I was the only reason he had come back. If it hadn't been for me, he would have taken Hedda and fled to Sweden instead of reporting for duty.

I whispered, "I'm sorry."

With a weak smile, he said, "Have you cried into your pillow every night?"

"Wailed," I replied, "and nearly gotten my head blown off because of it."

A grin flashed. For a second I saw the boy from Zethen, but just as quickly the hardened soldier resurfaced. He faced Captain Rothe and demanded he transfer us both, saying, "This front has eaten two years of our lives. That's enough, even for this bloodthirsty army."

"No more than I've given," Rothe replied. "Do you ever wonder why I'm still a captain, only commanding a unit? I don't play Command's political games, Schreiber. I'm a soldier leading a unit of soldiers. We fight other soldiers; we don't kill civilians. I've never let my unit be used by those *Einsatzkommandos* for their executions. So my superiors have made it clear I will never be transferred away from the eastern front."

Jäger asked what that had to do with him and Rothe said, "You are the unit's best scout. Possibly the best in the division. Your instincts have gotten us out of countless scrapes. I plan on surviving this disaster, Schreiber. You're going to help me do it."

When Jäger said he didn't care whether the captain survived, Rothe pointed out that if he died, the unit would be absorbed into another, possibly one with a commander who thought there were still battles to be won. Rothe said, "I'm not out to win, not any more. I'm out to live."

Jäger gave the captain a hard glare, then turned to me. We knew the captain was spouting treason, no matter how true. Rothe said, "How many members of the original unit are still here? You, me, Brandt, and three others. Six out of thirty. Most of the others are dead."

I cleared my throat and said, "Five. I forgot to pass the word. That shrapnel cost Geis his leg. He's being shipped home to Berlin."

"Where he'll get killed by a bomb," Jäger whispered. "What were we fighting for, Wolf? I can't remember any more."

Captain Rothe snapped, "Whatever it was, it's dead, Schreiber. Are you with me?"

Jäger stiffened and said, "Do I have a choice? I refuse to return to Hedda in a pine box."

Rothe added, "You know what will happen if anyone hears of this conversation."

A firing squad for three. Jäger turned away and I assured Rothe that no one would hear it from us. I told him, "So long as you're working to save the unit, and not just your own skin, we'll stand behind you."

Rothe nodded. As we walked away, I laid my hand on Jäger's shoulder and admitted that I'd never been so happy to see anyone in all my life. Jäger sent me a wry look and asked, "Not even Corny on a Saturday night?"

I laughed. I hadn't thought of the barmaid in months. Longer. No woman, no matter how eager, compares to the friend who guards your back. I sobered and said, "You should have run, Jäger. You should have taken Hedda to Sweden."

Jäger halted and clasped my upper arms and said, "Don't tell me to choose between the two of you, Wolf. She's my wife. You're my best friend. I won't turn my back on either of you." He gave me a long look and marched away.

I watched him go. I hadn't known he had actually married Hedda while he was home recovering from his injuries. Maybe I would get a letter in a month or six telling me the news. I whispered, "Congratulations," but felt jealous, wanting to have what he had.

I didn't have much time to enjoy Jäger's return. Every few days we were cycled to the front lines to face berserk Russians intent on driving us from their soil at any cost. We gave little to the fight, simply holding the line or retreating in the face of insane attacks.

Something big was being planned. We could see it in the way the officers swarmed around field headquarters. For us lowly foot soldiers, the sight was sobering. Frightening even. Our forces had been crushed at Stalingrad a few months before – a staggering defeat such as we had never experienced. Two hundred thousand dead; one hundred thousand captured. If this new operation was to be revenge for that, it would be fearsome beyond imagining.

Until we marched out, Jäger and I had hoped our unit would be one of the ones held back to guard the lines west of Moscow. They were shaky, but holding. It was not to be. With most of the rest of the Ninth Army, we moved south, toward a bulge in the lines where the Russians had punched through. Operation Citadel, it was called. The plan was to overcome the eastern flank and trap one hundred thousand Russians.

I woke in the early morning hours of July 4 and saw Jäger's empty bedroll. In the moonless darkness, I found him on the southern outskirts of our camp and crouched beside him.

"Why aren't you sleeping?" I whispered.

He said, "Who can sleep? They're out there, sneaking into position."

I knew he meant the first wave, the men initiating Operation Citadel. His next words, a quiet admission of fear, rocked me. I had never heard him say it aloud, though I had seen it in his eyes from time to time. You couldn't face the eastern front without feeling fear sometimes.

When I asked why, he said he thought it would go badly for us.

The eastern horizon was lightening to blue grey. The day would dawn clear. I asked if that was what he had talked to Captain Rothe about the day before.

Jäger said, "Yes. He passed my opinion on, but was informed by his superiors that his job was to do what he was told. Our buildup has been too slow. The Russians will be waiting. And the ground slopes down. It will be easy for them to see us coming."

I reminded him it was a pincer movement, that our best *Panzer* corps were getting ready to attack from the south. In the dim light, I saw him shake his head as he countered with how fiercely the Russians fought now, that they weren't going to throw down their rifles or surrender.

When had Jäger been wrong? In my mind, I saw rivers running a darker pink than now stained the sky. I settled down and peered into the semi-darkness. When we heard the first popping, he whispered, "Who will protect Hedda if I die in this battle?" I don't think he meant for me to hear, so quiet were the words, but they chilled my soul. I didn't reply.

Several moments later, the bombardment started. We both stood. I strained to listen to the rhythmic thumping and said, "Those don't sound like German guns. But it's too early for a counterattack."

Jäger replied, "Unless they knew when and where we were attacking."

A traitor? The thought made my insides roil with anger and fear. To betray your own people was unthinkable.

July 4 was one of the longest days of my life. To listen to the battle from afar, to know what was happening only from snippets of information, none of it good. We could see specks in the sky, circling like vultures. Airplanes. Whose, we could not tell. The wounded poured past our camp, first a trickle then a flood. The sight made mockery of the inspirational message the Führer had sent his troops, and which our commanding officers had read to us with zeal. He had urged us to make this offensive "a beacon of victory."

At supper, I went through the lineup behind Jäger and followed him out of the mess tent. We sat away from the others. To the south, smoke billowed over the battlefields. Was any kind of victory in sight? I asked, "Do you remember how his words stirred us when we were young?" We were only twenty-one, but felt ancient.

Jäger looked at me with a hollow gaze. He knew who I meant – our noble Führer. "We were fools," he whispered and stabbed a chunk of shrivelled meat. "He doesn't care about Germany. Or us. All he cares about is victory. Victory at any price." Jäger chewed his meat. In the distance, battle sounds droned and whined and thudded. He suddenly asked me to look after Hedda if he didn't make it.

"Look after Hedda yourself," I said. "If you die, I had better already be dead or you're in trouble."

That made Jäger grin. He said, "Both dead. Wouldn't that upset our captain?"

We were the reinforcements. On the second day, July 5, we marched behind our tanks into hell itself. The battleground was littered with smoking heaps of metal – I had never seen so many dead tanks in one place, and that after the first day's fighting. Corpses were scattered everywhere. The stench of oil, gunpowder and rotting flesh was overwhelming.

The tanks had to manoeuver through an obstacle course of death just to reach the enemy. We sheltered behind every crippled tank, fence, outcropping and tree we came across. We ducked behind an overturned truck just as the tank in front of us hit a land mine. The earth shuddered. Jäger pointed out approaching "flying tanks," those lumbering Russian bombers. Russian tanks advanced from the southeast. Behind us, our "door knockers" began their pointless thumping – the anti-tank guns had earned their name by being useless against enemy tanks. A German rocket – a *Nebelwerfer* – shrieked overhead, then another. We braced for the world to erupt into a chaotic mix of thunderous noise, flying shrapnel, exploding shells and blood. Always more blood. Only death itself walked without fear through that horror.

Tanks and airplanes were soon the least of our worries. Days of ferocious hand-to-hand combat flowed into one another. No matter what we threw at Soviet positions, we couldn't seem to make headway. Five, six days, and we had barely advanced ten kilometres, every centimetre of that distance soaked with blood. Always more blood.

We were exhausted, bruised, bloodied. We had nothing left to give. The dead seemed beyond counting. When the Russian counterattack came on the eleventh, our north line began to buckle. The south held only a little longer. Many of the Russian troops were inexperienced, easy to kill, but they were endless. Shoot one and fifty stepped into the gap. It was a flood we could not hold back. The official retreat was called for on the thirteenth; by the seventeenth we were in full retreat from the Battle of Kursk, called that because of the town in the centre of our objective area. Seventy thousand dead is the number I heard. So much for the revenge of Stalingrad.

K urt swallowed past a lump in his throat and studied Herr Brandt's features in the lengthening silence. The old man's eyes were shadowed a lead grey as they stared into the past – to the days when Jäger had won a medal for bravery and they both had survived one of the largest battles of the war. *Not a coward.* Kurt poured the last of his malt brew into the glass and downed it. The quiet thunk of glass on wood seemed to draw Herr Brandt into the present.

At a loss for words, Kurt said, "Sounds awful."

Herr Brandt's steel grey brows drew together. "Awful is too weak a word. It was full of horror, full of fear, full of terror and rage and death. Always death. You cannot imagine what it is to have death as a constant companion."

"I saw *Saving Private Ryan.*"

Herr Brandt snorted. "Make-believe is not life. I heard that movie was realistic. The sounds and sights of battle. But nothing compares to being there. Looking into a man's eyes as you fill his stomach with lead, knowing it is him or you. Kill or be killed, day after day, with death grinning as it sets its sights on you." He pushed to his feet and picked up his plate. "May you never have to experience it." He set his plate in the sink and plugged in the kettle.

Kurt joined Herr Brandt by the counter and turned on the tap. He squirted dish soap under the flow and picked up the folded dishcloth. "I didn't mean to insult you. You're right. I can't know what it was like. I had read that Kursk was a big tank battle. I didn't know infantry was involved." He immersed his hands in the hot water and began washing the plates.

Herr Brandt returned from the table with the glasses. "Infantry and tanks go together and guard each other. I used to harass Jäger about wanting to be part of a tank crew – at least they got to ride. There were so few trucks we almost always had to march. After Kursk, I didn't wish for that any more. I had seen too many tanks torn open by shells, their interiors gutted by fire. Sometimes tank crews were given refurbished tanks – they complained that the smell of death could never be scrubbed away."

Kurt inhaled the lemon scent of the dish soap to rid himself of the imagined stink of death. He delved through bubbles and warm water to fish out the cutlery.

The phone rang.

"I'm not here," Kurt whispered.

Herr Brandt gently swatted the back of Kurt's head as he passed by. In the living room, he picked up the handset and spoke loudly. "Hello Marta. Are you feeling better? No? Ach, that is too bad. Yes, yes, I understand. Not right now, I have company. Who? That is a rude question. I am old enough to entertain whom I please without informing you, young lady. Kurt? Frau Klassen told you he might show up here, did she? Yes, yes. I will certainly tell him when I see him. Yes, yes. I love you, too. Good night, *Leibling*."

The knot of tension in Kurt's neck unravelled when he heard Herr Brandt hang up.

The old man appeared at his side, quiet as ever. Kurt flinched. Herr Brandt leaned close. "You will talk to her soon, Kurt. Is that understood?"

"What did she say to tell me?"

A smile crinkled out from Herr Brandt's eyes. "I am supposed to tell you that you are a pigheaded boy. And she stressed the word, *boy*."

"What? Because I want to keep her safe I'm pigheaded?"

"You are arguing with the wrong person, young Schreiber." Herr Brandt unplugged the whistling kettle and set about making tea. "How have your dreams been?"

Kurt pushed the empty sauerkraut dish under the water with a *glub*. "Better. I think telling you about it helped."

"It has been helping me as well, I think. I should have talked to someone years ago."

Kurt said, "I know Marta wanted to hear about your wartime experiences, but some of it is...pretty gruesome. I'm glad that she hasn't been here."

"As am I, Kurt. It is easier to talk when it is just the two of us. One man to another."

Kurt grinned. One man to another. He liked the sound of that.

Chapter Twenty-Two

Friday afternoon, Kurt took the train to Stralsund on the north coast of Germany. He met four other exchange students and Jim, who had agreed to chaperone. They spent the weekend kayaking along the coast of Rügen Island. *So close to Peenemünde.* The whole peninsula was a national park now.

Weariness dogged Kurt's footsteps when he arrived back at the Klassens' late Sunday evening. His arms and neck and back ached. But he couldn't sleep. At midnight, he tiptoed down to Herr Klassen's den, glad he had permission to call home anytime he chose.

The telephone rang at the other end. 4:00 p.m. in Calgary. "Hello?" Grandfather's voice rasped. He cleared his throat and repeated the greeting with greater strength. "Hello?"

"*Guten Tag, Grossvater*," Kurt said. (Good day, Grandfather.)

A pause and Grandfather replied in German, "Kurt. It is late there. Is something wrong?"

"No. I couldn't sleep and wanted to ask you something." The line buzzed. Kurt took a breath and said, "Why didn't you ever tell us that you had won the Iron Cross?" *I would have known you weren't a coward. Peter's words would have been harmless.*

Grandfather sighed. "It was a different time. I was a different man. When I came to Canada I left that man behind."

"But you kept writing to Herr Brandt, to Wolf."

"A friendship of the heart is not so easily cast aside."

"What happened to it?"

"Our friendship? It is still there, still strong."

"No. I mean the Iron Cross."

The line hummed again. Kurt heard a muffled cough. Grandfather said, "That is a question for you to ask Wolf." Another pause. "Do you hate me, now that you know?"

Kurt scowled at the telephone. He had never heard such uncertainty in his grandfather's voice before. Guilt twinged. "I did, when I first found out you had been a Nazi soldier, but now that I've heard some of what you went through..." Kurt spoke firmly, "No, Grandfather, I don't hate you. I don't understand everything that happened, but I'm not sure I would've acted any differently. Except for the Iron Cross. I don't think I could have charged a tank, no matter what."

Grandfather chuckled. "We only find the strength to do such things when faced with them. I smell my toast. Thank you for calling. Say hello to Wolf for me." The line went dead.

Ask Wolf. Kurt laid the handset back in its cradle. He most certainly would.

"**H**ave you spoken to Marta?" Herr Brandt's thin frame blocked the doorway.

Kurt eyed the mat in front of the door. "No. But I want to talk to you."

"I am busy, Kurt."

A scowl crept across Kurt's brow. "Busy doing what?"

"Waiting for you to speak to Marta. Goodbye, young Schreiber."

The door closed in Kurt's face. He scowled at the door knocker shaped like a wolf's head. Its pewter eyes seemed to accuse him. "What are you looking at?" he muttered, then spun and jogged down the sidewalk.

Each day Kurt started out with the intention of speaking to Marta; each day he found some excuse not to. Mostly he spent his time avoiding Peter, who seemed to be tracking him. When he finally phoned over to the Fischers on Thursday evening, Marta refused to speak to him. Friday, after class, he saw her walking toward *Gunther's Apotheke*.

Knowing Peter couldn't be following because the Sports class instructor had held him back to discuss something, Kurt jogged up to Marta and matched her pace. "We need to talk."

Marta kept her eyes forward. "I'm busy."

Kurt snorted. "You sound like your grandfather."

She spun to face him. "Leave him out of this. This is about you and me."

"So let's talk."

"Only if you admit it."

"Admit what?"

"That you're being pigheaded."

"I have my reasons. Besides, you're the one refusing to talk...now." Marta spun away; Kurt grabbed her arm. "Please? Tonight?"

"I'm going to a friend's birthday party."

"On the weekend then."

Marta raised her brows. "Maybe." She tugged free and strode away.

Kurt lifted the door knocker and banged the ring on its brass plate. He tapped his thigh for a moment, then banged again. Finally he heard a muffled, "Yes, yes." He stepped back.

The door opened. "Young Schreiber. What do you want?"

"I asked Marta to talk. She's busy tonight, but we *are* going to talk before the weekend is over." He would turn her *maybe* into a *yes*. He hoped.

Grey eyebrows arched, just like Marta's often did. "What does that have to do with me?"

"Now can we talk?" Under the sharp blue grey gaze, Kurt's confidence began to shrink. "I was hoping you would..." When Herr Brandt didn't reply, Kurt sighed. "Never mind. I'm sorry I bothered you."

Kurt was on the second step when Herr Brandt said, "Perhaps if I talk to you now, I might be able to put off telling Marta. Far better she hears a short version from you."

His foot hanging over the third step, Kurt said, "You do tell a long and gruesome story. You wouldn't want her to start dreaming about the war."

"No. No, that would never do. Perhaps you should come in, young Schreiber, if you can manage to sit through another long and gruesome story."

Kurt pivoted on his heel. "But not boring. None of your stories are boring."

Herr Brandt leveled a wry look at Kurt. "Live through such days and you might come to appreciate times that are boring."

He peered over Kurt's shoulder. "Perhaps I will not invite you in after all." When Kurt started to protest, Herr Brandt raised his hand. "Give me a moment. It is a nice evening for a stroll. The breeze can carry away the stench of what is still untold."

They walked down the sidewalk at Herr Brandt's slow pace. He swung his cane forward with each step and chatted almost idly about the German retreat before the relentless Soviet army through the rest of 1943 and all of 1944. Units decimated and reformed, again and again. Food shortages. The retreat becoming more disorganized. And the three of them – him, Jäger and Captain Rothe – somehow surviving.

They wound up by the lake. Herr Brandt indicated the bench where they had first talked. After they were settled, Kurt stared at the water while Herr Brandt took up the story again. Kurt didn't see the water; he saw two young men and their captain, desperate to survive.

C aptain Rothe proved trustworthy. He struggled to keep the unit together and alive. He often chose safe retreat over desperate battle – unless an ss unit was in the vicinity. The ss remained fanatically loyal to the Führer and happily shot anyone who breathed a complaint about any Nazi leadership. The three of us never had reason to speak our feelings; we all knew our goal was survival. Not glory. Not victory. Just survival. The Russians did not make it easy.

January 1945: we were somewhere west of Moscow, being pushed toward the German border. The closer we were forced to our own soil, the harder we fought, but it did no good. Behind our lines, everything was in short supply, especially men. The Russians had plenty of everything, especially men. And their consuming hatred fed our growing fear.

Our unit had been separated from the rest of the Ninth during an attack and we were cutting across country, trying to rejoin our army. I don't know what day it was on the calendar. A frosty morning, the sun not yet risen, the sky icy blue. The ground crunched underfoot. Our trail across the barren field, as we knocked frost from brittle grass, was easy to track. We sought forest cover on the other side of a road.

We crouched in a ditch while Jäger scouted ahead to make sure the way was clear. I didn't know the other fifteen men who now made up our unit, remnants from other decimated ones. They all wore the same battle-weary expressions I suspected haunted my own face. Shadowed eyes and stubble-coated jaws. No one talked. There was nothing to say.

Jäger emerged from the wood thirty metres to the north. He started to cross the road, then froze right in the middle. A dark target against the white fields. I wanted to shout warning but sounds carried far in the pre-dawn hush. I willed him to get down.

Horror struck as Jäger dropped to his knees. *He's been hit!* my mind yelled. I scurried down the ditch, crouched low. Jäger still hadn't moved. I stumbled, scrambled up, kept running. When I got to him, I threw myself onto my stomach on the embankment.

He didn't respond to his name. I couldn't see any bleeding, no sign he was hurt. Below the brim of his helmet, his brow furrowed. I scanned the countryside, but couldn't see anything except the captain leading the rest of unit up the ditch toward us. Leaving my rifle, I darted into the road, grabbed Jäger by the arm and dragged him to the scant safety of the ditch.

I shook him hard and said, "What's wrong with you?"

Jäger pointed over my shoulder. I peered down the road, trying to see what had shaken him. Then I saw the marker, white painted on a flat rock. It was a normal-looking sign saying a village was five kilometres ahead. But it was the name. Not Polish. German.

We were back in Germany.

Behind me, Captain Rothe whispered, "What's wrong with Schreiber?"

I indicated the sign Jäger had spotted and said, "We're home, Captain."

"They aren't going to stop," Jäger said, his voice hoarse. "They're going to roll over the border. Roll over all of us." He lurched to his feet, said the forest was clear, and dashed across the road to disappear between the trees.

I slumped, trying to process what he had said. *They aren't going to stop.* It had always been a possibility, but now it was happening. The Russians were going to sweep into Germany, leaving destruction in their wake, and we were helpless to stop them. It was our job to protect our people and we had failed before the first tank rumbled across the border. For weeks I had suspected I didn't care about anything beyond survival. Now something stirred inside and I feared I cared far too much. Caring got you killed. I swallowed bile and exchanged worried looks with Captain Rothe. Was this crushing sense of helplessness, this weak empty rage, how other people felt when our armies had invaded their countries?

On the edge of the forest Jäger pressed against a tree, peered over his shoulder and said, "We have to stop them, Captain."

Rothe nodded. He looked as shaken as Jäger and me. Few of the others showed any response to the knowledge we were back in the Fatherland. They looked resigned as we settled in to wait for the Russians, desperate to keep them off German soil. Something had changed for the three of us. I saw it in Jäger first. The captain's eyes held the same knowledge and I felt it continuing to grow inside. It wasn't about survival any longer. Not personal survival. Now it was about the very survival of our country, of our towns and villages. Our families.

It wasn't long before we heard a distant rumble. We squinted into the sun rising over the field. A dozen tanks lumbered into view, heading for the forest in which we sheltered.

Captain Rothe swore and said, "This is suicide. Prepare to retreat."

Jäger growled and took a menacing step toward the captain, his rifle pointing at chest level. He said we had to stop them. Rothe swatted the *Mauser* aside and stepped close. He jammed his pistol under Jäger's jaw and repeated his order to retreat. When Jäger only glared, Rothe lowered the Walther a few centimetres and said, "We're at half strength. Our radio man was blown up two days ago. We don't know where the rest of the Ninth is. I want to stop them as much as you do, but we have to regroup, strike back from strength, not weakness."

I shouldered my way between the two men and told Jäger that dying in that forest wouldn't protect Hedda. His green eyes, sharp with pain, searched my face. He nodded. I guided him into the forest, away from the approaching mechanical thunder.

The next day we met another unit that had lagged behind. They had a radio and were headed to a town a dozen kilometres west where promised reinforcements were supposed to be waiting. We joined them, still not forming a full-strength unit. We entered the town wary, rifles ready, moving up either side of the street as if the enemy were waiting in the square. What greeted us was even worse.

We veterans clumped together and stared at the so-called soldiers lined up on the other side of the small square. Old men and boys. Mostly boys. I spat. The glob landed beside Captain Rothe's toe. I said, "What are we supposed to do with them? Babysit?"

Rothe's shoulders twitched.

A scrubbed, clean-cheeked boy, maybe sixteen, took two steps forward, flung his hand into the air in the Nazi salute, said *"Heil Hitler!"* His voice cracked. He flushed and fixed his gaze on Captain Rothe as he declared they were ready to do their duty for the Fatherland.

Rothe sniffed, but didn't move. Behind him, Jäger kicked the cobblestones and frowned his disgust. The silence became strained. I expected Rothe to do or say something. All the veterans stared at him. He only gaped at the boy still holding his arm in the air. No one else moved other than to shuffle their feet, so I strode forward and halted a metre away from the eager little Hitler Youth. He still even wore his HJ dagger on his belt. His nose wrinkled and I tried to sneer, knowing I stank worse than a herd of sheep. Had I ever been that young and innocent? Rage at the commanders who would send us children to fight hardened warriors leaked into my words as I said, "Ready to do your duty, are you?"

"Yes, sir!" he replied

"Are you ready to die?" His arm dropped; he appeared startled as I said, "That's what is going to happen to you."

I indicated the neat rows behind him and raised my voice. "All of you. Is that what you want?" No one would look at me; no one but the little fanatic in front of me.

The boy lifted his chin and said, "No cost is too great for the privilege of serving our glorious Führer. Herr Hitler says victory –"

The muzzle of my rifle touching his belt buckle silenced the boy. I whispered, "Never mention that name in my presence. That pig has failed us at every turn."

He shouted, "How dare you speak of our Führer that way! Your captain will shoot you!"

I spat again and whispered, "Fool." As I turned, movement flicked in the corner of my eye. I spun back and batted the boy to the ground with my rifle stock. He glared. His HJ dagger lay thirty centimetres from his fingertips. I kicked it away and strode back to the others. At that moment I felt brittle, like an antique glass falling off a ledge toward cobblestones. I knew we would use those boys, feed them to the tanks and let the Russians use them for target practice. We had no choice. We had made our choice over a decade earlier, when the madman had shone like a god and my innocence and zeal had been as pure as that boy's.

With our...reinforcements, we split into two units again, but stuck close to share the radio between us. We harried the advancing Russians. Strike and run. Hold where we could. But always we fell back. The Hitler Youth was in our unit, along with some of his buddies. They kept their distance from us, as if we were Russians in disguise. We used them as foragers, letting them be the ones to steal from our own people to keep us fed.

I tormented the little fanatic, took to calling him Zealot. If nothing else, maybe his anger would keep him alive. Despite our mutual dislike, he always seemed to end up near me during a fight. After a week he was still alive, though a few of his friends hadn't been so lucky.

Spring thaw hit in early February, stopping the relentless advance of the Russian tanks. It gave us time to dig in along the Oder River, the last barrier between the Russians and Berlin.

The Ninth had a bridgehead at Frankfurt on the Oder, east of Berlin. We were ordered to push north and break the Russian encirclement of Kuestrin. The night before the first push, I found Jäger pacing. He refused even to look at me. The captain waved me over. I crouched beside him, near a small fire that was mostly smoke, and we both watched Jäger trying to wear a trench into the packed soil. This was not the grinning friend who would do almost anything on a dare, who would lead me behind enemy lines just to find a coat. I whispered that I thought he was starting to lose his nerve. What a joke. We were all losing our nerve. Fear rode us hard; death trampled us if we faltered.

"I don't think that's it," Rothe said. "He's heard the rumour from units straggling in."

I asked which one. We didn't always have food, but there were always plenty of rumours to feed on. Rothe said, "What the Russians are doing in German towns they've overrun."

Word was Russian commanders were letting their soldiers do anything they pleased: loot, rape, kill. It didn't matter. Some said it was payback for the things that had happened behind the lines in Russia, for what we had done to them. Not me, I thought. I had only killed soldiers. Mostly, I knew, because

Rothe had always refused the duties that involved civilian executions. I didn't even dare wonder how I might have acted in a different unit.

Rothe asked how old I was. I said, "Ancient." In the silence, I realized Rothe wanted a serious answer, so I added, "I'll be twenty-two in April – if I live that long."

He said, "I thought you were younger than eighteen when you joined the unit. Or maybe I already felt old. I'm only three years your senior. I know what Schreiber is feeling. I have a wife and a five-year-old daughter. To know what the Russians are doing,...then think of them doing it to your wife or child... It's like getting kicked in the gut and the balls all at the same time."

I winced in sympathy and watched Jäger pace. Each day, the Russians were one step closer to Zethen. That was the unspoken cloud hanging over my friend.

The little fanatic appeared by my elbow and wanted to know what I was doing. I shoved him away and told him to go to bed. When he tried to talk about the Führer's latest message, I grabbed him by the collar and threatened to clobber him. He beetled into the darkness.

Rothe said, "I don't know why he likes you when you treat him like dirt."

I certainly didn't like him. It was like looking in a mirror that reflected myself six years earlier. I said, "I hope he's still alive after tomorrow. He thinks the skirmishes we've had these last weeks were real battles." I marched over and stepped in front of Jäger. I clasped his upper arms and told him he had to get some sleep if he wanted to save my skin the next day. When I gave him the choice of doing it willingly or getting cracked over the head, he almost smiled.

He said, "But then I'll wake up with a pounding headache."

I told him he wouldn't notice it over the artillery shelling. He relented and let me lead him toward our waiting bedrolls. It would be a short night.

We were up and approaching the Russian positions before the sun had risen, but the Russians knew our tactics. The world went from deadly quiet to exploding around us in a heartbeat. For some it was their last. Two of Zealot's friends fell in that opening push. The shock of full-out battle showed in his eyes, but he knew enough to stick close. We failed to gain Keustrin and the days melted together, a chaotic mix of thunder and death. Shelling. Tanks that shook the ground and buildings that crumbled. Hand-to-hand fighting. Bullets whizzing, shrapnel humming, hungry for flesh to slice. Smoke and burned powder and gasoline and always...the stench of death.

After that failed attempt to drive the Russians back, the Ninth held a front southeast of Berlin that stretched from Cottbus to Frankfurt and west. But the Russians were slowly encircling us. We drove them back here and there. But never enough. Our exhaustion began to tell. We were ordered to strike west, to stop the Russians going around us to reach Berlin. In the confusion, our unit got separated from the army.

We holed up in a barn on a convent grounds on the edge of a village. The walled compound gave us a false sense of security, enough to allow us to get some desperately needed sleep. The Russians were a safe distance behind us. We thought.

A familiar noise dragged me from sleep. The rumble of tanks. It was the middle of the night. I kicked Jäger, then Rothe. They roused the others. We squatted in the hayloft. Too tired to fight, we listened to the shouts outside the walls, the gunshots, the yells and cries of panicked village folk who were likely being rounded up from their beds or cellars. Zealot slumped against my arm and began to snore quietly. I moved away and he sank into the hay.

The sound of banging on the compound gate sent us to the hayloft door to peer down into the moonlit courtyard, hoping we hadn't been seen entering the barn. The hammering continued; nuns flowed out of the main building. One, carrying a lantern and holding herself like a queen, opened the gate to admit three Soviets. She had to have known a bit of Russian, for whatever she said stopped the men. The tallest one exchanged words with her while the others circled the compound, crossing each other's paths almost directly under us. The tall one waved his pistol under her nose. Jäger stiffened but, like me, only waited.

The men left. The nun who had faced them barred the gate and turned to her flock. We strained to catch her words. "Do not leave the compound, no matter what you hear. We will all go to the chapel to pray for our neighbours and thank God for sparing us the horrors of war."

I thought, for how long? How long until they tire of their sport in the village and return?

When the compound was empty, Jäger and I released our breaths. Jäger told the captain, "We might have an hour before it gets light. We go now or we won't be able to get out."

That thought was enough to banish any weariness. I clamped my hand over Zealot's mouth. He grunted surprise. I warned him to silence and he nodded under my hand. One by one, we dropped from the loft. Two skinny cows slept in their stalls. A few hens dozed, heads tucked under their wings, in boxes built into the third stall. Rothe grabbed one hen and wrung its neck before it could squawk. He handed it to Zealot and told him to guard our lunch. What would the nuns think when they found all the eggs missing, along with one hen? And all the eggshells in the loft? At the compound wall farthest from the village, the cries of terrified women followed us over the wall. When I hit the ground, I grabbed Jäger's arm. He was shaking.

"We're too few," I whispered.

Jäger's muscles corded under my touch. He said, "We're always too few. I hate this, Wolf. I don't know how much more I can take."

A few gunshots cracked. Terror spiralled out from the village to ensare us. When the last man was over the wall, I released Jäger. He led us through field and forest, past three Russian sentries. I was rearguard; the little fanatic, my shadow. The white chicken against Zealot's dark uniform must have alerted the third sentry after I thought we were safely by. A bullet whizzed past my helmet. I prodded Zealot into a run and shouted for the others to do likewise.

We eluded search parties into the afternoon, creeping through gullies, behind fences, under trees. In a narrow stretch of forest bordering a village, we ran into an ss unit under the pines. When Rothe explained the situation, they insisted on setting up a defence.

In the late afternoon, the Russians rumbled into town right into our crossfire. It was effective until they threw a company at us, three times our number. It became a house-to-house fight. We were running out of houses when the wall of the one I had just left exploded outwards, flinging me to the ground. The

Russians had withdrawn to let their tanks rout us out. It suddenly struck me that my shadow was missing. I scrambled for cover as another shell hit and debris rained down, then crawled to a pile of rubble with boots sticking out of it.

A chunk of wall, too big for me to move, had collapsed on Zealot's legs. He held the chicken against his stomach – I couldn't believe he still had it – and had a stricken look. The chicken's feathers were turning red from a gut wound he had suffered. He whispered, "Help."

There was nothing I could do. I pulled a potato masher from under my belt, and set it on the chicken. "Make the Führer proud. Blow up a few Russians when they find you."

Horror entered his eyes. I dashed away. His wail echoed through the street. The deep coughing of tanks drowned out his cry. Smoke and dust hid my flight out of the village. Jäger was waiting for me by the last house. He told me they were circling around, that the ss was set to slow them down, but our unit was retreating. He asked, "Where's Zealot?"

I whispered, "Dead or dying."

Jäger said, "Too bad." That was all the eulogy Zealot would get. Too bad. I agreed and raced across a yard. I vaulted a low fence and slipped into a forest, Jäger guarding my back.

The noose was tightening around Berlin: the Russian's goal, the place that would be our last stand. Too many Russians stood between us and the Ninth, so we headed in the direction of Berlin, our days a flurry of gun battles and desperate flights to safety. Only there was no real safety, just the mirage of something long gone.

We were a few kilometres east of Zethen Lake – almost home – when we happened upon a Russian advance unit. It surprised both groups. We all dove for cover and began exchanging fire. The noise drew more Russians. They came at us from the side and we were suddenly engaged in a fierce fight for our lives. One by one, members of the unit were picked off.

Jäger, Rothe and I had taken cover behind a stone wall. During a brief lull, we took stock and realized everyone else was dead. Rothe shot a Russian trying to sneak over the wall. The body tumbled to the ground on our side of the fence. The captain stated the obvious when he said we had to hold out until dark.

"An hour," Jäger said. "How's your ammunition?"

"Low," Rothe and I said in unison. Rothe sniffed, then added, "Make every shot count."

Jäger pointed behind us and said, "We'll have better cover in that house." It stood in the open, twenty metres away. We'd be able to see the Russians coming.

"Too risky to get there," Rothe replied.

We fell silent, spread out and continued to exchange sporadic gunfire with the enemy. They must have known we were waiting for dark, for they started to push forward. I was down to my last round. Jäger dropped his rifle and snuck along the wall to borrow the dead Russian's submachine gun. When he had it, Rothe motioned for us to run. The sun was down but it wasn't quite dark. It didn't matter – we were out of time.

We burst away from the wall, staying low, zigzagging. I couldn't hear the bullets, just my thundering heart. Dirt kicked up around me. Something scratched my arm. I dived through a window, spraying glass across an empty room.

Jäger yelled from another room. I poked my head into the hallway and pulled back as bullets sprayed through the open door. I charged, slammed the door shut, then dropped to the floor beside Rothe. I dragged the captain into the kitchen, painting a red path to where Jäger was using the Russian PPSh to pepper the field with bullets. He ducked, glanced at the captain and grimaced. Outside, the Russians stopped firing, probably to advance.

Jäger knelt on the other side of Rothe, whose eyes were open. His breathing was shallow. He was bleeding from several wounds. The door must have slowed him that half second too long. Jäger said, "Come on, Captain. Let's get you on your feet and out of here."

Rothe rasped, "Hit bad. Leave me."

My throat clenched. I said, "That wasn't our agreement, Rothe." Except for Jäger, I thought I was past caring who lived or died. Caring got you killed. I told him we'd get to the lake and find a boat. That our village was on the other shore and we could get him fixed up. I reminded him he had a wife waiting.

Rothe's bitter laugh turned to coughing. He replied, "No. I lived just west of the Oder. My town is in Russian hands. I failed her, Brandt." His face twisted in agony. He said, "I hope she's dead. I hope she made the Russians kill her instead of..." He clutched Jäger's hand and whispered, "Don't let them get your wife, Schreiber. Don't fail her like I failed Marien."

The captain sagged, his breath rattled, he stared over my shoulder. I looked, half expecting to see his wife's ghost. Despite everything, he had been a good man. He had kept his honour in brutal times and had helped us keep ours. I felt as if I had let him down.

Face contorted with anger and worry, Jäger took Rothe's pistol and its last clip. He handed me the Russian submachine gun. I fitted my *Mauser* in Rothe's limp grasp, in case he regained consciousness. We escaped out a back window as the Russians broke in through the front. A burst of gunfire chased us into the night. Growing darkness shrouded our movements, muffled our steps. As usual, Jäger led and I watched our backs. When we got to the lakeshore, we sheltered under some bushes for a brief rest. Around us, the forest was silent.

"I can't even remember his first name," I whispered. "Do you know what it was?" Jäger wanted to know what difference it made. I said, "I just want to remember his name."

Jäger thought it was Demetrius. He said, "I'm tired, Wolf. I can't do it any more. When I was home recovering from my injuries, Berlin was already being bombed. I didn't have the heart to go see it. I don't want to die defending a city that no longer exists." I asked him what he wanted to do and he said, "I want to go home. I want to try to keep Hedda safe. But how? The Russians will just kill me and take her anyway."

As I stared at the water, wishing for a moonless night, the moon's glimmering reflection faded to nothing. Clouds. I told him to take her away, as he'd wanted to when they first married. He said, "Where?" I replied, "Wherever the Russians aren't. Head west until you meet the British or Americans. They have to be better than who's chasing us."

"What about you?" he asked. I didn't answer. He said, "Don't make me choose, Wolf. If I go, you go."

I replied, "Has it ever been any other way?"

Chapter Twenty-Three

For two nights the Russians chased Kurt through his dreams. Or maybe it was Germans. Kurt didn't know, didn't care. All he knew was the terror of being chased. All he knew was his drumming heart, his screaming muscles, his rasping breath.

On Sunday, he really ran. Yesterday, Marta had been busy helping her parents. This morning there had been no answer at the Fischer house. Was she avoiding him? As he ran, Kurt puzzled over that and tried to let the run pound away his worry, but still his mind whirled. His steps became laboured.

Halfway around the lake he slowed to a walk. He caught glimpses of the lake between pine trees. The sailboats that had dotted the water earlier were scattering for shore as the wind began to rise. That seemed odd. To the west, Kurt saw a fork of lightning and understood. He peered at older houses, wondering if one of them had been the house in which Captain Rothe had died. Had these trees concealed Wolf and Jäger's retreat to the lake?

Kurt stopped at a little park that hugged the shore. Had this been the spot where two young soldiers had decided to resign from the war? A lot of soldiers had been hanged for deserting. The wind made Kurt squint; it whipped the water, frosting the waves with whitecaps.

Across from him lay Zethen. Herr Brandt had told Kurt that the bench where they had sat faced the spot where he and Jäger had come ashore that April night in 1945. Questions had boiled through Kurt's mind like the water on the lake was doing now. Herr Brandt had been reluctant to continue. Their war had ended that night, so the story was finished, he had said.

But it wasn't! Kurt wanted to cry. If Wolf had gone with Jäger, why was he still here, an old man in Zethen?

Kurt stood. The storm would be here soon. He needed to keep moving. He eased into a jog and kept to his usual route, circling the lake in a clockwise direction.

Few vehicles passed him. Around here, Sunday was better named "Outing Day" – the day everyone went somewhere, it seemed. Herr and Frau Klassen had gone to Potsdam to tour the palace with his cousins. If they were getting this wind, they were likely in a restaurant, enjoying *Kaffee und Kuchen* (coffee and cake). Kurt's stomach growled. Midafternoon and he hadn't eaten since breakfast. He sipped from the water pack on his back and kept going.

He rounded the south end of the lake and slowed to a walk. His heart wasn't in the run. He followed an empty path that skirted the lake between towns. Nothing but trees, and fields that were spring green with the promise of new crops. Around a curve he stopped.

Marta strode toward him, arms swinging as they always did when she had a purpose. The narrow band of trees offered little shelter from the wind; it tugged at her braid, freeing dark strands and whipping them across her face. She was flushed, as if she had been walking hard.

She was beautiful.

Kurt couldn't move. Marta drew near; her brown eyes sparked. She halted mere centimetres away. Kurt could feel the heat radiating from her body. She framed Kurt's face and pulled it to hers. She kissed him, then stepped back. Kurt still hadn't moved. He stared at her, blinking, shocked, unsure what to do or say.

Marta's lips thinned, then she said, "Tell me you never want to do that again." Her brows arched. Kurt swallowed around a lump of pain. Marta circled him. "Tell me you never want to laugh with me again, or roll your eyes when I try to tease you or share our dreams. Tell me that our friendship is over. Was it ever real to you? Was I ever more than a convenience?"

Kurt groaned. "Don't, Marta."

She halted, facing him again. "Don't what, Kurt? Don't feel hurt because you treated me like, like Peter Neumeyer treats people?"

"I'm nothing like Peter Neumeyer."

"Aren't you?" Dark brows rose again. Marta swiped at a strand of hair in her eyes. "You never gave me the choice, Kurt Schreiber. You decided what you thought was best for me, then dictated your decision to me. Isn't that what bullies do?"

Kurt tried to shove his hands in pockets that weren't there. His fists slid over the smooth material of his shorts and brushed thighs beginning to cool off in the chilly breeze. He shivered. "I was trying to protect you. It worked. Peter has left you alone."

"I can decide for myself what risks I want to take. You told Peter I wasn't a book to be passed from one person to another, but you −" Her lips pressed together for another instant. "You put me on a shelf and forgot about me without a second glance."

Kurt flinched. "I didn't forget. These last two weeks have been the loneliest since...since you decided to adopt this stray."

"I hate it when you call yourself that. Strays are lost and helpless. Is that what you are?"

"Without you I am." Kurt clamped his mouth shut, realizing how corny that had sounded.

Doubt shadowed Marta's eyes. "And what old movie is that from?"

"No movie." Kurt drank in her nearness, as if it was water quenching his thirst.

Marta laid her hand on his chest. "Let me decide who I want to be with, Kurt. Isn't that what your Rick from *Casablanca* would let his Ilsa do?"

"Actually,...Rick chose for her." Kurt squinted one eye, almost hating to say the rest. "He stayed behind when he forced her to leave Casablanca − to keep her safe."

Marta scowled and struck him on the chest. Kurt trapped her hand and held it there. "You're a lot stronger than Ilsa was, Marta. And I'm not strong enough to say 'go away' again, if you want to stay." He tucked a strand of hair behind her ear. "You're my best friend."

"Good." Marta lifted her chin. "Just best friend?"

Kurt smiled. "Well, I have to admit, I've never wanted to kiss any other friend, no matter how close. So what does that make you? My best...girl...friend?"

"I'd better be your only girlfriend."

They kissed. Kurt held her close.

Marta's muffled voice rose from his chest. "You're the first stray I've ever wanted to keep, Kurt. How am I supposed to let you go?"

He sighed into her apple-spiced hair. "My mom used to have a poster that said something like, if you let something go and it comes back, it's yours."

"And if it doesn't?"

"Maybe it will."

Marta stepped back and took Kurt's hand. They started down the path toward Zethen. A few minutes later, Marta broke the silence. "You've been talking to my grandfather again. I think the two of you are conspiring to make sure I don't hear about the war."

"That's right. That's how we like it."

She elbowed him. "Why?"

Kurt shrugged. "We're protecting you, I guess. It's what most men do, you know, for the women in their lives."

"Oh, that is such a sexist comment."

"Or maybe it's our way of showing we care." Kurt paused. "Your grandfather has seen and done things that you don't want to know about." Or dream about. "Just know it was awful."

"Tell me what he told you, Kurt."

He sighed, walked in silence for a moment, then began to tell her about those last desperate years on the eastern front. He kept it short, and as clean as possible – like an old black-and-white movie that bore almost no resemblance to the blood-red truth.

When he was finished, silence nestled between them. The wind huffed through the trees. Dark clouds gathered overhead. They were still over a kilometre from Zethen's southernmost houses. He really didn't want to get rained on, but Marta wasn't a runner, even if she could hike him into the ground. He began to walk faster.

A long arm whipped from behind a bush and grabbed Kurt's T-shirt, making him yell in surprise. Peter Neumeyer stepped onto the path. Had Neumeyer been following Marta? Kurt nudged her away, never taking his gaze off Peter's intense blue eyes. Something dangerous lurked there. As he readied for the blow, Kurt worked the lump in his throat. He couldn't even get his hands to raise to defend himself. A coward to the end. He tried to step back.

Peter hauled him close. "You have to help, Schreiber."

Kurt blinked. Help?

Peter's free hand pointed east. "Stephan. You have to help."

That wasn't anger in Neumeyer's eyes. It was fear. "What about Stephan?"

"His boat." Kurt could see the struggle it was for Peter to speak. "Turned over."

Marta and Kurt shared a concerned look. Peter clutched Kurt's arm, squeezing hard as he half led, half dragged Kurt toward the lakeshore. Kurt tried to loosen the iron grip, but it only sank deeper into his flesh. They halted at the water.

Kurt scanned the lake. "I don't see anything."

Peter released him and pointed a little to the left, to the dark green hull of what was probably a canoe, barely visible against the grey waves, half a kilometre distant and drifting away. Kurt thought he saw a head, but wasn't sure. The rest of the lake was deserted.

Kurt indicated the canoe on the shore beside Peter. "Why didn't you get him?"

The fear was naked now. "I don't swim." Kurt looked away from the pain in Peter's eyes. "I've seen you, Schreiber. You're a good swimmer. You have to help." Peter's voice dropped. "Stephan can't swim either. If anything happens to him —" His voice shattered. "He'll kill me..."

He. Kurt knew Peter meant his father. He clenched and unclenched his jaw.

The grip was back, tightening like a vise. "Please, Schreiber. We're not supposed to be here. Stephan is my responsibility. I know you hate me, but you can't let him die."

Kurt wrenched free, furious at the implication. Furious that Peter would be so stupid. Furious that he couldn't walk away. "Give me the life jacket." He stripped off his water pack.

Peter turned ashen. "No jacket. We...borrowed the boats. We didn't think..."

Borrowed. Stole. Kurt pushed past Peter. He grabbed the side of the canoe to shove it into the lake. Marta appeared on the other side of the boat. He scowled at her; she scowled back.

"This is dangerous, Marta."

"More dangerous if you're by yourself, Kurt."

He hated that she was right. They exchanged a long look, then waded into the water. While he steadied the canoe for Marta to get in, Kurt told Peter to go for help. Despite his hulking size, Peter looked like a boy — a scared, helpless boy. Kurt yelled, "Go!" He pushed the canoe into waist-deep water before he flung himself over the side. He settled in the stern.

Marta handed him a paddle. "At least there are two oars."

Kurt frowned. "Have you ever paddled a canoe?" The waves chopped at the boat, threatening to tip it. She shook her head. Kurt said, "Paddle on the right, away from the waves. I'll try to steer."

With the waves almost directly behind them, sweeping them away from shore, they made good headway. As they neared the overturned canoe, Kurt saw Stephan's head and arms. He clung to the hull, but he was sinking with each wave that crashed over him. Kurt paddled harder. Marta yelled for Stephan to hang on. Waves battered both canoes. Kurt struggled to keep his course. Behind him, lightning flashed.

And then Stephan disappeared. Kurt's heart lurched. He knelt in five centimetres of cold water pooling in the canoe and hauled the paddle through the water with all his might. With each stroke, he whispered, "Hang on, Stephan. Be okay."

They arrived at the capsized canoe. Marta pointed beyond it, where Stephan thrashed and tried to yell, water filling his mouth. His head disappeared, reappeared a metre away. Kurt and Marta paddled furiously. They reached Stephan but the waves carried him beyond arm's length. Kurt extended his paddle. "Grab it, Stephan!"

Terror filled Stephan's face as a wave hit him. Kurt leaned forward to lengthen his reach and yelled again. Arms flailed. One of Stephan's hands knocked the paddle, grabbed its edge.

A sharp yank unbalanced Kurt. He somersaulted into the water. He managed to hang onto the paddle and quickly resurfaced. Waves slapped at him. Thunder rumbled overhead. From the other end of the paddle, Stephan's eyes bulged with growing fear.

He'll drown us both, if I'm not careful. Kurt treaded water. The canoe hadn't capsized when he had fallen in. He struggled to side stroke toward the boat, one hand gripping the paddle. The canoe sheltered him from the waves.

It bumped Kurt's head. He grabbed its edge, urged Stephan to do the same. His yelling finally sank in and the boy lunged for the boat, almost tipping it. He disappeared. Dread gripped Kurt. He spotted Stephan floating face down, less than a metre from the canoe. A wave pushed the boat toward the boy.

"Pull him in, Marta!" Water filled Kurt's mouth and he sputtered.

Marta nodded and reached for the now limp body. Kurt scuttled, hand over hand, around the stern of the boat to hang onto the other side and counterbalance the canoe. While Kurt draped his arms over the edge of the rocking boat, Marta grabbed Stephan's collar and hauled.

Kurt worked his way down the side of the canoe. His legs were ice. "Give me one of his hands." Marta flipped a lifeless arm into the boat and Kurt reached across to latch onto the wrist. Marta got hold of the waistband of Stephan's jeans. They both pulled. Stephan flopped into the boat. Kurt lost his grip, sank under the water, bobbed up and grabbed the edge. He peered at Stephen's pale face, water dribbling from the side of a slack mouth.

Gripping the canoe, Kurt eased himself down, almost under the water, then kicked hard and pulled himself up. The canoe rocked as he fell across its width. He paused for a second, the gunnel cutting into his stomach. He swung one leg into the boat, then the next. A crack of thunder accompanied his landing in the boat.

Kurt straightened out. Marta handed him her paddle. He glanced around for his, then realized he had let it go instead of tossing it into the canoe. The waves hit the canoe broadside. Marta held onto the sides, her gaze anxious. Lightning forked.

One paddle. And Stephan still hadn't moved. Kurt worked to get the canoe turned so the waves were behind them. He shouted, "Is he alive?" He had to be alive.

"I think so. I don't know."

"Find out!" Kurt leaned into each stroke, paddling with an urgency that twisted his gut more tightly than Peter had gripped his arm. The waves were carrying them northeast. With only one paddle he was pretty certain they would be dumped if he tried to turn back to Zethen's shore. Following the wind meant well over half a kilometre of water lay between them and safety.

Marta knelt beside Stephan's head and bent over him. Kurt was relieved this canoe's bottom was wider than some. Marta looked up, stricken. "I don't think he's breathing."

Kurt could almost feel her growing panic. That wasn't like her. He yelled, "Then do something! You took that first aid course last winter, right? Through work?"

She nodded. Her eyes cleared. The canoe rocked as Marta positioned herself. Kurt saw welcome briskness in her movements. He focused on paddling and silently ordered Stephan to live. To breathe. The wind pushed at Kurt's back. The waves hit the stern, dulled by the point of the canoe's hull. The shore crawled toward them. Kurt glanced behind him, across the choppy water. If Peter had gone for help, he wouldn't know where to send it.

Marta remained hunched over Stephan, intent on the mouth-to-mouth rhythm of forcing air into Stephan's lungs and watching his expanded chest fall. Kurt stared ahead, glad to have a reason not to watch her lips covering someone else's, no matter the reason.

The lake seemed eager now to be rid of them, almost as eager as Kurt was to get off the water, with thunder rolling through the clouds. He angled away from a dock toward a grassy verge. The waves pushed them the last few metres. Marta shouted as the jolt threw her against the side of the canoe. Kurt jumped out and splashed out of the water. With Marta and Stephan still in it, he dragged the canoe onto shore, then hauled Stephan onto the grass.

Kurt lost his grip; Stephan dropped to the ground. A breath shuddered into Stephan's lungs with a high-pitched wail. His limbs spasmed and he started vomiting water. Kurt helped Marta from the canoe and hugged her. It started to rain. He whispered, "You saved him."

"No, Kurt," Marta replied. "We saved him." She stepped back. "You'd better run for help." She knelt beside Stephan and rubbed his back as he retched. "He still needs to go to a hospital. If he goes into shock..."

Kurt didn't wait to find out what would happen if shock set in. He had seen enough medical shows to know it was a word that meant trouble. He dashed toward the nearest house, a half block away, and rang the bell set into the gatepost. He held it down and stared at the house. No curtain fluttered. No one came to the door. He tried the next house. Nothing. He kicked the gate of the third house. Wasn't anyone home in this stupid town?

No sign of life on the street. Across the way, pine trees bent away from the wind. No houses for another two blocks on that side of the street. He rushed to the next gate. No answer again. Frustrated, he clambered over the gate and darted up the sidewalk. He pounded on the door, rattled the knob. He snatched a broom leaning against the door frame, walked to the front of the house and eyed the nearest window. Blood roared through his ears. Rain dripped down his neck. Kurt raised the broom. He'd pay for the window. He needed a phone.

"Police! Don't move! Lower the stick and turn around."

Kurt dropped the broom and spun. The policeman standing at the gate straightened. The officer who had given him a ride. Kurt smiled. "Am I glad to see you, Officer."

"That's not the usual reaction I get from housebreakers."

Kurt jogged to the gate. "No! I needed a phone. No one is home." He pointed to the left. "Stephan needs an ambulance. He almost drowned." Kurt scrambled over the gate. He frowned at the disbelief in the officer's face. "Please. It's an emergency." Kurt took a step.

The policeman grabbed his arm and hauled him around. His gaze drilled into Kurt, who held his breath and tried not to blink. The officer nodded and headed for his cruiser. He swung into the driver's seat; Kurt slid into the passenger's side while the officer radioed for help. Then he turned on lights and siren. Tires squealed as the car swung a tight circle.

Kurt pointed the way. The car bounced over the curb and cut across the grass to where Marta still knelt by Stephan, who was curled up in a ball.

Marta looked up when the car skidded to a stop. Kurt popped out. She said, "He's freezing." She rubbed Stephan's arm. Kurt joined her and rubbed the clammy denim covering Stephan's thigh.

"Get those jeans off him," the officer said. He pulled a silver blanket from the trunk of his cruiser. Kurt undid the zipper, then tried to peel the wet jeans off Stephan's clenched, shaking legs. The officer had to help him. By the time they were done, a siren sounded in the distance.

The policeman wrapped Stephan in the shiny material, tucking it tight. The flashing red of the cruiser's lights reflected off the blanket. Kurt sank back on his heels, the energy spewing out of him the way water had spurted from Stephan's mouth. He shuddered as the sideways drizzle pelted him with cold spray.

"Thank you, sir," Kurt whispered as he searched for a name tag. He wanted to know this man's name. Marta leaned against him and took his hand.

As if reading his mind, the policeman replied, "I prefer Officer Mielert over sir. Or even just Jurgen. You and your friend are the ones requiring thanks, Kurt Schreiber. You probably saved this young man's life."

Had he ever told the officer his name? "How do you know...?"

"Your name? I chatted with Herr Brandt the last time we met a few days ago. Though, at the time, I recall him being irritated with you. I hope you have settled your differences."

Kurt shared a smile with Marta. "Yes, we have."

The ambulance jumped the curb and raced across the grass, veering around a bench and a tree. The back doors burst open, a paramedic spilled out, hauling a gurney. In seconds it seemed, Stephan was strapped onto the mattress while a paramedic fired questions at Kurt, who briefly explained what had happened. As quickly as they had come, the paramedics whisked Stephan into the gleaming interior of the ambulance and the vehicle pulled away.

Kurt struggled to his feet. His legs shook. Lightning arced over the lake and thunder cracked.

Officer Mielert said, "You are soaked, too. I didn't realize you also ended up in the lake. I'll take you to see a doctor."

"I'm fine. I just need to rest."

"Don't argue with me. Get in the back. You too, young lady. Keep him warm."

Kurt didn't resist as Marta pulled him toward the cruiser. They climbed into the back seat. The officer slammed their door. As he drove away he said, "I always seem to run into you when I'm off duty. You're lucky I live near here. If I hadn't driven by and stopped you, you would have been charged with break and enter, no matter how noble the cause."

"Thanks," Kurt said, and he meant it. A charge like that and he would have been booted out of the country so hard he wouldn't need an airplane to fly back to Canada. He slumped against Marta and enjoyed the protective way she wrapped her arm around him. But not the way she poked him every few minutes to keep him awake.

After Marta called him, Herr Brandt got his neighbour to drive him to the hospital; they picked up Peter Neumeyer on the way. The Klassens still weren't home and Marta's parents were also gone for the day.

The doctor was satisfied with Kurt's condition and told him to go home. Peter waylaid him outside Stephan's room. Steel fingers dug into Kurt's upper arm again. Kurt scowled and Peter released him. Kurt rubbed his arm, already bruised from Peter's earlier manhandling.

"Stephan's going to be okay," Peter said. "They're moving him from emergency, but want to watch him overnight."

"Good." Kurt moved to step around, but Peter blocked the way.

"I owe you, Schreiber."

Kurt narrowed his eyes. The blue pair staring back at him looked sincere. "Maybe. But not for this. What you owe me is an explanation. Why did you call my grandfather a coward?"

Belligerence crept back into Peter's expression.

Kurt squinted one eye. "Tell me...and no one will hear that you were too afraid to rescue your own brother."

A flash of anger appeared in Peter's eyes, like a trout in a lake – and disappeared just as quickly. "You really don't know?" Kurt waited. After a moment, Peter said, "My great-grandmother, Oma Graumann, was here...during the war. She's still alive. At her birthday in March, Mom mentioned to her that you were visiting from Canada." He snorted. "I've never heard her swear like she did at the name Kurt Schreiber. He deserted. Took his bride and fled, while the rest of the town had to face the Russians."

Kurt waited, but the way Peter clamped his mouth closed suggested he was finished. That was it? That was the reason Peter's family had labeled his grandfather a coward? "You have no idea what he went through during the war, do you?"

"What does it matter?"

"That's a good question. Maybe you should ask yourself that very thing." Kurt sidled left and stepped forward so his shoulder was almost touching Peter's. "We're even, Neumeyer. Let's keep it that way. Leave me and my friends alone."

As Kurt walked away, Peter said, "I was wrong, Schreiber. You aren't a coward."

Kurt realized he no longer cared what Peter Neumeyer thought. He waved away the comment as he strode toward Marta and Herr Brandt, waiting by the exit. Marta gave him a smile. He returned it.

At his house, Herr Brandt plied the young people with hot tea and reheated soup while he dragged the whole story from them. He nodded throughout the telling. He patted Kurt's shoulder on the way to getting him more soup. "Yes, yes. So the younger Neumeyer will be fine, and you have passed your *Mutprobe*. Good. Very good."

Mutprobe? Kurt scowled. Oh, yes. Test of courage, like Wolf and Jäger had passed in the Hitler Youth. "It didn't feel like a test. Or courage. It was...what needed to be done."

Herr Brandt set Kurt's refilled bowl in front of him. "Yes, of course. That is the way with courage. It rises to the surface when it is needed, not before."

Kurt's spoon paused by his lips. His grandfather had said almost the same thing. He set the spoon down. "Why would Grandfather taking Oma and fleeing the Russians have bothered Peter's great-grandmother so much that over sixty years later it could still make her swear?"

"Without knowing who she is, I could not tell you. Did young Neumeyer give her name?" Herr Brandt sat down and sipped his tea.

Kurt thought for a few seconds. "He did say a name. Oma...Gaumann? No ..."

"Graumann?"

"Yes. That's it. Oma Graumann."

Herr Brandt set down his cup. "That explains a great deal."

Kurt sat back. "Well of course it does." He rolled his eyes.

Herr Brandt shot him an impatient glance. "But it does, Kurt. Their tale is remembered well by those of us who have always lived here. Peter's Oma, Liesl Graumann, hid and watched as several Russian soldiers raped her older sister. The sister was never right in the head after that. Later, the soldiers caught the younger girl and had their way with her, too. Both sisters ended up pregnant. The older one miscarried. The young girl raised her baby daughter alone and cared for her sister until the poor woman committed suicide. That daughter also had a child out of wedlock. Peter's mother, apparently. Frau Graumann is in the same facility as my wife. She still rages against the world, cursing the Russians who ruined her life and the Germans who didn't save her and her sister."

"What does that have to do with Grandfather?"

"Most knew Jäger had taken Hedda and fled west, though no one ever mentioned it to the Russians that I know of. She was one of the few who despised him for that, called him a coward and a traitor. Most wished they had done likewise."

"Why didn't you go with him?"

Herr Brandt sighed and stared into his tea. After a moment, he said, "I was going to until the very moment I walked into my house to change my uniform for civilian clothes."

Over his bowed head, Kurt and Marta exchanged glances. Pain darkened her brown eyes. Kurt asked, "What changed your mind?"

Herr Brandt spoke without looking up. "I walked into a shattered home. My mother was sick, pining for a man who had not loved her. She wept and told me how Father had mortgaged his successful factories to buy one in Warsaw, how his slave labour had evaporated when the Jewish ghetto was wiped out, how that and the bombing of his Berlin factories had driven him to despair and suicide. His secretary had found him in his Berlin apartment. Mother kept on about how it would all be fine now that I was home, and was the war finally over? I might have been able to walk away from even that if my sister hadn't been awakened by the noise and entered my bedroom. Eight months pregnant and her husband dead under a pile of Berlin rubble. I was all they had left. Their only protection."

Kurt heard the remembered agony in those words. He stared into his own mug of weak tea. "So you stayed to protect your family, and Jäger fled to protect his."

"I might as well have fled, for all the good I did."

The bitter comment drew Kurt's gaze. "What happened?"

"The Russians came. They were impressed with my criticism of Hitler and they chose to believe my story of having fought on the western front before deserting. But still they sent me to a prison camp." Herr Brandt's smile didn't clear the shadows in his grey eyes. "I was one of the lucky ones, released after only eighteen months. They wanted me to be their puppet running Zethen. I wasn't stupid enough to refuse. My mother had died of her broken heart, helped by pneumonia and the harsh winter of 1945–46. I had managed to settle her and my sister in this house before I was arrested, so at least they had shelter, but it hadn't been enough."

"You still had your sister to care for."

"Not for long. When she realized I was cooperating with the Russians, she pointed out that made me a traitor, and she searched for an escape from my vile presence. She married the first man who would have her. An engineer. He took her and her child to his home north of Berlin and we haven't spoken since. Zethen was all I had after that." Herr Brandt laid his hand over Marta's. "Until I met your grandmother."

"Frau Klassen said you often stood between the town and the Russians, saved them pain."

"Perhaps. But it was never enough." The telephone rang. Herr Brandt said, "Answer it, Marta. It will be your parents." When she left the room, he leaned toward Kurt, his voice low. "I learned nothing with Bertha. By the time I married my wife, I had regained my reputation as a Casanova. But it wasn't a reputation worth having, young Schreiber. Winning a woman into your bed does not win her into your heart." He pinned Kurt with a narrow gaze.

Kurt threw up his hands. "I won't do that, I...*respect* Marta." It was the right word. Herr Brandt nodded, his features relaxed. Kurt said, "What was the promise you didn't keep?"

The old man frowned. "That last night, I had arranged to meet Jäger in the cemetery. I got there ahead of him and Hedda, and watched from hiding as he laid his winter battle medal on his parents' tombstone – it was the first and last time he ever saw the grave. When I stepped into the open, still in uniform, he knew I was staying. The look on his face almost crushed my resolve, but even he could not fault my reasons. Before he left he gave me something of great value, which I promised to return as soon as my family was safe and I could rejoin him."

Kurt straightened. "His Iron Cross."

Herr Brandt nodded. Kurt released a breath that turned to a yawn.

From the doorway, Marta said, "You're going to fall off your chair soon, Kurt. Maybe you should stay here tonight."

"That was your mom?" Kurt asked.

"My dad. He's on his way over."

"Then I can get a ride to the Klassens'."

"They aren't home yet, Kurt," Herr Brandt said. "I would feel better if you stayed tonight. We can leave a message on their answering machine."

Kurt snorted. "I'm not going to slip into shock after all this time."

"Humour an old man."

Kurt couldn't find the energy to argue. He shrugged and let himself be herded upstairs. When he said he wanted to sleep in his grandfather's trundle bed instead of the guest room, Herr Brandt gave him a strange look. Kurt said, "Humour a young man."

T he dream returns with an explosion, slamming him to the cobblestones. Kurt scrambles to his feet, swinging his *Mauser* around, trying to spot the enemy. Dust clings to his grey uniform and he brushes at it. The street is empty. It's the street from the movie, but there is no sign of the little girl with the red coat, no sign of anyone or anything, not even signs of damage from the explosion. The apartment buildings lean toward him with empty eyes.

He realizes someone is watching him. Hunting him. He charges down the street, heart hammering, looking for an escape. Every door of every apartment building is boarded up. Who is chasing him? Russians? Germans? He doesn't know. He only knows he has to run, feet pounding over cobblestones.

The street dissolves into a Russian village. Kurt dashes toward the storehouse at the end of the road. Stones change into red-streaked mud that sucks at his boots. He struggles to reach the barn, slowing with each step. His mind screams, *Not the barn!* He continues forward.

Trees sprout from the ground in front of the barn. The peasant houses fade, becoming smoke on the rising wind. A pine forest clusters on the Russian steppe. The smell tantalizes his senses. Safety. If only he can reach it. Is that a lake glimmering through the trees?

Kurt reaches the first tree. A dark figure steps from behind the next tree and blocks his way, rifle raised. He stumbles to a stop and stares at the *Mauser* that will end his life. Behind it is a grey Nazi uniform. He squints at the face hidden by the helmet's shadow. The Nazi tips the helmet back. He gapes at the familiar face. His own face, topped by dark hair. His grandfather is going to kill him.

Kurt drops his *Mauser* and waits. Maybe there won't be any pain with the rifle so close.

The Nazi helmet falls to the ground. The *Mauser* joins his on the needle-covered earth. A hand stretches toward him. A quiet voice says, "Hello, Kurt. It's good to meet you finally. Wolf tells me you like to run. So do I."

He blinks. "Grandfather?"

"Call me Jäger."

Fear spirals away. He takes the hand, smiles at its warm, hard grip.

Jäger says, "Let's go for a run. Together."

Kurt looks around. They are in the park at the end of Friedenstrasse, by the bench where he first talked to an old man who thought he had seen a ghost.

Jäger points at the shore. "That's where we landed the boat the night we deserted."

"Wolf told me. He likes telling stories, once you get him started."

"Long and gruesome ones." A frown creases Jäger's brow. "It's over now."

"Yes, it is." A grin breaks across Jäger's face, making him look sixteen and free of worries. "Are you going to talk all night, or are we going to run?"

Kurt returns the grin. "We're going to run."

Epilogue

Kurt hauled Wolf Brandt's suitcase off the carousel, anticipating the surprise they were about to spring on Jäger. Kurt recalled his father's reluctant agreement when he had pleaded, "Make sure Grandfather is at the airport, Dad. I really, really want him there."

"Do you think seeing me will give him a heart attack?" Wolf asked in a loud whisper. Several heads swivelled at the sound of German, then turned away, uninterested.

"No," Kurt replied. "Dad has never said anything about Grandfather having heart trouble. He's just...tired of living without Oma, I think." He retrieved a cloth-wrapped object from an ouside pocket on a suitcase and handed it to Wolf.

They headed toward the exit, Wolf's slow pace a good one for Kurt pulling two suitcases. A crowd clustered in the lobby. Here and there people hugged or shook hands. Kurt noticed a blond head bobbing up and down. His sister, Emily. The little thief who had stolen his room mere days after he had left for Germany. Let her keep it.

Then he saw the wheelchair in front of his jumping sister, and the old man slumped in its seat. Kurt pointed him out to Wolf. The already straight spine straightened more as Wolf stuck his chin out and walked toward his friend, cane swinging, marking each step with a tap on the tiles. Kurt stayed a step behind, still amazed they had talked the Lufthansa personnel into letting an old man keep his much-needed cane with him in the cabin of the airplane. Much needed. That was a laugh. The wolf's head on the handle seemed to peek at Kurt with a sly grin.

Wolf halted. Kurt saw what had stopped him. The old man in the wheelchair had lifted his head, searching for a grandson. Instead he had spotted a friend who had been closer than a brother. Even from three metres away, Kurt could see Jäger's green eyes glittering. He pushed up from the chair, swayed slightly, waved away his son's help.

Weakness fell away with each step he took toward Wolf. He straightened; his steps became steadier, his shoulders drew back. Wolf moved forward to meet him. Kurt stood rooted to the spot. He watched Wolf reach into the pocket of his trench coat and press something into Jäger's hand. His eyes stung as he overheard words the rest of his family couldn't understand.

"Your Iron Cross, my friend. Forgive me for taking so long to return it. The Russians stayed a little longer than I thought they would."

Jäger laughed. "It is here. You are here. That is all that matters. You are *here* – after all this time. I hated myself for many years, leaving you as I did."

"We each did what we had to do."

The men embraced. Hard, like soldiers. Long, like best friends finally reunited. Kurt grinned, but didn't move toward his parents, unwilling to break the spell encasing them all.

They broke apart. Jäger pointed at Kurt, tears threatening

to spill down his weathered cheeks. "You did this! I would be angry with you if I weren't so happy."

Kurt nodded, smiled, and spoke in German. "You should use English, Opa. Your son is looking very irritated at not understanding what's going on."

Still in German, Jäger said, "Oh, you *are* a mouthy one. Just like Wolf." He winked. In English he announced, "Wolf Brandt, I would like to introduce you to my family. My meddlesome grandson you already know."

Wolf gave Kurt a smile. His English was thickly accented, but easily understood. "Very well do I know him. Almost as well as my granddaughter does."

Kurt flushed and gave Wolf a warning look. Kurt's mother, who had been circling the old men to get to Kurt, faltered, then continued forward and gave him a hug. He stepped back and smiled at her. "Hi, Mom. Dad." He accepted a hug from his father and tousled Emily's hair. She had grown. She gave him a dirty look and tried to smooth her hair back into place. Kurt squeezed his mother back when she gave him a second, longer hug.

Behind them, Jäger said, "Just how well does he know your granddaughter, Wolf?"

"It is nothing to worry about. He takes after you in that regard, not me."

"I should hope not." Jäger paused. "Are they like Hedda and me?"

At that, everyone stepped back from Kurt and eyed him curiously. It was family legend that Hedda had been the love of Jäger's youth, of his whole life. The heat burning Kurt's cheeks felt like it was going to peel skin.

Wolf chuckled. "On that one, my friend, we will have to wait and see."

Kurt's mother peered over his shoulder, searching the scattering crowd. "This granddaughter, she's still in Germany isn't she?"

"Yes, Mom," Kurt replied through clenched teeth.

"Well," his father said as he clapped his hand on Kurt's shoulder. "Then the little romance is over, isn't it? Just as well. Long-distance romances are hopeless."

Wolf's piercing gaze drew Kurt's. They exchanged a long look.

Jäger stepped up to Kurt. "What are the two of you planning, Kurt? I can see it in your eyes. And that wolf has a satisfied look about him, as if he's feasting on a secret."

"Later, Opa. This isn't the place," Kurt said in German.

His grandfather's eyes sparked with pleasure at being called by the familiar term – Kurt hadn't used it since Oma had gotten sick – instead of the formal *"Grossvater."* He replied in English. "This is a fine place. Out with it, young man."

With five pairs of eyes fixed on him, Kurt cleared his throat, uncomfortable with the expectant silence. He bit his tongue. The eyes bored into his composure, willing him to speak. He would never have survived wartime interrogations. But then, who knows? True courage only rises when there is real need.

Sometimes running was the smart thing to do – he had learned that the hard way. But his grandfather had taught him that it was always better to tell the truth.

Kurt cleared his throat again. "I've decided to apply to Humboldt University for next fall. I'll do my Math and Chem this fall like I had planned, working part-time. Then, come January, I'll work full-time to save enough money to go."

Jäger scowled. Wolf nodded his approval.

Kurt's parents looked at him curiously. His mother asked, "Where is that? Toronto?"

"It's in Berlin, Mom."

"You can't go to university in Berlin," both parents chorused.

"Can I keep your room?" Emily asked.

"Sure, Shrimp." Kurt faced his parents. "They take foreign exchange students at Humboldt, especially ones taking German studies."

"What will that get you?" his father said.

"Where will you stay?" his mother said.

Kurt stifled a groan. He knew they would react like this. He had hoped to have a little time to soften them up first. "It could get me a job at a university or college, or in an embassy or any number of things, Dad. It's what I want to do."

"He will stay with me when the time comes," Wolf said. "His living costs will be small."

"It sounds like the two of you have it all planned," Jäger said.

"We do," Kurt said. "Please don't get mad, Mom, Dad. I've made up my mind. I'll be eighteen in a few months so it's not as if you can stop me. I just...hope you'll support me. Maybe even be happy for me. I love it over there, Mom. It feels like...home."

Kurt cringed when he saw the tears welling up in his mother's eyes. He always seemed to say one thing too many. His father gave him a look that said they would talk later.

Wolf said, "The Schreiber house will welcome having a Schreiber walking its floors once more, if only for a few years. And so it should."

Kurt grinned. "Your bed is still there, Opa. Just think how happy the house would be having *you* to welcome back...if you decided to visit."

Wolf pointed. "You see that, Jäger? He grins like you, runs like you, brims with courage like you. How can I refuse him anything? Not even my granddaughter, if it comes to that."

Jäger scrutinized Kurt, red face and all. He nodded and turned to his friend. They started toward the exit together, past the abandoned wheelchair. In German, Jäger said, "Your grand-daughter and my grandson. That has possibilities."

"Yes, yes. More than that, my friend," Wolf replied in the same language. "It is fitting that lifelong friends should produce a lifelong love, do you not agree?"

Kurt stared after the two men. *What have I done? They're planning my life for me.* Marta came to mind. He missed her already. He wasn't ready to let those two old soldiers set a date, but he was eager to find out if his future included his best friend. He studied their backs, reminded of the end of the movie, *Casablanca*, when Rick says to the French policeman, "Louie, I think this is the beginning of a beautiful friendship."

He thought of Marta's dancing brown eyes and whispered, "I hope so."

ACKNOWLEDGEMENTS

Special thanks go to my husband, Michael, and my children, Nathan, Jason and Kristen, for being willing to fend for themselves when it was apparent that I was lost in the story and didn't want to be found.

And to my friends in Germany – Sabine Sattel, Kathrin Tordasi and especially Ellen Birkhahn – who answered an endless stream of questions, both in person and via email.

It seems odd to thank a town, but I must. Zeuthen is the real version of my fictional town – I took its location and its name, but dropped the "u," then made my own streets, filled them with fictional buildings and fictional people. Every person in my fictional town of Zethen comes strictly from my imagination and has no intentional counterpart in real life. I only know one family in the real town of Zeuthen. Thank you to Ellen and her parents, Dörthe and Jürgen, for welcoming me into their home and showing me the region's beauty.

In the historical portions of the narrative, I attempted to remain faithful to the facts. The larger events did happen as described, but the smaller events experienced by my characters happened only in the story. In two instances, I deliberately flirted with the truth: I don't know if there was a Reich Labour Service camp near Zinnowitz, or if there was a convent anywhere between Zeuthen and Frankfurt (Oder), but both exist in this story. Any other historical inaccuracies are solely my responsibility.

Thanks to all the members of my writing group, who are an ongoing source of support and encouragement. They read whatever I send them and always offer fantastic feedback. Many people, inside and outside the group, read and commented on *Run Like Jäger*. Of particular note are my first readers (Gisela Everton, who also corrected my German, and Catherine McLaughlin), and my last readers (Dymphny Dronyk and Angela Kublik), who all helped improve the story.

And, of course, I would never have needed to create this page if not for the wonderful people at Coteau Books. Particular thanks go to Barbara Sapergia for saying she was interested in publishing an unknown writer's first novel, and to Laura Peetoom for helping me polish it.